Hattie lit a cigarette shakily and lay back on her bed. Somehow, articulating her anger that afternoon finally crystallised many feelings about men which hitherto had been less definite in her mind. A steely resolve entered the inner citadel of her spirit. She'd use men as they'd always used her kind, for her own pleasure and without according them any particular respect. Hattie was filled with her perception of the accumulated womanly resentments of generations.

An Anger Bequeathed

By the same author

Engraving the Sky – Haiku and other poems
(1993)

An Anger Bequeathed

Bruce Leeming

Argyll
publishing

© Bruce Leeming

First published 1994 by
Argyll Publishing
Glendaruel
Argyll PA22 3AE

The author has asserted his moral rights.
No part of this book may be reproduced or
transmitted in any form or by any means
mechanical or electrical, including photocopy,
without permission in writing, except by a
reviewer in connection with a newspaper,
magazine or broadcast.

British Library Cataloguing-in-Publication Data.
A catalogue record for this book is available from the British Library.

ISBN 1 874640 70 X

Cover illustration,
typesetting and origination by
Cordfall Ltd, Civic Street, Glasgow G4 9RH
Printed and bound in Great Britain by
Cromwell Press, Broughton Gifford,
Melksham, Wiltshire SN12 8PH

Author's Note

The story of the early Murrays is based partially on events which occurred on one side of my family. However, Hattie and all the characters with whom she becomes involved are wholly imaginary.

BL

I do not wish them (women) to have power over men; but over themselves.

> Mary Wollstonecraft 1759-1797
> *A Vindication of the Rights of Women*

The woman's cause is man's: they rise or sink together.

> Alfred, Lord Tennyson 1809-1892
> *The Princess*

Val shrugged. "For forty-odd years I've been a member of an oppressed people consorting with the enemy . . . I'm part of the lunatic fringe now, the lunatic fringe that gets the middle to move over a bit".
It was good-bye she was saying, Mira thought.
Val had gone over the line.

> Marilyn French
> *The Women's Room*

1

IT WAS RAINING relentlessly in Rutherglen that Sunday. Upstairs in her bedroom Harriot Murray took off an old blouse and removed her brassière. Rummaging in a drawer for a favourite angora sweater, she caught sight of her reflection in the cheval mirror she'd had since childhood. How shapely her breasts were, hanging free. Slowly she caressed them with both hands, smiling in self-approval. She pulled on the sweater, made up her face with liberal eye-shadow and a purplish lipstick, then quickly brushed her auburn hair. There, that should do. Hattie was not especially tall but good skin and teeth, bold dark blue eyes and a better developed figure than most of her contemporaries gave her an undeniable presence.

She glanced out of the window. It was not yet five and the month still August but a lowering sky had already obliged the worthy residents on the other side of Oakside Avenue to switch on their house lights. Somehow this accentuated the square solidity of the red sandstone-faced villas. Hattie had lived at Number 47 all her life.

She sighed, staring down into the deserted street. Rainwater swirled prodigally along the granite gutters. Hattie tightened her lips. Her parents were probably reading in the silence below. Well, damn it, she wasn't going to sit meekly on her backside all evening being bored to death. She painted her fingernails, allowed them to dry, and about a quarter to six, went downstairs. Her mother was in the kitchen.

"Hello, dear. I'm just starting supper. Gracious, you're all dressed up."

"Leave me out of supper, Mum."

Charlotte Murray frowned. "But, Hattie . . ."

"Honestly, I'm not hungry. I thought I'd go over to Sheena's for a few hours. This rain depresses me."

"Have a sandwich at least. There's some of that salami you like."

"Oh, OK." Hattie felt unconsciously for her watch. Must have left it in the sitting room. She entered the room which was illuminated by a standard lamp only. In its pool of light her father sat reading a book of poetry.

Robert Murray took off his bifocals. "What's this outfit in aid of, Harriot?"

"I'm going out."

"On a night like this? Anyway, it's Sunday."

"Sheena McHugh always has a crowd in on Sunday evenings."

Murray snorted. "Yes, I can believe it. No doubt her parents are out gallivanting too. Once they've sat through a quick mumbo-jumbo of a mass in the morning I suppose it's party time for that kind. Absolute travesty of . . ."

"Now, Dad, if you're going to treat me to another of your anti-Catholic diatribes I'm afraid I haven't the time."

Murray's face was beginning to colour.

"Just you keep a civil tongue in your head, girl!"

"So it's all right for you to criticise my friends behind their back, but I mustn't say a thing to defend them?" Hattie's lower lip jutted defiantly.

Her father flicked the back of his hand dismissively at her. "I'm not arguing with you. I suppose it'll be drinking till all hours and I don't know what else with those sloppy, bearded creatures I've seen hanging around Sheena McHugh? Surely you've something more constructive to do?"

"As far as Sheena's concerned, her friends are my friends too. And I'll do what I like at her party. This is 1955 you know. Also, in case you've forgotten, I'm eighteen. In some countries that will soon give me the right to vote."

Robert Murray exhaled sharply in exasperation. He put his glasses back on and began to search for his place in the book on his knee. "Go on then. It's no use talking."

No it isn't, blast you, thought Hattie fiercely. I'll bloody well enjoy myself at Sheena's like *you'd* never imagine in a month of your rotten Sundays. If that Paul Horrigan's there tonight... exciting images jostled in Hattie's mind. She wriggled nervously as she went back to the kitchen.

"I hope your weren't arguing again with your father, dear?"

"Surprise, surprise. He never approves of anything I do. Listen, Mum, I think I'll do without that sandwich."

"It's made. Please eat it, Hattie. I expect you'll have some drinks and I'd like you to put something in your tummy."

Impulsively Hattie kissed her mother. "Dear Mum. I do love you. Why does he have to be such a misery?" She jerked her thumb towards the sitting room, the gesture filled with a mixture of anger and contempt.

Charlotte Murray ignored the rhetorical question. "Have some milk with your sandwich, Hattie."

"OK."

"You'll miss Charlie. He said he'd come over for a while this evening. Wants to collect a book from his room I think."

"It's all right for him, living over there in the West End with his Art School friends, even if they are some of Glasgow's real weirdos. I wish I was twenty one. Anyway, give him my salaams."

Behind Charlotte's understanding smile there was a bleak anxiety for the future.

Love Letters in the Sand. The muffled voice of Pat Boone crooned ingratiatingly inside as Hattie stood dripping on the doorstep of the McHugh house. She grinned to herself. No inviting warm beaches in the ancient Burgh of Rutherglen tonight.

"Come in, come in, Hat pet! My God, that's a monsoon out there."

Sheena shepherded her into the hallway and helped her off with her wet coat, then brought a towel from the bathroom.

"It's great to see you, Sheena. You don't mind . . . I mean . . . ?"

"Not at all, Hat. The boys were just complaining about uneven numbers. You'll be as welcome as the flowers that bloom in the spring, ho-ho!" Sheena winked naughtily.

"Who's here?"

"Sandy Watson, Hazel Ballantyne, Paul Horrigan and Willie Shields. Wiliam's mine so hands off! OK?"

The two friends giggled conspiratorially.

"Never fear, Sheena. There's plenty else for me to get my hands on!"

More giggles.

"C'mon then. Paul's brought a bottle of that clear malt whisky. Glenlivet or whatever you call it. It's lethal so watch your step. Your hair dry now?"

"Sure."

Hattie had to blink several times before she could identify the various bodies recumbent on cushions round the floor. Only a table lamp glowed weakly beside the record player. Pat Boone was now serenading *Bernadette*.

"Hi, Hat! Come down and see me some time."

It was Paul. Reaching up he took her hand firmly and pulled her to the carpet. Before she realised what was happening she was lying full length in his arms, a half mocking open-mouthed kiss planted on her lips. Immediately, Hattie was on fire. She ached to get on her back, to feel Paul's urgent fumblings with her clothes. The speed of her body's reaction shook her. She was sweating with lust.

But Paul rolled away abruptly. "Hang on. I'll get you a drop of the guid stuff. Hey, Hat, I like your sweater. Sexy."

He returned with a measure of the fiery liquor. They sat close together on the floor, ankles crossed, knees splayed.

"*Slàinte mhah!*"

Cautiously they sipped.

"So how's life with Miss Harriot Murray?"

"I get bored sometimes."

"It's an Arts degree you're doing isn't it? What happens after? Teaching?"

"Maybe, if I last the course. Are you going to stick it at the Tech, Paul?"

"Uh-huh. Another two years and I'll be a fully fledged textile designer. Hopefully National Service in the Forces will be a thing of the past by then."

Paul's conversational tone was light, easy-going, but as he spoke he held her tightly round the waist. His free hand slipped under her sweater, paused momentarily, then moved up to touch her left breast.

"Wow! No bra," he whispered.

Hattie was panting, making no effort to restrain him. All she could do was smile eagerly into Paul's eyes which were shining hungrily in the semi-dark.

He drained his glass and went stealthily to work with both hands. Hattie's nipples were hard as he stretched her out on to the floor again. This time Paul's probing tongue kiss was real and full of promise. He left Hattie's breasts and put his arms round her. "My God! You're something, Hat," he breathed earnestly in her ear.

"I'm getting very hot, Paul. It's this wool sweater."

He tensed at the implication in the remark and, as if to communicate his own stage of arousal, grasped Hattie's buttocks and pressed her hard against himself.

By now Hattie's mind was swimming. It had always been like this since that first time with Johnny MacGregor at the tennis club when she'd still been fifteen. They'd both been let down by singles partners, it was pouring anyway, and there was no one else in the clubhouse. Of course they'd mucked about for ages first and then Johnny had lost control before they'd really got started. But Hattie had never forgotten that first incredible excitement of abandoning herself to a man's rampant need. It had seemed the most natural thing in the world.

Nowadays she knew better how to pace herself, but the excitement of the build-up was even sharper. She thrust at Paul with slow accurate strokes.

"Steady, Hat, or it'll be all over for me."

They relaxed a little and Paul resumed his clandestine exploration of her breasts. She turned on her side and after a while, still in a half dreaming state, became aware of Paul's hard body pressed in behind her, his hand resting between her thighs, toying with her suspenders. But he was squeezing her breasts . . . what the . . . ? She didn't move. Her heart thumped. Jesus! There were two of them at her! Hattie was faint, near orgasm.

Paul suddenly realised what was happening. He sat up. "Is that you, Watson? Beat it, you bugger!" He leant down and pushed the other man away violently.

"OK OK, Paul. Hattie was just sharing the wealth a bit. Keep your hair on."

Paul glanced sharply at Hattie. "You didn't realise he was . . . ?"

"I certainly did not, Paul. My God! What d'you take me for? You keep your dirty hands to yourself, Sandy Watson."

She got away with it. Just. Sandy looked at her strangely in the dim light. But then he turned to Hazel and soon they were clasped in an apparently passionate embrace.

Paul kissed Hattie fiercely. "Listen, have a word with Sheena and see if there's another room, eh?"

Hattie nodded. With a little embarrassment she posed the question.

"All right, Hat, if you absolutely must. Just this once. Spare room, upstairs, second on the left. Leave it tidy, mind," Sheena laughed.

"When are your parents due in?"

"Och, they're over at my Auntie's in Whitecraigs playing bridge. They'll not be back much before midnight. You won't be long, pet!"

"Thanks, Sheena."

In minutes she was writhing with Paul on one of the spare room's single beds. He'd pulled off her sweater and his shirt and vest as soon as they were alone. Now he was alternately massaging her breasts and sucking the erect nipples or reddening her soft skin with rubs of his youthfully hirsute chest.

"You're beautiful Hat," he breathed in obviously genuine admiration.

She held him at arm's length for a moment and studied his physique, her eyes sweeping more than his exposed torso. "You're nice looking too, Paul." Her voice was thick.

He swallowed quickly. "D'you want the light out, Hat?"

"Not really."

"OK."

"Come close, Paul." He obeyed. "Lie on your back."

She undid his belt, his zip. Paul's eyes were shut tight. Hattie's were wide as she tugged off his trousers and underpants in one movement. She played with him, commanding that he keep his hands behind his head.

Paul moaned. "I can't wait much longer, Hat. Please, now . . . "

"Just a minute." In seconds she was naked and back on the bed.

"Listen, Hat, I haven't got anything . . . you know . . . "

"Lie still, silly boy." Deftly she removed a contraceptive from her handbag and rolled it on an astonished Paul.

"Christ! Where did you get that?"

"Never you mind. Just think of me as a good boy scout. Come on, Paul. You're *enormous*."

As he bent gratefully to his task Paul Horrigan again muttered, more to himself than his lover. "God, Hattie Murray, you're really something."

The rain had ceased and been replaced by a blustery wind. Hattie relished the freshness on her warm face as she walked home. Near Oakside Avenue she paused in the shadow of an overhanging holly tree. Ragged clouds raced past a yellow moon. She sat back on a low stone-garden wall, closed her eyes and replayed the reel of the last few hours. As a potent mixture of emotions swept through her she shuddered.

There was nothing like sex. She needed its obliterating thrill, its catharsis, often. All her prickling discontent dissolved in the act. It gave her an intoxicating sensation of wholeness, of being utterly in charge of her life. Afterwards, the serenity of body and mind were wonderful.

But was there something unnatural about her? Was it abnormal for a girl of her age to want intercourse regularly? She knew Sheena and some of her other student friends were no longer virgins but, well, they didn't seem so enthusiastic about sex. They talked about it all the time of course, and they had boyfriends too. They were always necking at parties, even pretty heavy stuff at times, but going the whole way appeared to be only an occasional outcome, and something which every attempt should be made to avoid. Often Hattie felt strangely isolated in the midst of her girlfriends. And she didn't have any particular boy to talk about. In fact, she'd admitted to herself some time ago that she didn't want to be tied, that one man for her was as good as another. She could pick and choose.

Dimly Hattie was aware that another factor had had a part to play too – her father. As a little girl she'd idolised her Daddy. With his stern ways and aura of literary refinement – he always had an appropriate quotation for her, however trifling the occasion – he was her hero. And she knew that he loved her, showing it frequently by bestowing little kisses on her lips or tenderly cradling her head against his chest, closely enough for her to feel the heavy beat of his heart. But slowly, as she approached adolescence, this intimacy unaccountably faded. Hattie was smitten by a nameless grief. Daddy became a distanced Dad, who would now kiss her on the forehead only, and that rarely. And he stopped embracing her.

She hid her pain. Indeed she affected a more or less constant jollity, laughing a great deal and developing a minor talent for mimicry. And then the parties started, young teenage gatherings of friends in neighbouring houses. Usually there were a few who were a year or two older, boys mainly, and Hattie found their company exciting. They in turn were amused by her attempts at impersonating the filmstars of the day, Dorothy Lamour, Jane Russell, even James Cagney, reacting with considerably more enthusiasm than did her father or even brother Charlie. Once or twice she took one of the boys home but the reception was always equivocal.

"Didn't you like Andrew, Dad?"

"What age is he?"

"Nearly eighteen."

"I thought so. Too old for you. Have you no friends of your own age?"

"Yes, but I prefer older boys. They talk more sense than fourteen year olds."

"Oh, no doubt. They know better what they're after and how to mislead a young girl. Oh yes, oh yes."

Charlotte spoke up, "Robert, I'm sure that lad Andrew was a nice boy. I'm sure he wouldn't . . . "

"Don't be naive, Charlotte. They all want the same thing." He turned to his daughter. "Hattie, look straight at me."

She did as asked. "Dad?"

"Have you and that young man been up to anything bad?"

"What d'you mean?"

Charlotte made to intervene.

"Let *me* deal with this," Robert said, silencing his wife with an outstretched open palm. "I think you know very well what I mean, miss. I'm talking about fumblings in holes in corners. I'm talking about men getting you to remove your underclothing so they can touch your secret places." He paused, eyes glittering. "*Now* do you understand me, Hattie Murray?"

She was near to tears. Almost inaudibly she replied, "Yes, Dad, I understand. But I've never done anything like that. Honestly."

Her father cleared his throat. "I'm glad to hear it. I saw a deal of licentious living in my youth. It starts, as often as not, with a lack of control at home. Hattie, you'd agree you have a happy home with parents who care for you, wouldn't you?"

"Yes, Dad."

"Well then, just you make sure to behave decently, whatever temptation the Lord may put in your way, and this will stay a happy and safe haven for you. Otherwise . . . "

In this and similar rows the final threat was never elaborated. Would she be beaten? Thrown out of the house for ever, or what? Eventually she perceived that these periodic outbursts were unreasonable in their overreaction, that their near-hysterical tenor derived from a deep sexual frustration, or a possessive jealousy, or an irrational attitude to the whole question of sexuality and pleasure. Hattie couldn't guess the truth and soon gave up trying to do so. It was a fruitless business.

All she did know was that the effect of her father's lectures was the reverse of what he said he intended. Necessarily she became devious with him about her movements and her increasingly passionate dealings with the opposite sex. Her ability to attract boys, to enjoy the thrill of their eager caresses, was inevitably conjoined in her mind with rebellion against a dictatorial father whose love for her appeared to have dried up. She considered that she was the winner, he the despised loser.

As the elation of the evening wore off, however, Hattie experienced a familiar stab of troubled insecurity. Was she different? Why *didn't* she want a steady relationship? Did she actually like men apart from what only they could offer physically? Hattie shivered. Merging black clouds now obscured the moon and occasional heavy spots of rain began to slap on the stiff holly leaves above her head. She hurried home.

When Hattie came down in her dressing gown for a late breakfast next morning, her father had long since left for the bank, where he was manager. Charlotte was reading the newspaper, coffee mug in hand. She looked up.

"Morning, Hattie. Good party?"

"Yes, Mum. Great. Have we any bacon? I'm peckish." Hattie did not want to be drawn into an analysis of the previous evening.

Her mother obligingly busied herself making toast and grilling bacon.

"I'm afraid your father didn't approve of the time you came in, Hattie."

"Really? It wasn't late. About eleven thirty? Before midnight anyway."

"Yes, well, maybe he felt because it was a Sunday that . . . "

"Och, for heaven's sake! Just because he turns up at Stonelaw Church doesn't mean we're Lord's Day Observance nuts or something. He makes me sick." Hattie recognised the shadow of pain her words brought to her mother's face. "I'm sorry, Mum. Forget I spoke. Just don't expect me to apologise to him."

Charlotte turned back to the cooker. "It's all right, darling. I understand. Try not to get excited. Your father can't help being a bit strict. We have to make allowances."

"Why? Why should everyone else have to defer to his notion of things? Especially when he's so often wrong or downright prejudiced."

"Let's not go over all that again, Hattie. Here's your bacon."

"Well, OK, Mum. But, quite honestly, I think if you'd stood up to him long ago he might be more reasonable now. Anyway, these days he's got me to reckon with too."

Charlotte smiled wistfully at her forceful daughter. "Bless you, Hattie. You can't realise what it was like for me in the early days. Robert was so strong, so mature. I was really just a girl. Never forget there's twenty one years between us."

"What you mean is he bullied you into submission."

"No, Hattie, that isn't fair. We found much in common.

Music, love of literature. It was just that Robert had such a hard life as a child. His father was a weak drunkard and your poor grandmother had a terrible time raising four children. I think she drummed it into Robert that he must always be firm and decisive, especially where his family was concerned."

Hattie ate her breakfast with evident satisfaction. Wiping her lips she took a mouthful of coffee and lent back in her chair.

"I never knew my grandfather but I'm sure I'd have crossed swords with him if I had. What was his excuse for treating my grandmother the way he did?"

"All I ever heard from your father was that he never really recovered from the shock of being disinherited."

"Oh yes, that's right. *His* father threw him out of the family home in Sweden, didn't he? That was a rotten thing to do."

"It's all ages ago, Hattie. Last century. Of course it's a sad story but it has its romantic side too, you know. I must tell you all I know about the Murrays some time."

But Hattie was scowling as she put down her mug. "I'm afraid I can't see men's weaknesses and cruelty as romantic, Mum." She already knew all she needed to know to be resentfully aware of her female forbears' sufferings at the hands of their men.

2

THE AGE OF PERUKES had not long drawn to its leisurely close in out-of-the-way corners of the kingdom like Nairn when Edward Murray was born in 1834. Eighteen years later, on a June morning full of dancing sunshine, he stood on the quay at Leith, about to take ship for Gothenburg. Queen Victoria had been on the throne fifteen years and the rising self-assurance of the age was well reflected in the handsome young man's face and carriage. Passers-by glanced with interest at a magnetic blend of refinement and bounding confidence in his gestures as Edward directed the stowage of his boxes.

A mere three months earlier there had been no thought of the stupendous adventure now before him. Indeed, it had been not at all clear what position he might obtain when his training in Bodle's Dundee shipyard was completed. Archibald Bodle was an old friend of Edward's father. One evening, two years earlier after dinner at Penick House, he'd agreed to take the young man on and teach him the business of ship's joinery. The Penick Estate, anciently established a few miles inland of the Firth, lay comfortably self-sufficient amid the rich grain lands of Moray. Besides farming, a main Penick crop was of high quality hardwoods from its two thousand acres of carefully tended forest, and it was the need to purchase fresh timber supplies that had brought Archibald Bodle up from Dundee.

After pudding Mistress Isabella Murray had left the gentlemen to their claret and talk of business. Although intelligent enough, she'd had no benefit of education and read and wrote only with difficulty. Bodle discreetly slipped the waist band button of his britches.

"Rob man, that was a grand dinner. Always the best at Penick, eh? You must be well content here."

Robert Murray smiled. "Aye, we're well enough, Archie." They drank in companionable silence. It was not yet dark. Murray inclined his head and glanced briefly through the casement. With satisfaction he observed the spectacular spread tail of one of two newly acquired ornamental peacocks as the bird paraded arrogantly on the lawn. "My only difficulty is Edward."

"So? I thought him a fine laddie last year when I met him."

"Betwixt ourselves, Archie, he's the pick o' the litter. But there's Hugh and Ninian before him and that's the law. Hugh will inherit Penick." He made a quick semi-circular motion with an upturned open-palmed hand.

Bodle detected a frustration in the gesture. "But Penick . . . surely there's enough here to . . . ?"

Murray shook his head. "Ninian and Edward could take on the farms but, really, there's a good living on that side for one only. Anyway, Edward's made it plain he doesn't want the farming."

"So what have you a mind to do, Rob?"

Murray looked up under craggy brows and held his friend's

eye. "I wondered if you could give the boy a training in your yard, Archie. He's extraordinary quick in the learning."

"Mmm." Bodle took stock of this unexpected request. Reliable young men with brains were hard to find. And those with the right social stamp, who could in time control the workers, were even less common. This young fellow might prove a valuable asset. He'd have to give a fair account of himself, having regard to the long-standing relationship between himself, Archibald Bodle, and his father. "I could maybe arrange something, Rob, if that was what you desired."

Before retiring the two men walked in the formal garden. A cool breeze came steadily off the Firth so they didn't tarry long outside. There was time enough, however, for the details of Edward's immediate future to be settled. Bodle reckoned he could teach him a sufficiency of the carpentering and commercial skills of his trade in two years for Edward thereafter to render him some useful service. He considered that it would be just to expect three years of productive work in return for his training, which meant he'd be looking for a five years' indenture.

Murray saw that since his son was now sixteen this would make him master of a valuable and expanding trade just as he reached his majority, to do with his knowledge what he would. Earlier that evening Bodle had regaled him and Isabella with amusing tales of his ship-owner customers, some of them Swedes and other foreigners. His business was clearly full of interest and prospering.

The two friends shook hands warmly on their agreement and went indoors.

At first Edward was resentful at having to leave Penick. It was hard to accept that a mere chronological accident had deprived him of a fine inheritance, but his ardent, questing spirit would not allow him to brood for long pointlessly.

Instead, he grew impatient to be away, to find out what Mr Bodle intended him to do, to discover his own path to an eventual place in society which he was determined would be at least as respected as brother Hugh's.

Rob Murray had said the lad was quick to learn and Bodle expected him to be eager to progress, but the phlegmatic shipyard proprietor was taken aback by the confidence and sheer energy of his new recruit.

"Now, Edward, just you do what my foreman, Mr Lawson, tells you and you'll learn quickly enough. Rome was not built in a day you know."

"As you say, Mr Bodle. It's just that I think I have the essentials of most of the carpentry and the finishing and . . ."

"In six months?" The traditional craftsman's disdain for rush and less than thorough work was in his tone.

"I have been here till nine every night except the Sabbath, Mr Bodle. And you've seen some of my pieces I think?"

Bodle had indeed been impressed by the speed with which Edward had absorbed Lawson's instruction, and the foreman had spoken highly of his application and quality of workmanship. It was not easy to hold him back. "All right, laddie. I'll think about it, but carry on with your job meantime."

"Yes, of course, sir. But I hope you'll show me something of the timber selection and buying soon."

Bodle gave a rare smile. "Just hold your horses, Edward. I said I'd think about the next stage of your training."

A year later Bodle was forced to admit to himself that young Edward had become a cuckoo nestling. Not that he wasn't damnably useful, almost indispensable. He seemed to be everywhere, to know what was happening in all areas of the business. Customers had somehow made his acquaintance and, if Bodle himself was absent for any reason, had begun to ask for him. While the boy, not yet eighteen, was popular with the men, who deferred happily to his easy air of authority, there were some of Bodle's immediate assistants who resented Edward Murray. Something had to be done. But what in heaven's name?

Towards spring 1852 a solution presented itself. The trade between eastern Scotland and Scandinavia, in particular Sweden, had been thriving in recent years. Dundee played its part and Bodle had made a trip to Gothenburg to examine the prospects for his company's services. It did not take him long to purchase a stake in a local ship-fitting yard, and neither he nor Herr Lorentsson had ever regretted their partnership. British and Swedish owners recognised the value of consistent attention on both sides of the North Sea and their patronage rapidly increased. Lorentsson now wrote to Bodle advising him of the Gothenburg yard manager's unexpected death and bemoaning his difficulty in finding a competent replacement. Bodle replied the same day offering him Edward on a three year engagement. He mentioned in passing the candidate's tender years but filled his letter with a description of Mr Murray's technical accomplishments and readiness for managerial responsibility.

Edward found a tutor, a retired teacher living in lodgings near the Gothenburg waterfront, and within weeks had enough Swedish to establish himself as Master of the yard workforce. They were a dour lot. Herr Lorentsson mentioned the identities of three possible trouble-makers and Edward made an early mark by insisting on the dismissal of all three.

After a year he felt able to make written recommendations to Lorentsson for the reorganisation and expansion of the business. He sent a duplicate of this document to Bodle who wrote back endorsing his suggestions. Edward worked unremittingly and drove his people hard. He became totally fluent in the language. In 1854 he was elected a Merchant Burgher of the city.

Sunday was his only time of relaxation. Morning service at St Andrew's Anglican Church at Hvitfeldtsplatsen invariably found him in his pew and he had recently been asked to read one of the lessons. He was becoming known. Sometimes the Lorentssons invited him back for luncheon. Over a glass of akvavit the older man spoke gently. "Herr Murray, you are doing a splendid job at the yard and I and Mr Bodle are well pleased. But you must not exhaust yourself, you know."

Edward was surprised. Lorentsson was a pleasant man of course but he was not given to intimacies. Was there another motive? "Thank you, sir. I much enjoy my work and am not over-taxing myself, you may be sure."

"Sometimes it is difficult to observe oneself, Herr Murray. You need a rest from your labours. Perhaps a month or two?"

Why was he pressing this? Surely he was satisfied? Edward looked round the handsome pine-panelled room. Fine paintings, a valuable French tapestry, Persian carpets, everywhere deeply polished mahogany, totems of a settled life and moneyed culture. It came to him then. Herr Lorentsson wanted him to go away for a while, to interest himself in other matters and to let the business be. Those last months he'd noticed a growing resistance to his suggestions for expansion and change. Herr Lorentsson was speaking again.

"You have been in Gothenburg for almost three years now, Herr Murray. Indeed, I feel you are one of us in many ways." He laid a kindly hand on Edward's shoulder. "Sometimes I find myself thinking of you almost as a son." He smiled sweetly. "Do forgive me." After a pause he persisted, "I am sure your parents and family would appreciate a visit after so long away from Scotland. Naturally, the company would finance a comfortable berth for you, and look forward to restoring you to your present position at the yard when you felt sufficiently refreshed to return."

Lorentsson's stout wife joined them as it was announced that luncheon was ready.

"You are very generous, Herr Lorentsson. I'll consider what you've said most carefully."

But it was not to be. That week a letter arrived from Edward's brother, Hugh, communicating the sad news of his father's death of a seizure. He'd been buried in the family plot at Dyke Kirk. Edward could expect to hear soon about his legacy. Hugh indicated that the estate had been doing well for some time and he expected his brother's settlement to be substantial.

Not many days later Edward learned the extent of his portion from Mr Lumley, the Murray's lawyer of long-standing. It was generous indeed and Edward quickly realised he was in a position to start a business of his own. Without delay he explained the situation to his Gothenburg bankers and obtained their support until the Scottish probate could be granted and funds released to him.

Through a confidential agent he took over a suitable waterside premises, then served notice on Herr Lorentsson. He wrote to Archibald Bodle thanking him for his five years' training and telling him he was now setting up in competition. Deciding to stay in Gothenburg he let it be known in the right quarters that he was looking for men. A foreman and his deputy defected from Lorentssons. Shrewdly Edward gave them a small share in the new business. E Murray & Co, was quickly in operation.

The next few years were a time of great fulfilment for Edward. Slowly at first, but steadily, he drilled his labour force and the organisation of his machinery to peak efficiency. He attracted the best craftsmen, kept his costs down and began to win orders at others' expense. Edward Murray became a prominent citizen of Gothenburg, respected by all, feared by some.

With his bank's enthusiastic backing he invested in a well positioned graving dock, and its long warehouses proudly bore his name in large letters which were legible from anywhere in the port.

Although whiskered in the fashion of the day and always looking serious, Edward was still just twenty seven. There was a lack in his busy life – a wife. This need he perceived to be social every bit as much as physical. He now owned a good house and was well looked after by his housekeeper, but he had started to entertain important guests and it was sometimes awkward to be without a lady of his own.

Apart from an early regrettable lapse with a group of newly elected burghers in a brothel in the old town, Edward had in effect taken his work to wife since his arrival in Sweden. Now he could afford to think more expansively. The time had come for him to go the social round appropriate for a gentleman in his standing, with a handsome woman at his side. As he allowed himself to dwell seriously on this thought, Edward experienced powerful promptings of long dammed sexual desire which he knew would not be gainsaid.

He did not find the Swedish women to his taste. Without doubt many were fine physical specimens, but they seemed to him coarse-grained, heavy in the bone. Sometimes their sing-song accent irritated him beyond bearing. He wondered if his jaded reaction might be bound up with the past eight years of toil in their midst. Whatever the reasons, Edward started day-dreaming of such Scottish young ladies as he could remember. In his heated reverie he pictured velvet-soft, cream and pink skin, alabaster necks, provocatively pouting bosoms, neat, slim waists, thick fine hair spilling over white shoulders, jet hair, white gold hair, long Titian red tresses. . . He determined to visit Scotland and return to Gothenburg with a wife.

Hugh had just celebrated his thirtieth birthday when Edward rode up the avenue of tall limes to Penick House. It was obvious that the estate was in good heart with evidence everywhere of careful husbandry. Edward noted stacks of long poles from pine and chestnut thinnings, to be sold for fencing and hurdles, substantial oak logs for the shipbuilders' yards, and large areas of sheltered new planting stretching away on either side.

All these works had of course been set on foot by Robert Murray. Edward found Hugh apparently uninterested in the agricultural aspects of Penick. Indeed, he did not appear particularly well-informed at all about the estate's business, preferring to leave these matters in the hands of MacKay, his factor. Hugh's attention was absorbed by hunting and the demands of the social season in the castles and great houses of the North East and the garrison town of Inverness. He'd married Alice Gordon who was a daughter of a noble house. She brought him no great fortune, but their union ensured an elevation in society which was greatly to Hugh's liking.

The two brothers soon found that their temperamental differences had increased with the years and that, really, they had little to say to one another. At twenty eight Ninian had not yet married. Edward was disappointed at his taciturnity – he'd been a carefree boy. It seemed that the management of the farms he'd been running for a year or two now taxed Ninian's energies. He had no conversation beyond crop routines, fluctuating grain prices, difficulties with labour. Ninian had become dull and Edward realised, with passing regret, that his second brother was not endowed with an abundance of brains.

Although Hugh's prattle and affectations annoyed Edward

he kept his irritation concealed. There was a mission to keep in mind and Hugh and Alice were likely to be essential to its speedy accomplishment. Edward confided in his brother.

"You've picked a fine wife, Hugh. I doubt I shall ever have such good fortune."

"And why not, Brother? From what you tell me you have much to offer in Gothenburg."

Edward gave Hugh a twisted smile of resignation. "True. A good house. A respected position and comfort. But I shall not find the likes of Alice among the Swedish women, Hugh, and alas, I know no young ladies hereabouts nowadays."

Hugh reached out and grasped Edward's forearm. He had always been rather impulsive. "Dear brother, this is nonsense! There are many ladies of our acquaintance who would be honoured to be paid court by Edward Murray. Won't you allow me and Alice to assist you with an introduction? If you do not object to my presumption that is."

"Object? Why would I?"

Hugh lifted his eyebrows and looked uneasy. "Oh, I don't know. It's just that you have always been so jolly independent. You might have felt offended that I . . . "

"Come, come, Hugh. I hope I also have the good sense to recognise a generous offer. I shall be much obliged if you and dear Alice will be so kind as to give some consideration to my situation."

Hugh beamed at the unaccustomed tone of Edward's words. He had soon mentioned a few possible candidates.

"I do not wish the extent of a dowry to weigh," Edward explained. "It is more necessary to me that she be a pretty specimen, willing to be cheerful in a foreign place. If I can state it plainly, Hugh, my lady must be no society gadabout, and she should at all times devote herself to my welfare. I need a settled domestic foundation to give me freedom to build up my business without distraction."

"I understand, Edward. I shall speak to Alice. I believe you may have described someone not far from here."

"Oh, what is her name?"

Hugh placed a finger on his lips. "Miss Jean Creighton."

3

AND SO, A WEEK LATER, Edward was presented to Miss Creighton at a ball given by her parents at their home in Elgin. He was captivated. Straight away he knew that this was his future wife. Jean was demure, even a little shy, but she had a way of looking directly into his eyes through averted lashes that momentarily confused him, although pleasurably.

They were partners in several dances, waltzes, reels, a quadrille, and Edward was not a little amused by Jean's quiet corrections as he stumbled over forgotten steps. They managed to converse a good deal and before the evening ended he had given her a full description of his house and life in Gothenburg.

He called upon her for tea. They rode round Elgin in the Creighton family fly meeting Jean's friends. Enchanted though Edward was with the society of this attractive young woman, it was soon clear to him that her educational development was limited. Jean's mind was quick enough but woefully poorly stocked. She'd not travelled farther than Nairn in the West or Keith to the East. But her graceful poise bewitched Edward. Shining auburn hair bounced in heavy ringlets on the nape of her neck. Her waist was small and her satin gowns had been cunningly cut to fit perfectly over her hips. Jean stood just shoulder high to Edward. He hungered to possess her.

After two weeks Edward raised the subject of marriage obliquely. Jean was not deceived.

"Eh, Mr Murray, you flatter me with such talk! And you in such a grand way there in Norway."

"Sweden, Miss Creighton. But I have proposed nothing to you yet. Of course, if I could be sure that you were of the same mind as I in this matter then, naturally, I would arrange to speak to Mr Creighton."

Jean looked sideways at him out of her bonnet as they walked in the garden of her house. Edward seemed rather old and serious sometimes, but then, would not all the young men she knew be like that before long? He obviously knew what he wanted to do in life, and his descriptions of voyages and foreign ways were thrilling. Jean had always wanted to travel. If she married a local man, even one with land or perhaps a title, her future life was not hard to predict. This was probably going to be her only opportunity for something different. Physically Jean was virginal, utterly innocent. It did not occur to her to take any such things into account. It was enough that Edward was a well set-up, strong gentlemen. God would decide if she was to bear his children.

After a long pause she said quietly, "Well, Mr Murray, Papa is usually in the library at this hour."

Edward stopped, turned to face Jean and grabbed her hands. He conferred a quick kiss on her gloved fingers and, smiling widely, exclaimed, "Ah, Miss Creighton, I thank you with all my heart. You may rely on me always to take good care of you."

She returned his smile shyly. "When we are alone you may please call me Jean or Jeanie."

"My dear young woman!" was all Edward managed in

reply. His thoughts were vaulting ahead, visions of conjugal intimacy and the need for immediate practical arrangements jostling with equal vigour in his mind.

Mr Creighton had a large family of daughters and was finding lately that his rents were no longer matching his expenditures. Mr Murray was most persuasive. Anyway, he came of a good family and clearly had excellent prospects in Gothenburg. After a convivial glass of Madeira together Mr Creighton gave his permission and enthusiastic blessing to the marriage. A few administrative details were discussed and it was finally agreed that the betrothal be announced immediately. Edward would go back to Sweden for six months and return in the spring for the wedding.

Jean's early impressions of her new country were of greyness. Moray had looked so bonny in May, abundant green lushness vying with the brilliant golds of gorse, celandines in the ditches and, in the meadows, dandelions and buttercups. The days had been sweet with the pervasive musk of burgeoning haws. But here wild flowers were sparse, the moorland grass in the hinterland a uniform, sun-exhausted, weather-beaten grey-green. Gothenburg's buildings too seemed to huddle in dull monotone.

Of course Jean realised she was wildly homesick, that the bustling Swedes with their unintelligible tongue were not really hostile. Indeed, Edward had employed a maid for her. Birgitta was most polite and solicitous, but they were able to communicate in only the most basic manner. As the months went by Jean did acquire a small Swedish vocabulary through necessity, mainly from Birgitta. But then her progress ceased. She knew nothing of foreign languages or how to go about learning one. This was the first occasion of discord between her and her husband.

"Now, Jean, if you're going to offer me the support which

is my entitlement you must bend your mind to Swedish."

"I find it so difficult, Edward."

"Then try harder."

Jean brushed away a small tear. "I heard that Mrs Bell, the Minister's wife used to give lessons to British people. I don't know if she still does it."

"Then find out, my lady. Please do not look to me to arrange everything."

"Yes, Edward."

"I expect to see some speedy improvement. We must start entertaining soon."

But Mrs Bell was not young. Her patience was minimal and poor Jean, in her desperation to learn quickly, became utterly confused. Her attempts to converse with friends of Edward's or their wives produced gaffes which caused either laughter at her expense or irritation. After a year in Sweden Jean convinced herself that she would never be able to speak Swedish.

As Edward's impatience increased at her inability to adapt quickly Jean withdrew into herself, and this cast a blight on their marital relations.

Edward had kept to himself on the ship coming over and for the first few days after their arrival. Then one night he'd come into her bedroom and taken off her nightgown. Naturally Jean had been embarrassed, even a little ashamed, but her apprehension melted in Edward's gaze of obvious admiration as he pantingly devoured her ripe twenty year old body with wide, shining eyes. Jean had no idea what to expect next and thought that her husband was merely being playful when he started handling her roughly, pulling off his britches and getting into her bed.

However, Edward's urgent fumblings soon turned to brute force as he found his wife silent and unresponsive. Jean was compelled to lie on her back and open herself to his will.

Then came a searing pain, as of an unexpected stabbing. Edward was breathing into her face now in great gusts of hot air as he lunged again and again. She bit her bottom lip in bewildered distress and thought she could not much longer forbear to scream when, suddenly, all was slackness and cooling sweat. She began to weep. Wordlessly Edward rolled off the bed, picked up his britches and left her.

Many black hours passed before Jean, aching and fearful for the future, fell into a troubled sleep. Thereafter, when Edward came to her bed she submitted to the joyless, always uncomfortable process as her bounden duty.

During their second summer at Gothenburg Jean found a perfect excuse to refrain from venturing abroad for anything much more than a shopping expedition with Birgitta. She had fallen pregnant. Only dimly did she connect her unhappy wrestlings in the marriage bed with this new excitement as she fervently thanked God for sending such a blessing to his unworthy servant.

For months Edward showed little interest but, as her time neared, he began to take notice of her condition.

"Now, Jeanie, don't you go reaching for things or straining yourself. You're carrying my seed and my heir and he needs all your care, d'you hear?"

She was touched to see him so earnest, and frankly surprised when he told Birgitta to place an extra cushion at her back. Even if Edward's attitude and actions were actuated by self-interest it was very pleasant to be pampered and to know that, at last, she was doing something important which pleased her husband. Gleefully she told him that she had sensed the baby kicking.

Edward smiled. "Aye, he'll be a lusty child I'll be bound. I'll see him when I return from Stockholm."

"Stockholm, Edward? What is this?"

"I must go. You know how I need to expand and diversify

the business? Well, the vegetable oil trade is very profitable these days and a caraway-seed crushing mill is coming up for sale here in Majorna. The owners have moved to Stockholm. I want to ensure the purchase. It's unfortunate that it happens at this time but the midwife is reliable." He rose to go.

Jean looked wistfully out of the window. "Edward?"

"Yes, yes?"

"How do you know the baby will be a boy?"

"Tush, woman! I know no more than you what the Lord intends. I merely hope. Now, see you take care to do your part."

It was four o'clock on a dark, rain-swept November afternoon when James Robert Creighton Murray arrived. He had traces of his mother's auburn hair and his father's large bold eyes. Jamie was a chuckling plump baby. Weakly Jean grinned at him. She could not even raise a hand in salutation, so profound was her exhaustion. A prolonged labour and complicated breech delivery had proved a devastating ordeal.

As old Dr Fleege put it later to Edward, "Your poor wife has suffered greatly, Herr Murray. We had to assist the birth with the knife, I'm afraid. Her wounds will take some time to heal. But it is the internal organs which most concern me."

"What do you mean, doktor?"

"I believe by her colour and aversion from certain foods that there may be severe damage to the reins."

"Eh?"

"The kidneys, Herr Murray. Sometimes we find this phenomenon as a result of childbirth. Not good at all."

"But Fru Murray will recover? She will not be affected permanently?"

"I would not like you to rely on that. If she is careful with diet and does not exert herself unduly, well, perhaps an equilibrium of the functions can in time be restored. But you must not think of further children. The risk would be too great."

Edward looked away bleakly.

"I see. Thank you, doktor."

Birgitta took over the baby and saw to his welfare while his mother slowly recuperated. Jean seemed to shrink, she stooped slightly and her skin took on a peculiar olive underblush. She early abandoned breast feeding James, and the services of a wet nurse had to be procured. But, for a few months, Edward's delight in his son eclipsed any other unease. Each morning he'd pick him up and walk him round the nursery before going to work, talking the while into the little blue-eyed face about the great things he'd do when he became a man.

Inevitably, however, his disappointment with his wife resurfaced. He'd chide her for being unable to be at his side at some reception or other.

"A gentleman has surely a right to expect his lady's support in society?"

"Oh, Edward, you know I would accompany you if I had the strength."

"Maybe strength comes from the right will, Jean. Can you not make the effort occasionally? I do not ask much."

"No, Edward, you are a good husband and I thank God every day for his providences towards me. But you must forgive me if I just canna do as you wish. I . . . I . . . " Jean sniffed and began to weep plaintively.

"Och, woman, stop snivelling! Look you to Dr Fleege's bottles."

There was outrage in the way he banged the door smartly shut. Why had this happened? Had he not worked hard all his life? Was he not entitled to some reward? Here he was shackled to a yellowing invalid wife who hadn't even the wit to learn the language of the country. And in matters of marital intimacy there was no pleasure to be had, if ever there had been. Jean seemed almost to be revolted by the act. He snorted angrily.

This last problem was soon solved. At a theatrical performance Edward met Olga Wilhelmsson. An impecunious but well-fleshed young widow, she looked at him knowingly over her fan.

"Your wife is not with you, Herr Murray?"

"Ah no, Fru Wilhelmsson. She is not well these days."

Olga quickly had the details of Edward's domestic situation, as well as a good indication of his standing in the business community. They were both intelligent and it did not take long for them to perceive each other's needs. She quietly agreed that he call on her and whispered the address before the entr'acte was over. A week later Olga became Edward's mistress, an arrangement which was to persist for long years.

Jean eventually suspected her husband of a regular arrangement elsewhere. She had no curiosity about the other woman's identity. Indeed, her overriding emotion was one of relief. Even though her health was poor and she knew that she was less attractive than she had been, still the chance of Edward's entering her room sexually rampant had been a nightly terror. Now it seemed she could be at peace on that score.

She took up needlepoint. Her father sent her from his library a box of the Waverley novels, and many happy hours she spent adventuring in the realms of Sir Walter's romantic vision. She continued to attend Sunday morning worship with Edward and this afforded her as much intercourse with others as she truly desired.

Little Jamie was the centre of Jean's limited world. He was a playful, inquisitive child and, while he was awake, the two women were hard put to it to keep him out of mischief. Jean taught him English, Birgitta Swedish, and his growing but hopelessly mixed-up vocabulary sometimes had them both doubled up with amusement. Jean wondered if she were over-indulging the little boy, but she had no immediate standard of comparison and she adored her son. Oh, how she loved him. Anyway, if anything, it was Birgitta who was more apt to spoil him by overlooking small misdemeanours and plying him with tit-bits.

James Murray grew up a clever youth but not a little devious, particularly where his father was concerned. He learned to reckon with the searching eye and sharp tongue from an early age and took care to ensure that he presented himself as occupied in pursuits which he knew his father approved. School work he excelled in and invariably he'd show great interest when his father took him round the dock or the oil mill. In fact, he was bored by Edward's long explanations and escaped as quickly as he could to lie on the floor of his room reading lurid penny-dreadfuls, loaned by Jan Bratt, his classmate. Jan's father was a ship's Master and brought these cheap books from London.

Privately tutored as well, James was modestly well grounded in English, French and mathematics before Edward took him into the business at sixteen. He started the young man on a five year apprenticeship closely resembling his own twenty eight years earlier. The joinery foreman confided to Edward that James could be a skilled craftsman but that he lacked patience. Father and son had a private talk and James's application improved.

However, when he was moved to the ship-fitting side his inherent lack of interest became apparent. He was reported for being absent on a number of occasions. Edward remonstrated with him and received promises of reform. But when, in increasing embarrassment, Edward had once more to summon the boy to his office for questioning about absenteeism and then smelt liquor on his breath, he lost his temper.

"Go you home and sober yourself, you insolent whelp! I'll talk to you when I've done my day's work."

That evening in the Murrays' spacious drawing room Edward stood, intent on securing his son's compliance once and for all. James sat upright, a contrite enough expression on his face. His mother simply looked frightened.

"Well, sir, what have you to say for yourself? Your mother and I would like to know when you started on the akvavit."

"Of course it's my error, Father, but one of the men on the job where I was pushed me into drinking it."

"*Pushed* you? Have you no will of your own? Don't you know your name is Murray? Man, it's up to you to set the example, not to copy that of others. When I think . . . "

Jean broke in, her heart thumping painfully. "Edward, James is still only seventeen. Don't you think we could . . . ?"

"Only seventeen? That's age enough to know how to behave. He's grown now. You gave him years of damned mollycoddling in that nursery. Maybe that's what's wrong now. No backbone, eh, Jean?"

She dabbed her eyes, a familiar sensation compounded of guilt, inadequacy and something like shame at her husband's unsympathetic insensitivity rising to overcome her.

"Edward, let us be fair. James . . . "

Brusquely he pushed aside his wife's ineffectual pleading with a backhanded thrust of his arm. "Quiet, woman. Let Master James speak for himself." He turned his exasperated gaze on his son. "Why have you been on the absentee list again? Too busy at the drinking, is that it, my mannie?" His voice rose in irritation.

James had never been able to stand up to his father in this sort of confrontation. He hung his head.

"I'm sorry, Father."

Jean felt the tears coming but she burst out, "Jamie, Jamie, speak up, my dear! Tell your father you've made a mistake. Aye, a bad mistake. But you'll not fall into that trap again. Go on now, James . . . please."

But the young man's brain was in turmoil. The very propinquity of his father in a rage was enough to shatter his thinking processes. It always had been. His strong desire was to get out of the room at the earliest possible moment. It also occurred to James that what he wanted more than anything was a deep draught of spirits. The mere thought was balm.

"You make me sick in the belly, boy." Edward's voice hissed. He looked from the miserable recipient of his derision to his whimpering wife. Bad skin, rheumy eyes, rounding shoulders, shrunken breasts. God! the woman hadn't even the art to dress well, to attempt at least to disguise her unloveliness. She looked twice her age. Fleetingly Edward wondered if she'd live many more years. "You are no help to me, madam. And as for you, sir, I give you due warning that if you displease me in this way again *I will disown you.*"

The final words, with all their terrible import, rang out in the appalled silence.

4

As the 1950s moved nearer the next decade, to the youth of Europe the recent World War seemed an irrelevance. It was something their parents' generation had allowed the nations to blunder into and its main consequences, from the viewpoint of seventeen to twenty one year olds, had been a lack of good things to eat or bright clothes to wear. Now rationing was a thing of the past, the shops were filling up, man-made fibres and plastics had been introduced. Military conscription had been scheduled for termination. Everywhere among the young there was a rising spirit of excitement, and their fun-making had a new, thrilling edge of iconoclasm about it.

Harriot Murray joined in enthusiastically. Among her peer group at university and outside it was regarded as axiomatic that the views of anyone over thirty on any subject must be suspect. This outlook naturally created tensions at Oakside Avenue. A series of unresolved disputes between Hattie and her father had produced stalemate. Eventually, their communication, by unspoken mutual consent, was confined to practical matters of daily routine only. But a bitter enmity smouldered between them.

Charlotte and Hattie maintained good relations but mother did not automatically endorse all daughter's opinions or, more important in Charlotte's view, her behaviour.

"Hattie dear, I wish you wouldn't go out of your way to provoke your father. You're not going to agree on most things so why not just leave it at that?"

"But I would, Mum. He's the one who stirs it up."

"Yes, well, I mean there's no need to *advertise* some of your friends' lack of respect for convention. Your father comes from a hard background where drinking and loose living were simply not acceptable."

Hattie threw her hands heavenwards. "I know, I know. Do what you like, hurt anyone who can't hit back *as long as you're not found out*. Oh, and don't miss church on Sunday. Well, Mum, my generation thinks that that's a stinking philosophy, and we're not going to adopt it."

"You know I do really understand, don't you, Hattie?" Charlotte sighed. "It's just that I'm going to have to live with Robert long after you've left." Charlotte was in her chair in the sitting room. She'd been reading before her daughter came in.

Hattie enquired, "What's the book, Mum?"

"This? Oh, it's just a light historical novel. Good on detail though. Regency."

"Have you ever heard of *The Second Sex* by Simone de Beauvoir?"

"Yes, but I've not read it. Have you?"

"Sheena just lent it to me. It's absolutely fascinating. The author lays it all out how women have been systematically abused and exploited, really since civilisation began. It makes my blood boil."

"Sounds too extreme for me."

Hattie turned from the window where she'd been standing. "It's not extreme, Mum. It's the truth and, with due respect, women will have to take hold of their own destinies if they're ever to cease being chattels."

"But women have all sorts of freedom nowadays. Plenty of good jobs. Economic independence if they really want it. They can avoid having babies even if they're married. Hardly 'chattels', Hattie."

"All that's the least of it. Surely you wouldn't deny that there's active discrimination against women? *That* hasn't changed."

"Maybe so."

"It *is* so, and women will have to become really militant if they're going to do anything important about it. You know, get protective legislation on the statute books and so on." Charlotte was surprised at her daughter's passion as she swept on. "If some of the women in this family had stood up for themselves in the past they'd have been a damned sight happier. Instead of just giving in to all that male dominated religious rubbish about the woman's preordained role of submission, etcetera. I mean, ignoring present circumstances for the moment, look at my grandmother's life. If that wasn't a case of the exploitation of a good woman by a real chauvinist male pig I don't know what it was!"

"Poor old Martha. But things were different in those days, Hattie."

"That isn't good enough, Mum. Why did she have to put up with her husband? I know divorce was almost impossible then, but she'd have been better off walking out on him, wouldn't she? At least she'd have had some peace."

"We can't ever know the full story, dear."

"Rotten men."

Charlotte looked closely at her daughter, at her flushed cheeks, her down-drawn brows. "Hattie, don't you like men?"

The question caught Hattie off guard. "I adore them! . . . I mean . . . I mean, well, they obviously have their biological role to fulfil. I suppose there's pleasure in that, sometimes." She was quickly regaining her balance. "But the sexual side has nothing to do with women's rights. That's the real issue today and, d'you know, Mum, I feel the fight that's now starting is every bit as much a duty towards those past unhappy women as a struggle for our own position in the future. A matter of avenging them. Something like that anyway."

Charlotte loved her daughter. With a mother's insight she'd known for some years that Hattie had been behaving in a way that bordered on promiscuousness. It troubled her but she felt inadequately experienced to challenge Hattie. The youngsters seemed to grow up so quickly nowadays. At twenty four Charlie sometimes seemed tired of life, almost to have experienced too much. She worried about her son too.

"Hattie darling?"

"Mmm?"

"Promise me you'll always take great care of yourself."

"Oh, *Mum*!"

Eighty years earlier another anxious mother had exchanged confidences with a loved child.

"Jamie dearest, you'll have to mind what your father says."

"Yes, Mama."

"He quite meant that about disowning you, you know. Oh, Jamie, that would be a calamity I couldna withstand. If you should go from me, my darling son, I should not want to live on." She brushed her eyes with a new linen handkerchief, then blew her nose genteelly.

James was well accustomed to seeing his mother in varying states of distress. It made him angry, and doubly fretful at his impotence. "Mama, I think I hate Papa."

"Jamie! You must not speak such a thing. He is a fine

man, well respected in the town. Besides, he provides us with everything."

"Yes, and he's unkind to you inside this house."

"Jamie. I will not hear any more. I have my duty to Edward and my vows. We should pray for guidance from the Lord as to how we must behave." She perceived the weakness in her son's face, the pettish pouting lips. "I love you, Jamie dear, and I'll always stand by you, but you'll have to avoid the drinking. I canna defend you if you disobey your father in that."

"Yes, Mama. I love you too and I promise to attend to my training at the yard. Now!" He jumped up suddenly. "Here comes Mr Jeremiah Blackwood, ship-owner and high civic dignitary from Greenock."

James proceeded to entertain his mother with an impersonation of a recent Scottish visitor, an absurdly affected and pompous personage, to E Murray & Co's yard. Soon they were both laughing loudly, a recognition of mutual dependence underlying their amusement.

James had been shocked by his father's threat of disinheritance. He set himself to persevere in his five year apprenticeship, but a coolness between father and son became habitual. Jean's health deteriorated further and there were long spells when she was forced to take to her bed. Frequently Edward did not return home at night, but he never failed to arrive at his desk as usual in the morning. Nothing was said about this.

James Murray grew into a man of twenty four, tall, slim and dashing, his pale skin and auburn hair marking him out among his Swedish comrades. He wore his clothes with a careless grace.

There was no shortage of women in the old town whose company could be bought by the hour, and James and his merrymaking friends enjoyed comparing their experiences with these girls, who were mainly of illiterate country stock. But it was the dangerous glamour of the seaport taverns which drew James. The rank smell of stale drink and lysol emanating from a freshly swabbed out den in the morning had his pulse thudding. He yearned for the relief a few glasses guaranteed. In half an hour he could forget the overpowering presence of his father, the pain he felt at his beloved mother's misery, the eternal, endless grind of work in the yard.

He had learned to take less potent wine and to disguise its smell by eating fish and spiced meats. But, on holidays when he felt safe, James allowed himself an unrestrained bout of drinking. He was young, in the prime of health, and he had a hard head. But after a number of hours at the bottle with a succession of jovial companions James would fall into a helpless stupor.

On such occasions the innkeepers would simply drag him through to a back storeroom to sleep with the rats on straw and sacking, a not unusual service to good customers. One fateful day, however, the tavern was to be closed for handing over to a new owner. Since there seemed to be no one to assist him James was unceremoniously dumped outside in the lee of a warehouse.

One of Edward's own men discovered him and ran to tell the Master. Edward called out his carriage and drove hurriedly to the spot. By now the young man had been roused sufficiently by passersby to be squatting with his back against the wall. Hatless, his clothes covered in mud and sawdust, he presented a sorry sight. Edward was incensed. He and the groom manhandled James into the carriage and drove home.

The broad-backed groom carried him upstairs to his room, dropped him on the bed, loosened his cravat and pulled off his boots. The older man shook his head. "May the good God help you now, my son."

An Anger Bequeathed

Jean had been alerted by Birgitta to what was happening. She emerged blinking from her shuttered bedroom, already weeping in fright. Edward met her on the staircase.

"Edward, oh, Edward! Don't be hard on Jamie! He's worked well for you. It's just a wee weakness he has now and then. It's probably my fault. Maybe I've over-indulged him. Oh, Edward . . . for my sake, Edward . . . *please* now . . ."

"Shut your whining woman! Well you may blame your mollycoddling of our only child *now*. It's too late, too late." He made to brush past her.

She grabbed at his sleeve. "Do what you will to me, Edward, but don't harm Jamie. You wouldn't send him away, Edward . . . ? Surely . . . "

He shook her off impatiently. "I'll do as I always said I would. He'll not disgrace me again. I'm going to see Advokat Leffler this very hour."

"Advokat Leffler? The lawyer?" Jean's eyes were wide with terror. Edward *was* going to disinherit James. She knew her husband. Nothing would stop him now. Her mind spun, out of control. From her throat came an agonised ululation. Her small hands beat the air in defeat.

"Birgitta!" Edward's shouted summons brought the trembling maid to the upper landing. She was white with apprehension.

"Sir?" she whispered.

"Help your mistress back to bed and give her a strong draught of laudanum. She's no good to anyone."

The formalities were quickly completed. James had one brief meeting with Advokat Leffler to sign papers, one with his father.

"You'll be out of this house by Sabbath next and return on no pretext whatsoever. I trust you have no doubt in the matter?"

"No, Father. I will say again I regret my actions, but there seems to be nothing I can do to make amends."

"No, and, by God, I shall give you no further opportunity to disgrace this house!"

James felt nothing for the angry man before him. His remorse centred entirely on the ailing woman upstairs. Her abject desolation at his imminent departure was pitiful. It was too cruel. James made one last bid for clemency.

"Father, I believe I can forswear the drinking. It has been like a madness these past years. If I thought you really wished my reform, I should try damned hard to serve you honourably."

Edward's face was expressionless, implacable. "The Murrays are a proud family of breeding and strength. We shall remain healthy and command the respect of society so long as we are always prepared to cut out rotten limbs. You, sir, have made it quite plain to me that you are such a cankerous growth. Now leave me, if you please."

Somehow Jean found enough money for James to purchase a passage to Dundee. It was impossible for him to stay in Gothenburg and she hoped that her family, or Edward's, might help him. It seemed the only course. Faithful Birgitta secretly sold some of Jean's jewellery and this provided the young man with enough to live on for a few months. After an achingly tearful leave-taking of his mother he set sail from Sweden in May, 1889. As he took a last look at the city of his birth his father's name stared balefully from the graving dock buildings. E MURRAY – the large white letters seemed to reach out and smite him in final reproach.

His weeping mother's voice came to him again.

"Ah, Jamie! I'll not bear your absence, my dear dear son. You're the only one in the world to love me."

He tried vainly to comfort her, saying without conviction, "I'll return one day, never fear. We'll meet and be happy again, precious Mama."

The distressed woman shook her head hopelessly. Then she spoke more frankly than ever before. "No, Jamie, it'll not be, dearie. Your father will do for me before long. Because I'm sickly he's no use for me, so he'll just oppress and bully me till I'm gone and he's free to marry again."

The young man, despite the misery of the occasion, was taken aback. "But, Mama, you've always defended him as a good man?"

"Aye, well, Jamie, I've done my best to be a loyal wife to Edward, even to making some pretence for your sake, my darling laddie. But now it's not necessary any more. I married a cruel tyrant, Jamie, and you should know the truth of my opinion before you go."

Then Jean was crying helplessly again. Her son put his arms tenderly round her shoulders. "Oh, Mama," was all he could utter through his own tears.

Eventually Jean regained her composure. "Edward Murray has never shown me any husbandly feeling, Jamie. He never wanted me save as mistress of his grand house and to bear his children. I don't think he's a notion of *love*." Her hands had started to shake. James helped her take a draught of medicine. A look of resignation settled on her weary face. "If he'd been the least wee bit kind after I fell ill I could have borne my lot. But he was not, Jamie. He shouted at me and scorned me. He made me afraid of him."

Jean's sallow face was becoming quite red and James felt anxious she might swoon. It had happened before. "Mama, please don't vex yourself. No good will come of it. Won't you lie down?"

"I will have much time for rest when you've gone, Jamie. What I want you to know is that your father never gave me any Christian love. He's despised and abused me but I've had no means to fight him these long years. Every day I feel so angry, and it makes my sickness worse. It's a devil's trap I'm in, Jamie. But I'll have to go to my grave without redress. Remember this, my dearest son, and treat your wife aright when you find her."

They embraced for the last time, their bitter tears mingling.

James went below deck and set himself to face the lonely voyage.

Arrived in Scotland, he called first on Archibald Bodle. On reflection the reception did not surprise him.

"You must think me mad, laddie. Not only have you disgraced yourself from what you say, but Mr Murray is our main competitor. He took all he could from me and then cold-bloodedly proceeded to steal my clients. It's over thirty years ago and I'm finished with the business now, but I've never forgiven that act of ingratitude. No one connected with Edward Murray can expect any favour of *me*. Good day to you, sir."

Mr Creighton in Elgin was a very old man and in chronic debt. The family house had been sold and he lived, a confused widower, in a small cottage with a housekeeper. His sons-in-law felt no obligation towards James. One found his accent highly amusing.

Uncle Hugh had agreed by letter to receive him at Penick but, as James trotted up the lime approach avenue astride a black filly hired in Forres, signs of neglect were everywhere. In the young plantations weeds abounded. The avenue itself was badly rutted and as Penick House came into view its peeling walls and broken balustrades underlined the ruinous condition of the estate. James slumped in the saddle. He was suddenly very weary.

At least Hugh was welcoming. "Well, James my boy! Here you are, good as your word. Give your mount to Finlay and come in."

As their friendly conversation proceeded James wondered about his uncle's attitude. Had he not liked his father, Edward? Perhaps been jealous of his successful enterprise? Maybe now he was covertly pleased at Edward's discomfiture? Then, Hugh had not had a son of his own of course. Whatever lay in the background James relaxed for the first time in months as the courtesies and hospitality of a great house lapped around him. Later, his aunt, Alice Murray, joined them for tea but she seemed distant and did not reappear for dinner. His cousins were married and living in other parts of the country.

James explained his situation, putting the best face on it he could. Words like 'disowned' or 'disinherited' were not used. Gradually Hugh saw that his nephew was in fact desperate for help and, in particular, for money.

"It is sad but true, James, that I am in no position to assist you. Ninian's crops have been deplorable for two seasons now, and the timber market is unbelievably depressed. The new iron ships, you know, and cheap logs from the Baltic. I suppose I should have foreseen it all, but my interests have been more social . . . I don't know which way to turn . . . damned avaricious creditors."

James's head was bowed. "I'm sorry to hear of your difficulties, Uncle Hugh."

"Yes. But of course you may stay as long as you please at Penick, James. Come now, have another charge of this excellent cognac. We may not chance together again." Hugh Murray's skin shone with a pink glow bestowed by the regular bibbing of choice clarets.

"I'm afraid I have to keep a strict rein on myself with cognac and the rest, Uncle Hugh," said James, ruefully refusing the proffered decanter.

Lying in a narrow, cold turret room that night James was possessed by an unearthly sadness. In the weeks since his arrival in Scotland he'd become disorientated. Daily he wrestled with a gnawing thirst – but why struggle, for whom? Who cared? Truly, he belonged nowhere.

He left Penick next morning and, reaching Forres at noon, bought a third class railway ticket which would eventually land him in the great shipbuilding city of Glasgow. As he rattled miserably southwards his disjointed thoughts oscillated from English to Swedish and back again. What would he do on arrival? Where would he lodge? Would he find employment? So low was he in spirits that James Murray could have been persuaded only with extreme difficulty that among Glasgow's teeming thousands there might be one tender heart, uninterested in the errors of his past and willing, nay eager to lavish upon him care and affection without stint.

5

THE CITY SEEMED extraordinarily busy and accommodation was not to be had at any price. Moving south-eastwards, following word of mouth recommendations, James was at last taken in by Mistress Craig who kept a small rooming-house in the Trongate district. He expressed his surprise at the crowds.

"Aye, but it's always the same in July, Mr Murray. The Fair of course."

"Fair?"

She looked sideways at her new guest. "You no Scotch?"

"Well, I was brought up in Sweden, but my parents are from Scotland."

"Sweden, eh." Jemima Craig had barely heard of the country. "I thought you were foreign. You speak funny."

James inclined his head courteously with a smile. Jemima's toil-worn hand flew to her throat in a momentary confusion. She was not at all accustomed to the beguiling manners of fine gentlemen in her house.

"Now, please tell me about this fair."

"Och, it's the Glasgow Fair. Every year in July there's holidays from work and shows and too much eating and drinking. Some Bishop invented the caper hundreds o' years ago, so they say. It's a good excuse for they youngsters to meet up on the Glasgow Green and misbehave themselves in the bushes."

James laughed out. It was impossible to tell from the expression on her face whether Mistress Craig approved or disapproved of this supposed dalliance. If he'd had to guess, James instinctively felt that his landlady had probably entered enthusiastically into the spirit of the Fair on the Green in her youth.

At all events she made him more comfortable than he'd been for two months. He ate heartily and his clothes were laundered. After a few days in the Trongate he was refreshed and even, unaccountably, optimistic.

"Mistress Craig, I think today I shall visit Glasgow Green." He placed his hand on his heart in mock solemnity. "But I promise to comport myself with perfect decorum."

Her reaction, it amused James to observe, was that of an anxious mother hen. "Now you mind yourself, Mr Murray. Watch out for cutpurses and rogues. And they lassies, Mr Murray, they're cunning hussies that'll take you for all you're worth, just for hoisting their petticoats and cocking their shameless bums."

James smiled at her earthy warnings as he strode down the Saltmarket towards the river Clyde. Soon he was one of a vast crowd in carnival mood. Entertainments abounded on all sides – small circuses, wrestling and boxing booths, booths selling beer, pies and oysters, tents showing wax effigies and a variety of performing animals. Squeals of excitement mingled with the distinctive cries of itinerant vendors. It was a hot day and James stopped to eat a mutton pie. He allowed himself a tankard of ale.

A knot of young women was doing likewise, giggling constantly. James could see they were working girls and supposed that this day of freedom must be an annual treat. They joked with each other and flirted with the young men dispensing pies. James noticed that one of the girls did not speak much. She grinned at her companions' foolery but didn't appear to participate. He drained his tankard to move on. The quiet girl caught his eye and smiled straight at him. Her teeth were white and regular, her unflawed skin pale and, neatly pinned under a straw hat, her hair was a glossy black. James smiled back, lifted his hat politely and walked away.

He dismissed the girl from his thoughts. She, however, kept him in sight. Her keen seamstress's eye had noticed small differences in the stitching of his clothes. The crown of his hat seemed fractionally taller, more convex than was usual. And he seemed so gentlemanly, but alone. Normally that type of young man went about with a pack of cronies, drinking and generally making their presence felt. Her curiosity was aroused.

It was by a freak-show booth, where a two and a half foot dwarf and a twenty eight stone fat lady were on display for a penny, that James realised with a pleasant start that the smiling girl was again standing close by. It would be such a relief to have someone to talk to. Again he raised his hat.

"It's a fine day for the Fair, don't you think, miss?"

Was there a sudden faint suggestion of colour in her cheeks? If so, she replied levelly enough.

"Indeed, sir. Have you no companions with you?"

"No. I am alone."

She discerned a strange intonation in his speech.

"You are not Scotch I think?"

"I am, but my life has been spent in Sweden."

"Oh, I see."

James was much affected by the quiet composure of this young woman. Her features were good and he could now see that she had a handsome physique under her well fitted fine cotton dress. Surprised at the urgency of his need, he felt all at once a compelling desire to know more about her, to tell her about his own plight. If he didn't say something quickly she might at any moment be lost in the shifting crowd. Already the other girls were strolling away.

"I . . . perhaps I may . . . ah!" He felt himself unable to speak further.

To his delight he felt his forearm gently touched.

"Will you tell me your name, sir?"

He took off his hat and bowed, if almost imperceptibly.

"James Murray, miss. At your service."

She laughed with pleasure at his formality.

"I'm Martha Byrnie. But I have to leave now."

"I must see you again, Miss Byrnie!" he blurted out.

"Must, Mr Murray?"

"I mean, I should be most pleased if you would permit me to call on you."

Martha's face betrayed an amused detachment no longer. Her large brown eyes seriously appraised the man before her, almost it seemed she could already see into their future life together.

"My place of work is Maclehose & Co, the dressmakers in Albion Street. On Tuesdays I finish at 4 o'clock. I could be at the staff door in the back lane at that hour if you wished it, Mr Murray."

James's heart leapt. Today was Friday. "You do me an honour, Miss Byrnie. I shall not be late."

They smiled boldly at one another. Then Martha was gone with a brief wave of her linen-gloved hand.

James had already established that unless one belonged to the Joiners' and Carpenters' Guild it was highly unlikely employment could be had in the Clyde shipyards. He was quickly made to feel a foreigner when he did manage to talk to two different foremen. And, of course, there was no one here to speak for him, no friends or relatives already in the yards. Apart from these disabilities there was something else. James was obviously a gentleman, and the worthy Glasgow craftsmen felt awkward with him. They could not understand what he was doing in their midst.

It was not many weeks before Martha understood everything. He was a bachelor with no family in Glasgow. His money was running out and he needed work. She also learned that he'd quarrelled with his father.

"I just cannot understand why you should have been cut off by your father, James. 'Cut off with a shilling' it's termed, I think, in this country."

"My father is very hard, Martha. I did not please him."

"But that doesn't call for what he's done to you."

"You don't think so?"

Reluctantly, over several outings when they'd walk together and visit teashops, James confessed about his former drinking.

"Well, I'm sorry to hear it, James, but you're no drunkard. My Heaven, half the men in this city are drunk as dogs at least once a week! Aye, workers, gentlemen and all. I don't see you merited that treatment."

"Bless you, Martha dear."

"Edward Murray sounds a wicked, cruel tyrant to me. Too full of his own pride to allow some weakness in others. Did he behave well towards Mistress Murray?"

James felt an old pain at his heart whenever he thought of his mother. "He is not kind to her either, Martha. She is not a well woman and I think he regards it as an affront to him."

"Poor woman. I presume he nevertheless takes his carnal pleasures as he pleases?"

"It seems you can look uncommon deep, Martha. Yes, it was well known he kept a widow woman. But it was never spoken of."

Martha and James were seated at a small tea-table. She folded her arms and, leaning forward on her elbows, looked directly into his face.

"Oh, aye. And no doubt he was a stoop o' the Kirk too? Damned old hypocrite!" She paused for emphasis. "Now look you, James Murray. If you've a mind to make a go of things with me you'll have to convince me you're a quite different brand of man."

Her forthrightness took him aback a little but he admired her spirit, her underlying steadfast character. And she flushed most becomingly when she spoke with passion.

"I don't know how to convince you, Martha. All I can say is that my father's example is the very last one I shall follow in my life. Especially where my wife and children are concerned. I believe a husband's duty is to be considerate in his domestic dealings. Oh, Martha my dear! If God will bless me with the good fortune of a loving wife, that lady shall find me the truest and gentlest man on earth." Tears stood in James's dark blue eyes.

Martha was touched to the quick of her tender soul. "Jamie darling, you mustn't greet." She held his hand to steady him. "I believe you with all my heart."

Before that evening was out it was understood between them that, once James had found work, they would arrange to marry.

Martha took him to Mauchline in Ayrshire to meet her family. They were friendly but rather shy of him, and James realised anew how different was their class from the one in which he would have moved in normal circumstances. Martha's Uncle John was a joiner in the town. He was impressed by James's knowledge of carpentry, and when they left for Glasgow again they took with them a heavy chest of part worn or discarded tools.

Mistress Craig allowed James to post a small notice at the entrance to her premises and by Christmas he was regularly being called about the district to do small repair jobs. He began to overhaul his regular expenses by a reasonable margin. Martha and he were married and moved into a one-roomed tenement house in the new year of 1890.

Martha continued to work at the dressmakers, but she was soon pregnant. In August she left Maclehose & Co and a few days later Isabella was born, a very small baby who needed all Martha's day and night attention in her struggle to survive. Before the end of November the harassed mother was again with child and, as the months went by, she wondered if her great girth could mean more than one new life. Twins were not uncommon in her family she knew. William and Hugh arrived on a sweltering night late in July after a long and exhausting labour.

In the morning as the midwife cleared up the room Martha asked for James.

"He went out, Mistress Murray. About nine o'clock I believe."

Martha lay weakly till perhaps eleven. The babies woke and needed suckling. She managed and then fell back into a deep slumber. At two she awoke and tended the babies again. Now Martha was whimpering unhappily. Where was Jamie? Why had he not stayed with her? Was he hurt? She prayed as uncontrollable tears slid down her sweating face, from her chin down her neck and on to her swollen breasts where they mingled with her milk.

At three James burst into the room. He was dead drunk.

"Jamie, Jamie! What are you doing?" She had smelt the harsh whisky fumes as soon as the door opened.

"I just been celbratin' . . . the twins . . . ha-ha! Met some friends in the Popinjay. Very, very generous!" He collapsed in his chair by the fireplace.

"Jamie, please get me a cup of cold water. I'm that dry I..."

"Right, Queen Martha. Just a wee minute now." He swayed at the sink but managed to fill the cup and carry it over to the bed. As he stretched out his arm, however, he stumbled and spilt most of the water over his wife.

She took the cup and gratefully moistened her lips with the residue. "Jamie, why did you drink so much? You've never got in this state before." She was too weak to be angry, merely sad and puzzled.

James started some garbled explanation about the proper way to welcome children into the world, but was overcome by alcoholic nausea. There was no time to get out to the landing. He just reached the sink where he vomited horribly and repeatedly.

"Sorry, Martha... I... sorry..."

"Just clean up the mess, please."

He did his best but the whole area of the sink and floor had been soiled. Eventually he gave up and slumped back in his chair. Almost immediately he was in the grip of an ugly, stertorous, open-mouthed sleep. Martha looked at him in shocked pain. The stench of stale vomit sickened her. The babies were again demanding suck. Martha wept silently, her mind filling with nameless fears for the future.

It had been a bad relapse. They faced his weakness frankly and James gave Martha his word that he'd keep out of public houses henceforth. But she noticed that he became listless, half-hearted in his attempts to find jobs. Their income dwindled and Martha was compelled to take in neighbours' laundry and garments to mend in her frantic efforts to feed and clothe the children.

They fell behind with the rent and their credit ran out with local shopkeepers. There was the shame and indignity of a 'moonlight flit' to another part of town, the Partick district, as they sought in desperation to escape debts they simply could not meet. James notified his parents of the new address in Rosevale Street. A month later he received a letter from the family lawyer, Advokat Leffler, who stated, baldly, that there were three matters he was taking the opportunity of communicating to James.

> *His mother, Fru Jean Murray, née Creighton, had died of renal failure and other complications on March 30th, 1893.*
>
> *His father, Herr Edward Murray, had had the honour to be appointed Consul for Brazil at Gothenburg, in recognition of his standing in the community and his promotion of Brazilian produce, such as caraway seed etc, in the Swedish and overseas markets.*
>
> *Herr Murray was engaged to marry the widow Olga Wilhelmsson at the Anglican Church of St Andrew in Gothenburg on September 10th, 1893.*

The letter was like a hammer blow. Somehow, as long as his adored mother lived, James had felt that there was ultimately firm ground in his life. Although formally estranged, he still belonged in a deeper sense to his family. With Mama gone now he was curiously rudderless. And his father's continued prosperity and social ascent was in such stark contrast to his own situation that James experienced sharp, painful excesses of shame.

Martha comforted him. Intuitively, but helplessly, she understood his unhappiness. He started to drink again, but took care not to come home in a seriously intoxicated state. This in turn meant that increasingly he returned late at night, having slept off the worst effects of cheap wine or whisky in some sordid shebeen. Martha chided him, but more in sorrow than real anger. Her handsome, educated husband was now losing his beautiful auburn hair, his eyes were bleary, and his speech was roughening. She knew his health was deteriorating.

For a year or so they stumbled along, saying little to one another. In the tiny one-roomed 'single-end' slum apartment, with its cavity bed and iron range for heat, cooking and hot water, when they could afford coal, the three children kept up a ceaseless, querulous din. Little Isabella had developed a worrying cough. Fear of eviction for late payment of rent haunted them.

Perhaps as part of a despairing last effort to reach out to the James she loved, to try to win him back to a braver address to their hard life together, Martha used her still comely body to show him that he was yet a man. Back-weary and swollen-fingered with constant sewing, laundering and carrying the children about, she forced herself nevertheless to respond enthusiastically to James if he showed the slightest inclination to lovemaking.

Inevitably, in mid 1895, Martha again found herself pregnant. Such were their financial straits, there could be no joy in the impending arrival. The burdens they already bore were too heavy. To Martha's dismay James's reaction was to descend to an even lower plane of despondency, deaf to her pleadings that he get out and seek work. Perhaps, she urged, he could now qualify for Glasgow citizenship, maybe guild membership and a regular job in the shipyards. James simply walked out of the house, uncongenial as it was, festooned with other folks' washing and noisy with childish complaints. In minutes he'd plunged hopelessly into a sea of raw, unrefined whisky.

Robert was born in April 1896. A day or two later as Martha, despite herself, chuckled over the vigorous tugging of the black-haired infant at her breast, there was a commotion on the stairs and a heavy-handed knock at the door. She broke out in a sudden premonitory sweat. In the doorway stood a thickset Highland policeman she knew well from the dismal streets of Partick.

6

HATTIE AND HER STUDENT friends had sat their finals. The caressing warmth of summer was in the air and they were euphoric. For good or ill there was nothing more to be done now but await results. During the balmy long evenings Hattie felt restless, incredibly sexy. Most of the crowd had paired off in the last two years but she still prized her freedom, although it did mean she was sometimes isolated. Hell, it was just 1957 and she was not yet twenty one. There was plenty of time – even if she was about to become a Master of Arts!

Tonight, however, she was on a double date. Sheena was going steady with Willie Shields, and Sandy Watson was picking them up in his father's car before collecting her. They were driving in to Glasgow to see a Japanese film, *The Seven Samurai*, that was all the rage and then going for an Indian curry to one of the new places that were opening up everywhere in town. Hattie put the finishing touches to her makeup and lit a cigarette while she waited.

Her hand shook as she put the lighter back into her handbag. It should be a good evening. She was looking forward to it. But, secretly, Hattie was impatient for afterwards. She'd make sure Sheena and Willie were dropped first, then get Sandy to drive somewhere quiet. She'd already had a few heavy sessions with him, but only at necking parties. Anyway, Paul Horrigan was usually there. But Paul was away doing a holiday job as purser on the Clyde steamers, so this was a golden opportunity to find out what Sandy was made of. She didn't doubt he had a lot to offer. Hattie stuck her tongue out at herself in the mirror, giggled nervously and took a long drag on her Capstan Extra Strength.

The emotionally powerful film and the exotic meal kept the quartet in high spirits and Sheena suggested they come in to her house for a nightcap. Quickly, Hattie feigned fatigue and they decided to call it a day. Sandy deposited Willie and began to head for Oakside Avenue.

"I've magically revived, Sandy. How about you?"

"Uh-huh. I feel great."

"There's a quiet wee lane on the other side of Overtoun Park. Why don't we drive there for a while? We could discuss the film."

"What film?" Sandy laughed as he reached across and squeezed her thigh.

They slipped into the dark cul-de-sac, unlit and overhung by trees from the park. Sandy switched off the lights and, without speaking, they got out and moved to the back bench seat. In minutes Sandy was sitting in his underpants, Hattie on his knee, her skirt hitched up round her waist. They kissed and explored each other with abandon.

"Christ, Hat! I'm sweating like a bull."

"I can smell you, delicious man!"

"Hang on!" He rolled down a window. That's a fraction better. We'll have to keep our passion sotto voce or all the voyeurs in the area will be homing in on us."

Hattie was not listening. She slithered to her knees and removed Sandy's underpants. In the dim light she examined him closely. "You're beautiful, Sandy," she whispered hoarsely. Taking him in hand she tongued him to a pulsing erection.

Sandy moaned. "Go on, Hat. A bit more please. God, that's sublime!"

"Oh no you don't, my boy! Just think of something else for a moment. Hattie's going to get her share too."

Rising slightly she lent over to her bag on the front seat and fished out a slim packet.

Hattie supposed she'd known all along that a really serious clash with her father was eventually going to be unavoidable. It occurred one Saturday after lunch in the usual, chronically strained atmosphere.

"Your degree will be through soon, Harriot. Can you tell me if you've formulated any future plans yet?"

"I thought I'd wait till I definitely know the result." She already knew this was going to end in disagreement. It was just a question of how vitriolic or otherwise her dear father turned out to be today.

"Do you doubt you've passed?"

"No, I suppose not."

"Well then?"

Hattie took a quick drink of water. Charlotte was clearing away plates and cutlery to the kitchen for washing.

"I've told you before I don't want to teach."

"Yes, we've been treated to a steady flow of negativism for the last year or two. When you've deigned to speak on the subject at all that is. What I'd like to know is when you propose to earn a living and how. Don't you think I'm entitled to ask?"

Nervously Hattie ran her fingers through her hair. She felt very much like a cigarette but her father didn't approve and so she avoided lighting up in his presence. Charlotte had picked up the thread of the conversation. She too could see the looming risk of a row.

"Robert, there do seem to be plenty of jobs available these days. I'm sure Hattie will find something suitable."

"Then let her speak up."

"I'm pretty sick of book work, Dad. I need a rest from it. Maybe I could do something in one of the big department stores for a while."

"A shop assistant? Surely you can set your sights a bit higher than that, girl?"

"I only meant temporarily. Sheena has a friend who's just finished at St Andrews. She's working in the bar at Cathkin Golf Club."

"Pulling pints for those idlers," Robert exploded. "What a reward for years of self-sacrifice by your mother and me that would be." His eyes narrowed. "Perhaps the girl has other objectives? No doubt the golfing gentlemen are always on the lookout for a woman who is free with her favours."

"Robert! That's a *terrible* thing to say." Charlotte could now smell real danger in the air. "Hattie was just talking about the sort of holiday jobs she might do."

"I know, Charlotte, but the truth always hurts, doesn't it, Hattie?"

"I don't know what you're talking about, Dad."

"Oh yes you do. D'you think I'm blind, and stupid too? Don't you realise I know full well what you're up to, coming in at all hours, lying in bed half the morning. In some quarters of society there are nasty words to describe that kind of behaviour. I find it utterly disgusting the way you and your 'friends' go on. Nothing but pleasure-seeking in your silly heads. My God! If you'd only had half the hardship some of us had to put up with in our youth you'd sing a different tune!"

Robert was breathing hard after this speech. Charlotte

was about to try another peace-making intervention but Hattie waved her aside. This was hopeless. Her mother was too brow-beaten to stand up for her. Charlie had opted out. Why should she sit around here just waiting for her ill-disposed father to attack. If only he knew it, it was his treatment and peculiar, Victorian attitude to sex as much as anything that had made her rebel. Hattie felt quite self possessed.

"Would you please explain what you mean by 'that kind of behaviour'?"

"Whoring!" he exploded. "Like a woman of the streets, a prostitute!" His eyes were blazing.

Hattie stood up. She addressed Charlotte who was now crying in vexation. "That's it. I don't see why I should stay here and listen to any more of this. Excuse *me*." She left the dining room and went upstairs.

Presently her mother tapped on the bedroom door.

"Now, Hattie darling, you must calm down." Charlotte's anxious eyes were red. "Your father got carried away. I'm sure he didn't mean half of what he said."

"Well I'm afraid I'm not, Mum. His vocabulary may be limited but his opinion of me is *very* clear."

"He's a man of extremely strong feelings and opinions about how people should behave, Hattie. His own difficult childhood had a great effect on his character, you know."

"I don't see that that justifies making everyone else's life a misery."

Charlotte sighed, pulled a small handkerchief from her cardigan cuff and dried her eyes. "Because of his own father's weakness, and then his absence, Robert really became head of the house when he was quite young. I suppose he had to be tough, and it's left him intolerant of people who just seem to drift and behave . . . you know . . . sort of self-indulgently."

"Prostitutes like me, you mean?"

"Oh, Hattie, don't *say* that!"

"*He* did."

"Yes I know but I'm sure . . . "

"Forget it, Mum. Mr Murray and I have been on a collision course for a long time. Today we collided. QED."

Charlotte reached out and took her daughter's hand. "What will you do, Hattie?"

"Not sure yet but I must move out, Mum. You do see that?"

"Yes, Hattie. I understand."

"I think you've been the only reason I've stayed so long, Mum, but I've got my own life to think of. I'll be twenty one in no time." She smiled sadly at her mother who was showing signs of breaking down again. "I'll see you often, I expect. I just wish you'd tell him where to go sometimes. Was he *always* like this?"

The first hard blow of a malevolence that was to dog Robert Murray's young years fell only a few days after his birth. While he hungrily drew sustenance from his ill-nourished mother's breast PC MacPhater came up the close in Rosevale Street and into the cramped Murray dwelling.

"Mistress Murray, I have a message of sadness for you."

"Yes, Alasdair? Tell me quickly."

"It's James . . . an accident, I'm afraid. One of them accursed horse-buses in Dumbarton Road. Too fast they go."

"What happened, please?" Martha was impatient to know the worst.

"It seems that James had been in Molly Flanagan's place. They say he was walking like a blind man, not minding his safety at all, at all. The poor man just fell under the hooves and wheels. They got him up to the infirmary in Byres Road pretty quick though."

"And is he . . . "

But PC MacPhater was shaking his big head.

"I'm told he was with his Maker before the doctors could get a right look at him. Ach, Mistress Murray, I'm that sorry. And you with the new bairn and all. May the Blessed Virgin herself watch over you in her graciousness."

Thus began a long chapter of back-breaking toil and unrelenting poverty. For a time Martha grieved for her lost husband, but it was the memory of a man who had vanished years earlier that she truly mourned. As the months went by, even that fond memory was erased by the ceaseless labour of sewing, laundering and tending the four children. Soon Martha felt only a burning resentment at her plight. What right had James had to drink himself into an early grave? What of her and the brood of children he'd fathered? Why should she be condemned to a life of misery on account of his cruel selfishness?

As the older children grew Martha was compelled to push them out into the mean streets, there to consort with the urchins of the district. She made one more trip to Mauchline but her parents had aged and the family was almost as poor as she. Little Robbie was her one comfort. Bright-eyed and quick to understand he gave his mother no trouble once he was past the infant stage. In no time, it seemed, he had learned to help Martha fold up and bundle the laundry. Often she'd impulsively hug the serious little boy.

"Ah, Robbie, what would I do without you, my dear? You're more good to me than your father ever was." Her reward was a puzzled smile from her son.

"Mama, why did Papa die?"

"You know, Robbie. He had an accident."

"Is it right he was drunk?"

"Maybe. He had a little weakness that way. But just you

remember, Robbie, that your Papa was a fine gentleman. He was one of a good family and I want you to grow up a gentleman too."

Little Robert, looked round the drab room. "Yes, Mama. I promise to remember." The sight of her tear-filled eyes made his own smart.

Martha saw to it that all four children attended the elementary school, even if on occasion they had to bear the humiliation of arriving shoeless. But only Robert showed an interest in schoolwork. At thirteen Isabella had been found to be suffering from tuberculosis and the disease rendered her apathetic. The twins, Hugh and Willie, were eager to quit school as soon as possible and, at fourteen, found jobs as sweepers-up in a Govan shipyard.

The years dragged by and Robert went on to the Higher Gràde School aided by the sacrifice of the twins' meagre contribution to the household. He studied constantly, supplementing his knowledge by borrowing books from the public library and reading the daily newspapers displayed there.

At seventeen Bella died and Robert wept silently for the hopeless wreck of his kindly, wistful sister's life. The twins became men and moved out into nearby lodgings. Now Robert and his mother were alone. She was never failing in her encouragement of the adolescent boy in his studies. The servitude of years had taken its toll and Martha, suddenly lined and stooped, gladly ceded her domestic position to Robert. He took over their careful budgeting, ensured they did not pay a penny more than necessary for supplies, insisted that laundry customers pay more, exacted maximum credit terms from the small shops in their quarter of Partick.

The Great War came and engulfed the community. Hugh and Willie volunteered. Soon they were swaggering about the district in the dashing MacKenzie tartan trews and khaki tunics of privates in the Highland Light Infantry. But the glamour was short-lived and they were quickly taken off to a training camp in Yorkshire. Robert's eyes had never been strong and Martha was intensely relieved to hear that he would not be acceptable for military service. It appeared that he had badly strained his sight through years of study by the single guttering gaslight on the wall at Rosevale Street. He finally left school and obtained a beginner's post in the British Linen Bank.

Robert was determined to progress rapidly. Apart from his own ambition he was eager to earn enough to relieve his mother of the drudgery of doing other people's washing. He observed her bent back, her now permanently red, swollen hands, rivulets of perspiration running down her deeply etched face, and ached with sympathy and love. These painful emotions were shot through with a virulent hatred, if seldom openly expressed, of his wastrel father, the cause of his adored mother's degradation.

In 1915 came the national disaster of Gallipoli. Robert returned from the bank one evening to find his mother slumped at the ironing table, a telegram open before her. The War Office deeply regretted to inform Mrs M Murray that her sons, Hugh and William, had both been lost in the Expedition, fighting bravely for King and Country. Martha never recovered properly from this last cruel shock.

Robert was doing well. He'd been promoted to the post of assistant teller and his income at last was sufficient to enable his mother to give up the laundering and mending. But she didn't seem to know what to do with her new-found leisure. The respite had come too late. She'd pull her old Paisley shawl close round her shoulders and sit for long hours when Robert was out, looking vacantly about her. Martha's spirit had been broken. As the war neared its end she died silently one night in the cavity bed, utterly worn out in body and mind.

Robert's grief was unassuageable. For weeks he wept at night in the darkness of the room at Rosevale Street. He wished desperately that his mother were alive, that he could again comfort her, perhaps buy her a small gift. He heard Martha's voice quite clearly. "Now, Robbie, just you mind, your Papa was a gentleman. You have good blood in your veins. The Murrays are a high-born family. We may have come down in the world but that doesn't change things. You stick in at the bank. The cream always rises. You'll see."

He would smile to himself for a moment but then his mother's ravaged face would materialise vividly. Robert's bowels melted with tearful pity.

Eventually, he found an emotional equilibrium again and took up his bank work with new vigour. But it was not enough to fill his hours, to satisfy his questing mind, so he spent much time at the library reading a wide variety of books on many subjects. After a time he decided that literature drew him most and, in particular, poetry. He discovered Robert Burns and set himself to study the poet's life and everything he'd ever written.

A year after his mother's death Robert left Rosevale Street with no regret and took lodgings on the edge of the district of Kelvinside in the genteel West End of the city. He decided that this move should mark an important turning point. At twenty three, already a stern scholarly man, he made a solemn pact with himself, his determination granite-like, to succeed in life.

7

Two years earlier, in a distant English village near the country town of Burton-on-Trent in Staffordshire, a daughter had been born to Herbert and Harriot Browne. By 1920 little Charlotte had two baby sisters to play with in the meadows behind their cottage, Millie and Edwina. Herbert was a loving father, Harriot an efficient housewife. The Brownes were a happy family.

As a warehouse clerk at the local Ind Coope Brewery Herbert Browne's wage was low, but their needs were not extensive and country living was cheaper. Even so, Harriot had to budget carefully. Herbert was so vague, always dreaming about books and all that poetry he read. Not that he couldn't sometimes take his head out of the clouds and be quite strict, especially with the children. Harriot thought that there were many worse husbands she might have married.

As the eldest child, Charlotte was the first to discover the financial restraints her father's small income and swelling library imposed on the rest of the family. She was obliged to walk the three miles to and from school in Burton.

"Father doesn't earn much, Lottie pet, so we must all save what we can. Anyway, it's much nicer to walk in God's fresh air than to sit in that stuffy old bus, now isn't it? Look at your pretty complexion."

"Yes, Mother."

Secretly Charlotte wished she could take the bus, especially in winter, but well, there it was. She'd have to make the best of it. Her route was mainly past farms and along thick hedgerows. By the time she was nine Charlotte could name all the wild flowers in the district as they appeared each season. Her sisters were not really interested and just skipped along together behind her, intent on their own little games.

But as soon as Charlotte reached school her mood changed and she entered into her classes with enthusiasm. She loved the work, science studies and mathematics particularly, and was often top in those subjects. Millie and Edwina teased her for being a swot when she took pains in the evenings with her homework, but there was another element behind their censure. Charlotte was showing signs of growing into a beautiful young girl, tall for her age with wide-set dark eyes, delicate skin and lustrous golden hair cascading down her back. Only in needlework and knitting was there harmony, and the younger girls were glad enough of their sister's guiding hand.

Herbert noticed his eldest daughter's academic cast of mind but was disappointed that her inclination was not towards literature.

"Science, chemistry, engineering, medicine and the like are all very necessary, Lottie, especially in today's world. But only in great writing, and most of all poetry, can we find glimpses of the truth of things. It would please me if you also gave your attention to the English mistress, anyway as much as to science and mathematics."

"Yes, Father, I will."

"I'll draw up a list of works by fine authors and poets and you may read your way through it. They will all be in my collection."

Charlotte's interest in things scientific continued unabated as she matured but she also dutifully followed the literary path indicated by Herbert. By the time she was sixteen Charlotte Browne was an outstanding young woman, cultivated and good-looking, who was liked but feared a little too by her peers and teachers. There was talk of further education, scholarships, perhaps even Oxford. It was all utterly thrilling, and so buoyed up was she that even her sisters' derision about being a blue-stocking could do nothing to diminish Charlotte's hunger for the pursuit of knowledge. The prospect of going on to do real scientific research in fully equipped laboratories Charlotte found intoxicating.

She had one more year at school. Nothing and nobody was going to stop her passing out with as high marks and as much honour as she could possibly achieve.

Herbert was a gregarious man. Lack of money didn't trouble him much since the activities he favoured involved little expenditure. These were literary in character. The main forum in which his wide reading found focus was the East Staffordshire Literary and Dramatic Society, and through its weekly meeting he met several people of standing in the local community. His profound knowledge, particularly of poetry, saved him from any feelings of social insecurity. Indeed, many of the members seemed to find his gentle ways most charming. He looked the part too, always wearing a smart Norfolk jacket, from the top pocket of which depended a large silk handkerchief. His iron-grey hair and Vandyke beard lent him a grave authority when declaiming.

The chairman of the literary section was George Beaton, an energetic, if somewhat dilettante Scots doctor who had come to Burton as a young man. Originally the locum position was for a month only, but this had had to be extended owing to the sudden illness of one of the partners in the practice. In the end he'd stayed on, married a local girl and settled in Staffordshire. Now, forty five years later, Beaton was retired and able to devote his time to two main passions, trout fishing and poetry. Deriving from an old Edinburgh family he had inherited sufficient assets over the years to allow him now to travel widely and visit friends in many places.

One September evening in 1933 Beaton spoke to his fellow committee member after the weekly meeting at the Station Hotel.

"Well, Browne, what did you think of that?"

"Mr Knightley was certainly an enthusiastic lecturer but, to be frank, George, children's poetry through the ages is not a favourite subject of mine."

"Quite. I'm afraid a great number of these literary circuit wallahs are rather desiccated gentlemen."

George had bought his friend a glass of ale in the hotel bar. They drank thoughtfully.

"True literature is not such a cosy matter. It should shake one out of the rut. Even provoke revolutions. Stir up the reader at any rate."

"Mmm." Beaton looked into the middle distance. Slowly an idea formed in his mind. "Herbert, how are you getting on with that Burns collection I lent you?"

"Very well. I like the vernacular poems best. As long as the glossary does the translation work for me!"

"Yes. Rab's ventures into polite English lack pith. The love poems and his political pleas, *A man's a man* and so on – he needed his native Scots tongue to express those sublimities."

"But the thoughts were international, George."

Beaton took a deep draught of Ind Coope's best bitter

beer. "Come January twenty-fifth the Bard will be honoured in clubs all over the world. D'you think the worthy members of the East Staffs L and D could be induced to do the same?"

"What a capital idea, George!" Herbert's face registered sheer delight at this characteristically unexpected suggestion from his always surprising friend. "But you'd need to find an expert to interpret the verse. Unless you were thinking yourself to . . ."

"Ah no, Herbert. I love Burns but I wouldn't presume to lecture on him. No, I'd invite someone qualified to come down from Scotland."

"You know such a man?"

"Last time I was North I heard him speak in Glasgow – *Burns the Enduring Champion of the Oppressed* – or some such title. Profoundly inspiring address. I had a long talk with the man. He's contributed some fine analytical pieces to the *Burns Chronicle* too." Beaton's mind was already planning the Burns Supper. "I'm sure he'd accept if he's free."

"What's the man's name, George?"

"Oh, eh, Murray. Robert Murray."

In the wake of the War there was an acute shortage of able young men in the British Linen Bank, as in every area of industry and commerce. Robert's serious approach to his work and a natural agility of mind had ensured rapid progress through banking examinations and up the promotion ladder. As the Twenties blared the population's relief at the establishment of millennial peace, he worked steadily, ignoring the jazz age. Colleagues shimmied and Charlestoned in the evenings, humming the latest tune next morning, but Robert Murray was to be found studying either in his room or at the library.

He'd joined the Hillhead Parish Church and attended

mid-week meetings as well as Sunday services. He became a sidesman and was much respected in the congregation. When eventually he was asked to be one of those who read the lessons Robert felt proud. He remembered hearing that his grandfather had done the same in the English Church at Gothenburg. Robert often wondered about Edward Murray and his household, but the fact that his own father's wilful behaviour had deprived him of a rightful inheritance and, much more importantly, of an automatic position in the community, always edged his curiosity with bitterness. He never forgot his mother, Martha's, constant reminders of his pedigree, but this was no help as he struggled internally with a sense of social inadequacy. The brand of the slums was not easily eradicated.

The pugnacious egalitarianism of Burns made a natural and powerful appeal, particularly as the poet's political protest was conjoined to lines of ineffable beauty. For Robert, as well as being industrious to a fault, concealed in his nature a deeply romantic element. That he had recoiled in horror from alcohol in his earliest years, that at thirty five he was a celibate virgin he considered not at all inconsistent with his whole-hearted embracing of the poetry of one renowned for energetic tippling and womanising.

In 1929 Robert was sent to a branch of the Bank in the Dennistoun district of the city. It was further promotion and he was delighted to discover that the Manager, Mr Alexander Currie, shared his poetic enthusiasms. Sometimes the Curries would entertain their serious bachelor friend to supper, after which there would be readings. Whitman was a great favourite of Currie's. His hosts soon became aware of Robert's sympathy for and encyclopedic knowledge of the life and work of Burns and, through Mr Currie, an introduction to the Glasgow Ballad Club was arranged. Robert began to compose some verses of his own, and was thrilled to have one accepted by a local newspaper.

He now deputised for Currie if he was absent from the bank, and Robert found that he commanded the co-operation of the staff and the respect of the customers without difficulty. It was the beginning of a happy few years of consolidation.

One day in the summer of 1933 Currie called him into his office.

"Robert, sit down. Tea?"

"Thanks, Alec."

"I had a call from MacVey at Chief Office."

"Mr John MacVey? Yes, I met him once."

"Well, he's looking for a new manger. A vacancy's coming up over at Rutherglen next year."

"Next year's a bit away."

"Oh, they plan well ahead, Robert." There was a pause. "You can maybe guess why I'm being consulted?" Murray said nothing. "They've got their eye on you, Rob."

"I'm pleased to hear that. And will you recommend me, Alec?"

"I already have. There's only . . . "

Impulsively the younger man thrust out his right hand. "I . . . I . . . may I just thank you sincerely. It's very kind of you to . . . "

"All right, Rob. You've earned the chance and I'm only too pleased to do anything to help. There's just one matter." Currie poured more tea into both cups. "To put it bluntly, MacVey made it clear that they prefer their managers to be married."

"I see."

Currie let him think for a minute or two. Then, "What can I tell MacVey, Rob? I said I'd call him back, on a strictly confidential basis you understand, by the end of the week."

Murray didn't hesitate. With not the vaguest idea how he would redeem the pledge he replied evenly, "You can assure

Mr MacVey that I'll be a married man before 1934's out."

Currie looked closely at the earnest man before him. "Can you confide to an old friend the name of the lucky lady, Rob?"

Expressionlessly Murray stared back. "Not yet, Alec."

"No. Of course these things are very private. I understand, Rob." But he again looked curiously at his subordinate. A good man Robert Murray but strange in some ways, strange.

Soon after this Robert was the speaker at a Ballad Club meeting. Discussing aspects of his beloved Burns' poetry he greatly impressed the audience with the freshness of his approach, and afterwards, at question time, his total grasp of the subject became evident to all. It was a triumph. Now, a month or two later, here was a letter inviting him to give the Immortal Memory oration to a literary club in Burton-on-Trent – he'd never even been south of the Border! Dr Beaton had certainly been flattering about his talk, but Robert had not dreamed that meeting him would lead to this adventure. Next day he arranged to take a week's leave in the latter part of January.

Autumn slipped away. In the dark winter mornings, as he sat huddled in his black topcoat and homburg on an early tramcar to Dennistoun, Robert experienced uncomfortable sensations of pounding energy which made him perspire. His life was surely on the verge of a giant step forward. In the church he was now on the Kirk Session, an elder. What he needed was an uplift financially and socially to match those achievements, and this was now within his grasp in the next few months if he could secure the Rutherglen managership.

Although this earnest, sober man had for years successfully sublimated any sexual urges through habits of industrious activity, there were of course times of lonely privacy when fantasies of the naked female form taunted him. Saint Anthony-like he'd sometimes wrestle in the night with insistent, gnawing desire. Not infrequently he'd awake in tumid desperation, just in time to know the thrusting power of his sexuality as he surrendered to voluptuous spasms of release. That Christmas, often alone in his room listening to selected musical programmes on the wireless, Robert realised for a certainty that the key to his future happiness, his business progress, even his health, lay in taking a wife. On Ne'erday 1934, when he called in the morning by custom for ginger wine and shortbread, the Curries thought they observed a new lightness of step in their guest.

He prepared his address with great care, keeping in mind that the audience would be largely unfamiliar with Burns. Poetic illustrations of his points he chose for their intelligibility to an English ear. Judging by the applause on the night, his speech was thoroughly understood and appreciated. George Beaton had procured the services of a London Scottish piper and himself gave the *Address to the Haggis* with gusto. Mrs Beaton had organised the fare and the occasion was generally agreed as likely to prove the best event of the L and D's calendar that winter.

Beaton introduced Robert to the members after the formal proceedings. They were a pleasant, unexceptional lot he thought, until Mr Browne was presented.

"Herbert Browne, Mr Murray. A good friend of mine who knows a bit more about the Bard than most of these Sassenachs!"

They laughed together. Browne soon confirmed Beaton's remark with a couple of searching questions about the folksong origins of some of Burns's poems. Robert answered with his usual authority. Mr Browne was obviously someone he could happily converse with, perhaps he'd see him again before returning to Scotland. But Robert's eyes were elsewhere. A striking young woman with a glory of long golden hair and finely coloured skin was approaching.

"Ah, Lottie. Mr Murray, this is my daughter, Charlotte. I brought her along tonight instead of her mother. Mrs Browne's not so keen on poetry."

They shook hands. How cool her grasp was, somehow gentle and firm at the same time.

"I hope the dialect wasn't too hard for you to follow, Miss Browne?"

"Not at all, Mr Murray. You made it wonderfully clear."

She smiled widely, generously, revealing strong white teeth set regularly in healthy pink gums. As her face relaxed again she moistened her lips with the tip of her tongue. Robert was seized by a violent attraction to this girl. He swallowed quickly and politely returned her smile.

"I think maybe one has to come to England to appreciate just how foreign Burns can seem."

And if Charlotte Browne had merely nodded graciously and passed on at that moment that might have been an end of it. But she'd not followed her father's literary agenda for nothing.

"Of course I know what you mean, Mr Murray, but Burns is perhaps better understood than you imagine. Look at our John Clare for instance. And he lived in Northamptonshire, south of here."

"John Clare? You mean the author of *The Shepherd's Calendar*?"

"Yes. He knew his Burns all right and modelled a good deal of his poetry on Burns's. He even used Scots words sometimes. Sir Walter Scott and he corresponded."

Robert was astounded. Not only was this information of riveting interest but that it should be imparted by this poised young beauty excited him profoundly.

Herbert Browne could not fail to notice the flattering

effect his daughter was having on this outstanding, if austere Scotsman. Before the evening's proceedings concluded it was understood that Robert would call on the Brownes the next morning.

8

SINCE THE FINAL BIG ROW with her father Hattie had felt paralysed. Her reactionary determination to leave home had given way to a miserable indecision. It was not that she lacked courage, just that she didn't honestly know where to go, what to do. Her mother tried to use this space to take the heat out of the situation.

"Hattie, I think if you just said 'sorry' to your father we could forget those intemperate words. I can't stand this unnatural silence much longer. It's killing me."

Hattie looked with sorrow at her unhappy mother but, despite the aching pity in her heart, her own spirit was undaunted. "I can't do that, Mum. I'd be betraying myself shamefully. It's up to *him* to apologise."

Charlotte dabbed her red eyes. "Yes, I suppose you're right. But he won't of course. Never would."

"And why not, for God's sake, if he's in the wrong? He's just a fallible human being like the rest of us. Mum, tell me, if he was always so arrogant how did you come to marry him in the first place? I mean, it's not as if you were some kind of Hindu peasant woman handed over in an arranged marriage or something."

"No, I wasn't."

"From what you've told me you were really bright, with university in prospect when you met."

"Oh yes, I was bright."

"Well?"

Charlotte sighed, closed her eyes and shook her head. "Robert was very persuasive you know, Hattie. He was thirty-eight to my seventeen. A mature, handsome man, with a great gift of the pen too."

"You mean those love poems? You showed them to me once but I can't remember them. Pretty old-fashioned stuff weren't they?"

"Maybe, but to a vulnerable young woman in 1934 who'd never been anywhere they were overwhelming. I remember some of them by heart." The familiar lines sounded again in Charlotte's head.

> *I leave this place tomorrow, dear,*
> *A barb is in the fleeting hours;*
> *The Trent's soft murmuring charms my ear*
> *While, in a dream, I linger here,*
> *Within these lovely bowers.*
> *Goodnight, beloved, shrine me in your heart*
> *As you are shrined in mine. – How bright*
> *The stars are shining, how the soft winds breathe*
> *The melody of love! – Goodnight.*
> *Sleep, loved one, in a trance of happy dreams*
> *Be darkness richer than the light;*
> *May dawn awake you with a thought of me. –*
> *Sleep, my beloved one. Goodnight.*

Again Charlotte shook her head.

"But he was so much older, Mum. I'm not saying he wasn't sincere, but couldn't you see . . . well . . . that he was just unsuitable for you?"

"Yes, Hattie, I wasn't blinded. In fact I fought hard for my independence."

"So? It wasn't the Victorian era."

"I had to reckon with my father too."

"But you've always said he was a kind man? Grandad's always seemed a nice old softie when I've met him."

"I know, but we were short of money. And I had two young sisters needing clothes. Anyway, I wanted to study science and Father didn't really approve."

"So he decided to marry you off?"

"It wasn't cold-blooded like that, Hattie. But he *was* enormously taken with Robert. After all, a well set-up professional banker with prospects who was also a literary man must have seemed terribly impressive. To a humble clerk like Herbert Browne anyway."

"Did you discuss things seriously with him?"

"I *pleaded* to be allowed to go on to university, Hattie. But it was no good. Robert and Father had made up their minds."

"Jesus wept!"

"Hattie, please don't swear."

"Oh, Mum! I just can't stand your *passivity*. Why didn't you run away? Or slash your wrists? Do *something* to stay free?"

"I nearly did run away. But then . . . "

"Then what?"

"Oh, I don't know. Robert is a very passionate man, Hattie. Every minute we were alone he was embracing me and asking for little favours. Physical intimacies. I suppose in the end he got me pretty worked up. I really knew nothing about sex then, but what with Robert pulling and Father pushing I just gave in I suppose."

Hattie frowned, her face suffused with anger. "What did

Grandma think about all this chauvinistic horse-dealing?"

"Poor mother. She never had any say in things. Nothing important anyway."

"There you are. Your whole life decided in a few days by two totally self-centred men. And since then you've been subjected to nearly a quarter of a century of exploitation. That kind of behaviour merits the rope in my opinion."

"Hattie! Try not to be so *extreme*. And what do you mean 'exploitation'? Robert has worked hard at the bank, and he's written some fine poetry too. We've had a good enough life."

"And you? What of *your* potential have you realised."

"I've two children."

"Anyone can do that. But you had *talent* which was sacrificed to enable *men* to follow their own bloody stars. I call that exploitation, Mum."

Charlotte looked at her daughter's vibrant, intelligent face, her fearless eyes. She was right of course. A bit unfairly black and white no doubt but, fundamentally, right in her assessment. Charlotte's life stretched behind her. She saw Robert working at the bank or writing in seclusion, the children moving through the various phases of their growing up. S*he* was only a shadowy background figure ministering to everyone else's needs, without personal preoccupations. Weakly she smiled. "Hattie darling, I just hope you'll find a happy path and do everything in life you want to do."

Hattie's heart was thumping. She wasn't finished. "We don't have to go into it, but the other massive injustice is sexual exploitation. Men have always taken their pleasure when *they* felt like it and women have been expected to oblige, whether they wanted to or not. It's written into religion and the Law, but that doesn't make it morally right."

Charlotte remembered the terror of her early days with Robert. Although the theoretical facts of life had been clear enough to her, on a personal level she'd truly not known what to expect. At times he'd seemed to her like a wild animal in his demands. She'd tried to make allowances for a torrent of pent-up desire, but he'd seemed insatiable. The first year or two he'd come home from work at lunchtime several days a week to tumble her into bed. Sometimes he'd take her as soon as he got in, on the kitchen table.

She was frightened by his red penis, his driving maleness. There had been no pleasure in those confrontations and often she'd realised she was in fact being raped. But Charlotte had been brought up to be obedient, never to forget her solemn promises, and so she did her best to smile and to hide her hurt. Secretly she felt guilty and inadequate. Years later, spring cleaning, she'd stumbled on notes for a poem he'd hidden with some papers. She was pierced to the heart.

> *She gave him all she could, but it was never all he asked,*
> *And he could never guess indeed how much of her was masked.*
> *She gave her lovely body, coldly chaste but full and fair,*
> *That she might grant him, for sweet love, a child to speak for her.*
> *An early breath of frost will chill the garden's finest flowers,*
> *And only love can tempt them back to decorate the bowers.*
> *But though he loved with passion rare and waited many years,*
> *Yet never came in fullest flood the gush of generous tears.*
> *He never knew the joy of love,*
> *The soul-surrendering gift of love,*

*Love's rapture warm, responding, full –
Instead, obedience, beauty cool.*

"I think relations between men and women, in that sense, can be very complicated, Hattie. I wouldn't want to generalise."

"Well I'm afraid I would, Mum. When I think of the generations of women in this family alone and the way they were treated by their men, I get wild. I mean, you and your mother have been used and abused, whether you admit it or not, haven't you?"

"I've told you before, Hattie, Robert's upbringing gave him a strong sense of the male role in domestic matters. His own mother encouraged him to take a firm hand and give a lead. As you know, your grandfather was weak and . . . "

"Just because Martha Byrnie had the misfortune to marry a drunken layabout in Jamie Murray, have we got to allow her son to walk all over us as he pleases? Not me anyway, Mum."

"Oh come on, Hattie. Be reasonable."

"Is my dearest father reasonable with me? Was Jamie reasonable with Martha? Come to that I'll bet old Gothenburg . . . what was his name . . . ?"

"Edward Murray. And Jean."

"Right. Edward. I bet he was anything but reasonable with Jean. In fact isn't he the one who kept a mistress?"

Charlotte stared wearily out of the window. "Yes, Hattie, that was Edward."

"Well, Mum, if that isn't a rogues' gallery of selfish, chauvinistic bloody men I'd like to know what it is. I'm really sorry you're stuck with it, but you'd better take it from me that yours truly is not going to be beholden to any member of the opposite sex – *ever*!"

Charlotte's eyes were again misting. She'd had to admit

painfully to herself some time ago that her son, Charlie, had reacted to his father's domineering regime by seeking the company of gentler souls. That he was by now fixed in a homosexual way of life she didn't doubt. Had she done wrongly in the past by shielding him from Robert, by giving him too rich a measure of maternal love? She ached for Charlie. And now Hattie. Could she take care of herself, avoid the aridity of spirit which Charlotte felt certain would be the inevitable sequel to prolonged promiscuity? Many of these opinions and protests were intellectually quite coherent of course, but life was more complex. Would Hattie, dear Hattie who'd been such a bright affectionate little girl, would she come to grips with the realities of the world before it was too late? Charlotte allowed herself to weep a little before leaving her daughter's bedroom.

Hattie lit a cigarette shakily and lay back on her bed. Somehow, articulating her anger that afternoon finally crystallised many feelings about men which hitherto had been less definite in her mind. A steely resolve entered the inner citadel of her spirit. She'd use men as they'd always used her kind, for her own pleasure and without according them any particular respect. Hattie was filled with her perception of the accumulated womanly resentments of generations.

That morning Sheena McHugh rang. They met in a coffee bar.

"Come on then, Sheena, what's this big news? Are you engaged, or pregnant, or both, or what?"

Sheena giggled. "You've got a one track mind, Hattie Murray. No, I've got a job."

"Big deal."

"In London."

"So!" Hattie raised her eyebrows and slowly exhaled a stream of smoke to emphasise her surprise and interest.

"I didn't tell you I'd applied in case it came to nothing. Anyway, I went down last week for interview and got the OK this morning. It's great, isn't it, Hat?"

"What's the job?"

"Oh, in London University's Central Library. They're apparently going in for a large-scale reorganisation, so they've taken on a few arts graduates to help out. Actually, it sounded really interesting."

"Congratulations, my old china. And are they paying you a fortune?"

"This is where maybe you come in, Hat. No, it's only peanuts, a beginner's money. But I have to live and that means sharing a flat with someone."

"You mean you and I . . . ?"

"I don't fancy moving in with a complete stranger. You're always saying you want to get away, Hat."

"Sheena, you've saved my life! Count me in. When do we go?"

"Steady now! I have to report for work on the tenth of next month. We could shoot down on the overnight bus. Cheaper than the train. One day should be enough to find a place and sign a lease if we get our skates on."

"Where on earth would we start, Sheena? London might as well be outer Mongolia as far as I'm concerned."

"Earls Court seems to be the best bet. There are plenty of house agents around. Listen, can you mange financially, Hat?"

"I've got a few bob in my piggy bank. Enough to tide me over till I find a job. Oh, Sheena, this is fantastic! Thanks a million."

"It'll be lovely to have you with me in the big bad city, Hat."

And so, not many weeks later, the two girls were established in a small two-bedroomed flat in Bramham

Gardens, SW5. Hattie worked for a while as a waitress in a café patronised mainly by students. Then, after two interviews, she was taken on by a publishing house as a trainee in their children's books division. London was new and exciting but an element was missing. Hattie brought the subject up.

"Sheena, I enjoy your company very much but don't you think we need some trousers round here?"

"Amen. But who?"

"Well, there's a rather gorgeous character I've passed the time of day with in our thriller section. Very pukka type but decorative. Beautiful long legs."

"Oh, Hat!" Sheena laughed out in delight. "D'you mean you'd simply go up to him and say, 'excuse me but you're taking me out next Friday'?"

"More or less. And why not? Especially if I offer to split the cost."

"I suppose so."

"And can Central Library produce a suitably endowed young man for you?"

"Well, there's Alan Foster. I've had a coffee with him in the refectory. He's no oil painting but he's fun. I like him."

"Right. You ensnare your Alan and I'll tackle Nicholas. Next Friday sound good? We'll just eat here. Let's see what they're made of, Sheena."

It was an amusing evening. The girls enjoyed laying a smart table in the kitchen, chequered cloth, candle in bottle, and preparing a spicy spaghetti dish. The young men seemed to fill the cramped room, especially Nicholas Whiteford whose six feet three inches simply couldn't be accommodated at the small table with any degree of comfort. There was much laughter.

Over coffee it emerged that Nick's family lived somewhat grandly in Somerset. Alan's father held an appointment in local government in Leeds. Both men were clearly taken with their new, slightly madcap Scottish girlfriends, and it was agreed they'd all meet again the following week, venue to be decided. Before they left Hattie found an excuse of something in her room she wanted Nick to see. Once inside she boldly embraced him and offered her open mouth for his kiss. As he bent his head to meet hers Hattie saw in his wide open eyes a mixture of apprehension and lust. He was a virgin. She just knew it. The thought was teasingly aphrodisiac – in seconds she'd touched him lightly and confirmed that he was already rampant.

"I say, Hattie, you're wonderful! I wish I could stay a bit."

"Yes, so do I, Nick, but I've got to consider Sheena. I'll talk to her. Maybe next time."

"Oh, yes please."

There was no difficulty with Sheena. Both girls wanted to make the most of their freedom. And so the following Friday evening by ten thirty they'd paired off into the bedrooms. Doors were kept ajar and occasional leg-pulling remarks were shouted back and forth. But while Sheena and Alan were merely curled up affectionately on the bed leafing through Sheena's photo album, a few yards away much heavier intimacies were in progress. In fact Hattie had taken off her sweater and bra. Nicholas was minus his trousers. Soon the compelling need was for skill in avoiding bedspring creaks while making rapid, but stealthy love. Nick had little control and so the risk of giving themselves away was short lived. Throughout, Hattie amazed her panting partner not only by providing him with a contraceptive but by continuing to chat with the others as if nothing in particular was happening.

It was not long before the charade ended and Nick was spending Friday nights at Bramham Gardens sleeping with Hattie. The trouble was that although Sheena's friendship with Alan Foster was warm enough they were just not ready to emulate the other two. By midnight Alan would take his leave. Inevitably, tension developed between the two girls. Sheena became withdrawn and Hattie resented her attitude. Whether her frowns stemmed from disapproval or simple jealousy was unclear to Hattie.

Matters came to a head one Saturday morning. The quartet had consumed a large curry meal at an Indian restaurant the previous evening and drunk several pints of German lager to slake raging thirsts. The fiery food had not agreed with Sheena and at 6 a.m. she sat on the WC in diarrhoeic misery. Anxiously she eyed the defective door bolt. Then – horrors! In burst a naked Nick in desperation to urinate.

"Sorry, old girl! But needs must I'm afraid."

So saying he turned to the washhand basin and, hand on hip, proceeded to relieve the pressure on his bladder with a grand insouciance. Sighing luxuriously he shook himself dry and departed with a cheery grin to the other occupant of the bathroom.

But Sheena was not amused. She had been mortified by the incident and lost no time when Nick had gone to criticise his public schoolboyish lack of sensitivity. Hattie felt herself included in Sheena's shrill complaints and realised, as she defended Nick, that she'd have to leave the flat.

9

HATTIE MOVED TO an even smaller place in Weymouth Mews, Marylebone. She'd have to be frugal, but the propinquity of sweeping white Nash terraces on the edge of Regents Park, the chic of Harley Street and Manchester Square, the rather bohemian atmosphere of the High Street – all fascinated Hattie. She experienced a surge of optimism, a feeling that somehow she'd finally arrived, that doors were opening and that she could do anything she chose with her life.

She was promoted and entrusted with the writing of simple children's book jacket blurbs, and it was a thrill to see her words in print on publication day. When she was busy Hattie was happy. But most of her colleagues seemed to be from the Home Counties and to return home at weekends. Nick played cricket in summer and shot in the winter. There were interminable Sundays to be endured on her own. Sheena and she had managed to patch up things and sometimes they'd walk in the park or meet for a simple supper together. But their interests were diverging. Sheena was looking for stability and a husband; Hattie's ambitions were not fully formed. She was open to everything, her horizons limitless. They stopped seeing each other at all regularly.

One grey Sunday afternoon in November Hattie threw down her newspaper. She'd begun to reread items.

"Christ! I'm bored," she announced to the empty room. In the silence her words sounded awesomely incantatory. Hattie shuddered. She needed action and, yes dammit, she hissed through clenched teeth, a man. Suddenly she thought of the Tropicana coffee house in the High Street.

All was light, gurgling espresso machines and thudding juke box music in the overheated Tropicana. Hattie sat at the counter, lit a cigarette and ordered a coffee. At a table against the wall she noticed a white-blonde student type on his own. Their eyes met. Hattie smiled. He returned a grin but looked down again at his magazine. She surveyed the other customers one by one but found no faces to interest her particularly. Looking back to the wall table again she was surprised to see that the blonde young man had left his seat.

"Excuse please. Can I sit here?"

It was the student.

"Yes, of course. I thought you'd gone."

"No. I went to lavatory, then I think, 'pretty lady smile to me so why not I speak with her?'"

Hattie laughed at his quaint language. "Why not indeed?"

"Excuse my English, please. I am Norwegian come to London for engineering studies."

"Really. And how do you like London?"

"Much. But now I finish. Leave tomorrow. Six months course over."

"Perhaps you'll come back."

"No. I stay in Norway. Please, I am Pietersen, Karl Pietersen." He offered his hand. "You?"

"I'm Hattie Murray. Hello Karl."

She took his hand. His grip was so firm it almost hurt. There was a pause. "It's hot in here. How about some air?"

"We walk together? Thank you! I like very much. Many

months I have not walked with a lady."

"Where on earth have you been?"

"In factory hostel. Too dull."

"Oh dear."

They meandered up the High Street and into the park. Darkness was descending. On a bench they tried to converse but Karl's English made this more of a trial than a pleasure. They got up and began to leave the park. It would be locked up soon. Just outside the gates in the Marylebone Road their hands accidentally touched. Hattie grasped Karl's fingers in an instinctive friendly reaction. She was not prepared for her new friend's response. Grabbing her by the shoulders he spun her round to face him and kissed her forcefully. In the gathering darkness she sensed his coiled strength.

"Steady now, Karl!" she stammered.

"But I love you, Hattie!"

"Oh, for goodness sake. You . . . "

"I must make love with you. Now please."

Hattie swallowed hard in an effort to display some composure. "You're crazy, Karl. You just met me."

"Tomorrow I leave. Maybe I never see you again."

"Well, come on and I'll give you something to eat at my place. But no promises except that. Understand?" Hattie tried to laugh.

"You have house here to sleep?"

"A very small flat."

On the walk to Weymouth Mews Hattie elicited from Karl that he lived in Bergen and, although still only twenty, had had a surprising number of girlfriends. However, he solemnly advised her, he was currently quite free. Fleetingly Hattie wondered at the sheer quantity of Karl's inamoratas.

Hattie poured two mugs of instant coffee. While they drank this she learned that Karl's intention was to make his way out to Heathrow and sleep the night there, on the floor if necessary, before catching his flight at 0930 hrs.

He put his mug down empty. "Now we make love, Hattie. Where is your bed?"

"My God, Karl, you're to the point! Don't they teach you how to approach a lady in Norway?" Hattie smiled at him maternally.

"I am sorry if I say wrong. But you do not remember it is six months since I have touched any womans." His face was blank. He was absolutely serious.

Hattie realised it was pointless to fence with him. Either she told him to go or they got on with it. In one glance she took in the thick blond hair curling on his wrists, the sturdy neck, the strong, perfect teeth, the powerful thighs straining his corduroy trouser legs. "Come on, Karl. Let's make up for lost time."

His body was as hard and muscular as she'd expected, and as she watched him undress a wave of frantic longing to be possessed by him swept her to near fainting. But now he was on her, biting her nipples and unceremoniously spreading her legs. She cried out, "Don't hurt me, Karl! Stop biting."

He lifted his face and kissed her, his tongue pushing down her throat till she gagged. Then he had entered her, thrusting long and deep, time and time and time again till Hattie lost track of events. For the first time in her life she'd found a really practised lover and she abandoned herself wholeheartedly to him. He brought her to orgasm several times but still didn't give himself release. On and on he hammered at her. His control was incredible.

"Oh God, Karl, please come now!" she pleaded, anxiety and ecstasy equal in her small voice.

But Karl paid more heed to Hattie's eloquent thighs which she clamped ever more eagerly around his hips. Finally, in a paroxysm of lust, he disengaged sufficiently to heave his shoulders under the backs of her knees. Gripping Hattie's buttocks with vice-like fingers he forced himself into her more deeply than before, and in this position lunged repeatedly until he had to give way to his own obliterating, scalding orgasm.

From start to finish he uttered not a sound apart from hoarse breathing. Now he simply rolled on his back and promptly fell asleep.

Hattie was floating in another realm where huge pink waves crashed and brilliant lights of every colour flashed and pulsed. The air was balmy and exotic, thick-feathered birds nestled warmly against her bare skin. Only very slowly did she return to reality. In the bathroom it took her a while to minister to herself. There'd been no time to use a contraceptive, even if Karl had been prepared to, so she wanted to make sure she douched herself as effectively as possible. Soon she was sleeping as deeply as the golden stranger at her side.

Not for long. The first Hattie knew she was already penetrated and Karl was hard at it, his libido evidently undiminished. At first it was painful, for she was raw, but as the love juices began to flow Hattie clung greedily to the body swinging above her. Oh Christ! It was going to be even better this time. The session was mercifully shorter but the grinding, explosive climax no less shattering.

It was the same in the greyness of five in the morning. Hattie awoke to feel Karl's hard penis head being pushed between her lips. She reached out and switched on the bedside light without moving her head, and looked up the length of his blond-hirsute torso. Kneeling, he tightened his knees against her ears and gave a rare smile.

"Please to give him little suck to say good-morning."

Raising her head from the pillow Hattie obliged generously, and in minutes they were again locked in a tight, conjoined embrace. Karl was less dominating this time. He allowed

Hattie to squat over him, first facing and then reversed. She held on to his toes for leverage and did not object when he dug his fingers into her already bruised buttocks. The voluptuous waves she was generating at will, as she flicked her rump up and down on his ramrod-stiff penis, crowded out everything else.

It was too late to sleep again. Another cup of coffee and Karl was gone with his bag to the airport. There had been no exchange of telephone numbers, employers' names, nothing. As Hattie washed and again doctored herself before going to work she knew that her behaviour had been highly unconventional, to say nothing about morals. An unknown man picked up in a coffee-bar and taken straight to bed – wow! How had it happened? Was she normal? Apart from an aching tail she felt normal enough.

After breakfast of juice, muesli, sliced banana and more coffee she felt full of energy, euphoric, and several times caught herself grinning as she savoured her secret adventure.

Travelling in the tube later she remembered Nick and almost laughed out. How could she stomach his apologetic, inept efforts at love-making after Karl? OK, Karl was some kind of throwback, a beast, and it wasn't surprising that he couldn't find a nice young Norwegian lady to stay the course! But Nick – oh dear. Hattie determined to give him his marching orders without delay.

They met in the office reception foyer.

"Oh, hello, Hattie. Good weekend?"

"Fine. You?"

"We were down at Shamley Green. A village league fixture you know. Well, actually, I got a six."

"Oh, well done, Nick!"

He acknowledged her congratulations with sheepish pleasure.

"Are we all right for Friday evening, Hattie?"

"As a matter of fact, Nick, I don't think so."

"Oh. Something come up?"

"Not really."

Nick suddenly coloured. "You don't mean you... surely...?"

"Look, this is neither the time nor the place for this, Nick."

Looking crestfallen he enquired quietly, "Could we have lunch and talk it over?"

"I've got a meeting."

"Oh."

He looked so miserable that Hattie said over her shoulder as she made for her office, "Give me a ring in the evening at the flat if you like."

He called that night.

"Oh, it's you, Nick."

"Hattie, I can't believe you're giving me up. I've thought and thought about it but I can't guess what I've done wrong."

"You've *done* nothing, Nick."

"Well then, can't we...?"

"Listen, our relationship was never for ever, was it? We're free agents, aren't we?"

"Yes, of course, but I thought, well at least I hoped that you rather liked me, Hattie."

"I think we need a change, Nick. That's all."

Hattie thought she heard a sniff on the line.

"That's a bit callous, Hattie, isn't it? Is there no chance we could...?"

"Nick, it's not going to help if we prolong things."

There was a long pause.

"Hattie I won't be able to stay in my job, seeing you every day and not being able to..."

There was a muffled sob.

"That's up to you of course, Nick. I don't really think

you have to leave. You'll get over . . . "

"But I *love* you, Hattie darling! I don't know what I'll do without you."

"You'll go on playing cricket and shooting defenceless birds, Nick. *And* you'll find a nice new girlfriend in no time."

There was a burst of weeping. Then eventually, "Hattie?"

"Yes, Nick? Do cheer up."

"I'll never meet anyone like you again." Then he was crying again.

"I'm putting the phone down, Nick. Get a grip of yourself."

Groans of distress were still emanating from the earpiece as Hattie replaced the receiver. Weak fool, she thought, suddenly filled with contempt.

Nick was as good as his word. He resigned from his job the following day.

Hattie went home for Christmas. She didn't really want to, but her mother was pressing and the prospect of the festive season largely on her own was not appealing. She found her father more morose than ever. Too many harsh words had passed between them for a happy relationship to be re-established now. He did show an interest in Hattie's work in the publishing world, and they were able to discuss it with some animation. However, since Hattie volunteered no information about any other subject, the customary tension between them quickly returned.

Hattie knew that her father guessed much about her relations with men and condemned her behaviour. For his part, Robert Murray realised that his spirited daughter nursed a root and branch disapproval of most of what he believed in. Although she couldn't know the half he recognised too that she blamed him totally for the unhappiness in her parents' marriage. And no doubt for Charlie's pathetic way of life too. They had ceased to argue. It was bitter stalemate.

"Dad doesn't improve, Mum."

"He's had a lot to contend with lately, Hattie. Don't be too hard."

"What's the problem then?"

"Robert's always wanted to make a top job in the Chief Office before he retired."

"He's still talking about that? He's barely a year to go."

"I think he'd resigned himself to missing it but a vacancy came up last month. Someone retired unexpectedly. Robert applied. He got on the short list."

"But he wasn't picked?"

Charlotte shook her head sadly. "No. They chose a slightly younger man. MacIntosh."

"It's not the end of the world, is it, Mum?"

"Of course not, but it wounded Robert badly. It seems Mr MacIntosh had a rather fancier education than Robert. He's a member of the Clyde Yacht Club, plays golf at Haggs Castle and so on. Robert never took up golf. His poetry was his world, but it's not everyone's cup of tea of course. It seems hard after twenty five years of faithful service here in Rutherglen. All through the war with a skeleton staff too. It would have given a nice lift to our pension."

Hattie wanted to be fair. It was too bad her parents weren't going to get a consolation prize, but then maybe there were others who didn't care for Robert Murray's dour, holier-than-thou ways. Maybe his ultimate career failure was not so surprising. All she said was, "I'm sorry about it, Mum, but he mustn't expect me to change any of my attitudes just because he's been bilked of a job he wanted."

"No, dear."

Hattie was helping her mother with the preparation of the Christmas Day turkey. Her eyes watered as she chopped an onion.

"What kind of skive is it Charlie's on in New York?"

"I don't fully understand, Hattie. There was a group of Americans at the art school earlier this year and Charlie's gone over to spend Christmas and New Year with them. I think the idea is that he stays at their college on an exchange basis for a month or two. He somehow talked the authorities into funding him."

"Enterprising."

Suddenly there was an unearthly scream from the sitting room. "CHARLO . . . TTE!"

Charlotte dropped her wooden spoon and rushed out of the room. Hattie followed.

"ROBERT!"

10

IT WAS A RELIEF to get back to London. During the holiday Hattie had met Sheena briefly but she was seeing Willie Shields again and talking about giving up her library job. It was amazing how they were growing apart. Hattie was eager to meet a wider circle of people in London, the more foreign the better, to expand her horizons. Sheena seemed too timid, in an irritated sort of way, to jump new social fences, and Hattie could see clearly that she would soon be married and settled in some comfortable suburb. Rutherglen had suddenly become claustrophobically provincial.

But it was her father's seizure which had dominated everything. They'd got him to hospital quickly and it had only been a mild attack but, even although he was home before the New Year, the doctor counselled against a return to work. There was some residual numbness in his left arm.

The worst aspect from Hattie's point of view had been her discovery that she was incapable of genuine sympathy when he was helpless and in some pain. Of course she did all she could to help and visited the hospital with her mother each day, but her instincts were those of an uninvolved nurse or health visitor. Worse still, when he came home Hattie's solicitousness had melted away and been replaced by a barely concealed resentful anger. It seemed to her that he had had things his own way all his married life and was now going to place an intolerable new burden on her mother. Charlotte was only forty three but she was ageing quickly. Robert could live another ten, twenty years, probably increasingly infirm, and it grieved Hattie to think that her mother might never achieve any degree of freedom while she was young enough to enjoy it. Her father's soulful glances from his chair in the sitting room infuriated Hattie.

There was a staff reshuffle at the office and Hattie was given some minor editorial responsibilities. Through this new work she met Kate Loxton, an author of charming storybooks for the seven to nine age bracket. Kate was also trying to have an adult novel published but was fortunate in having gained early acceptance with her children's books. She was still just twenty nine.

Soon after they met, Hattie and Kate had lunch together in a smart new bistro just opened near the office.

"Thank goodness for someone not *hopelessly* distanced from their own childhood to edit my little books, Hattie. Miss Jones was nearly a *hundred*."

"I'm really thrilled to be doing your work, Kate."

"I think we'll get on splendidly."

For the first time in her life Hattie tasted moules marinière. Kate held up her index finger and two waiters sprang forward. She smiled archly at them both.

"I don't need *two* of you!" The white-jacketed young Cypriots grinned happily at the joking double entendre. "Just one of you bring us a nice bottle of Chablis, please."

The meal was fun. Kate and Hattie found common ground straight away. At one point Hattie expressed surprise that such a startlingly attractive woman as Kate had avoided marriage so far.

"Marriage? Good God no, Hattie sweet! Friendship, yes. Slipper routine, absolutely no. Not to put too fine a point on it, I regard men, as they might term it in HM Forces, as 'us ladies for the use of'. Lord, that's not a particularly felicitous phrase, is it?"

They laughed as the slightly nervous waiter recharged their glasses. After sorbets and over coffee Kate produced a slim silver case containing small cigars. Hattie accepted one. She was an eager listener and Kate expanded in the flattery of Hattie's avid attention.

It transpired Kate had in fact been married at twenty one, a disaster which hadn't lasted a year.

"Poor Jeremy. He was really as queer as a coot, and the whole business must have been a terrible trial for him. I was climbing the walls at the end and I think he wasn't far off doing himself in. Thank heaven we had the sense to quit, even though everyone disapproved in 1951. We were so naive."

She described amusingly various subsequent adventures, always involving a man. Kate was a spell-binding raconteur. Eventually she broke off with, "And what about you, Hattie? you're twenty three. I'll wager you've not been hiding your light under a bushel. A bonny, sexy lassie like you."

Hattie said enough to make it clear she was no stay-at-home, but she was honest enough to say, "The trouble is I don't know many people in London, Kate. I'm a bit lonely at weekends especially, to tell you the truth."

Kate made a mock frown and clicked her tongue. "Well, that'll never do, will it? We'll have to put things right straight away. I've some friends I know you'd enjoy." She ground out her cheroot. "Just leave it to Aunt Kate, Hattie."

Two days later she rang the office.

"Hattie sweetheart, it's Kate. How's your engagement book for next Thursday evening?"

"Oh hello, Kate. I've nothing fixed. I . . . "

"Splendid. A friendly gathering appears to be developing at my place. Would you care to come along?"

"That'd be lovely, Kate. Where do you live?"

"Holland Park. Number 7 Queens Place. About nine. OK?"

"Yes, fine. I'll look forward to it. Oh, Kate?"

"Yes, Hattie?"

"What should I wear?"

Kate laughed breezily. "Anything at all. Silk pyjamas if you fancy them."

Hattie fantasised a good deal about the party, and when Kate met her at the door of her tastefully furnished two storied house it looked as if the evening was going to be fully up to expectations. Hattie's eyes widened at Kate's outfit, a long, diaphanous Greek-looking tangerine affair. It was evident Miss Loxton was wearing little else. She'd also let down her thick black hair.

Kate grinned delightedly at her young friend's amazement. Putting one hand dramatically behind her head, the other on a hip she bobbed her ample breasts. "Treats for the boys, my dear."

In fact the other guests proved to be a considerably more demure lot. The first man Hattie spoke to was a stockbroker, the next a Naval Commander on leave, the third, a rather lugubrious individual, appeared to be a newspaper journalist specialising in the Arts. Two of the women had been at Cambridge with Kate – one was personal assistant to a senior merchant banker, the other married and not working. Another girl of about Hattie's age was in advertising and had in tow a male colleague who, more colourful than the rest in pink velvet trousers and sporting a small gold ear-stud, apparently rejoiced in the sobriquet of 'Cocky', though his name was actually John.

"What? Oh, the nickname. I got it at school for reasons best left to your imagination. Little boys can be *horrible*, don't you think?"

"So can big ones."

Cocky Thompson snorted in amusement. "Well, there's cheeky!" And before Hattie knew it this slightly piratic individual had bent forward and bestowed a moist kiss on her cheek.

Kate kept the party going and her guests circulating. She flitted about like an exotic bird, making sure she contrived frequent body contact with the males, who were duly discomposed. It occurred to Hattie that Kate might prefer a greyish backcloth against which to perform.

"And when did you descend on the Metropolis from dark Lochnagar?"

It was Cocky again, his rather swarthy face close, a warm hand comfortably pressed for a moment in the small of Hattie's back. She told him something of her history, finishing with an indication of her job.

"So that's how you met Kate. My firm know you lot professionally. Special promotion campaigns, book fairs, that kind of thing. Maybe you and I'll need to collaborate one day?" He looked straight at her under lowered eyebrows with an innuendo she realised she could react to or ignore.

Without hesitation Hattie winked and shot back, "I'll look forward to that, Cocky."

He understood. "Listen, Hattie, my humble abode is not so far from here. Maybe we could tell each other a bedtime story after this? I've got some real Blue Mountain beans."

Hattie replied with a smiling pretence of shock. Then, "What about . . . ?" She nodded quickly towards his partner.

"Sally? Oh, not to worry. She and I are very much in the

just-good-friends category. She's got her own car."

By eleven they were actively planning their escape from the party. The warm room, several drinks and many intimate brushes had brought them both near the boil.

"Oh, let's beat it, Hattie. You tell Kate you're overcome by fatigue. I'll follow almost immediately. Just wait round the nearest corner. We can walk. It'll do us good to cool off!"

"I can't wait to taste that Blue Mountain coffee."

"Oh, *you*!"

Hattie glanced around for Kate but she was not in evidence. It seemed she'd gone to answer a ring at the door. In a moment she reappeared with a large woman who did not look like a party-goer, blazered and grey skirted as she was.

"Ladies and Gentlemen," Kate announced to the party, her hands held high for attention, "meet Drusilla Slingsby-Gore!" There was a frisson of excitement. "Come and say hello, Dru. I'm glad you made it."

"I nearly didn't, Kate dear. We had a very fine meeting at Hammersmith which simply went on and on."

Hattie was struck by the magnetically mellifluous quality of this heavily built woman's voice as Kate led her round by the hand to meet everyone.

"Who's that, Cocky?"

"Don't you know? The Hon Drusilla is one of the leading lights in The Movement."

"Movement?"

"Yes, The Women's Movement. You know, Feminism and all that?"

"Yes, I see." Of course Hattie knew about the Feminists who were becoming increasingly vocal in their demands for equal rights for women, but she'd not yet had contact with any activists.

"Kate's pretty involved. I think everyone here is a sympathiser at least. The ladies have some strange allies, sometimes with rather strange motives maybe. I suppose I'm a sort of non-paid-up honorary member myself."

"Really?"

"Mmm. There's no discrimination in our firm. Just merit, which is an unarguable leveller. Or should be. Naturally some females try to . . . "

It was Hattie's turn to be presented.

"Dru, this is a new friend from Scotland, Harriot Murray. Hattie, Dru Gore."

They shook hands. Although she was not particularly tall the woman's physical presence was formidable. Amazonian was the word that first occurred to Hattie – or perhaps more of a trim Russian discus thrower, she thought. But the refined, carefully modulated voice and gentle handshake were very feminine. The combined effect was disturbing.

"Welcome to the wicked South, Harriot! I hope we'll see you at our meetings soon. We need all the hands," she paused to smile engagingly, "*and* the brains we can find for the cause."

Everything about this woman's physique seemed double the norm. Her hips were decidedly outsize, her bust huge, probably in the forty five inch league thought Hattie with an internal snigger. Her big flawlessly olive-skinned face was fascinating. Below a wide brow, great brown eyes danced with intelligence. Her slightly squat nose was strong, and between the full lips of a generous mouth large white teeth shone healthily. Her chin positively jutted – from one angle it looked massive and square, from another softly rounded, feminine. It was slightly cleft.

Despite these weighty attributes the overpowering impression was one of neat-waisted, light footed bounding vigour. Drusilla's curly dark brown hair was cut short, unfussy.

Hattie guessed her to be about 35.

"I'll ask Kate about your meetings."

"That's fine, Hattie. Just come and listen." She patted Hattie's forearm in a kind, sisterly gesture. "We'll have you in armour in no time!"

Then that caressing, controlled laugh again before she moved on. Hattie had to shake her head. There was something hypnotic about Drusilla Slingsby-Gore.

"Quite a specimen," observed Cocky Thompson.

"She certainly is."

Hattie was relieved to feel Cocky's exploratory fingers again pinching her bottom, to get back on to terra firma.

They were in the small hallway of his flat half an hour later. The Blue Mountain coffee was forgotten as they fell on Cocky's capacious, black silk-covered sofa. They kissed and wrestled in increasingly urgent need till he called out, "Halftime, Hattie! I'm as hot as hell. Just a minute while I put on something less tropicalising. I'll see if there's something for you."

He returned in a thin, Paisley-patterned dressing-gown which, rather than concealing, tended to make obvious his preparedness for the fray. He found Hattie stripped to bra and pants.

"Well! Noel Coward himself. Come here, Cocky."

And she quickly discovered the probable reason for the horrible little boys' nickname. They made love energetically, smiling gleefully at one another as their bellies slapped ever faster. Both were accomplished lovers, hungry to defer the climax.

The morning session was rushed since they both had to get to work and Hattie needed to call in at Weymouth Mews en route for a change of clothes. They agreed to meet again soon.

For months Cocky filled Hattie's horizons. He was not

only a superb bed-partner but tremendous fun to be with. He was also highly artistic. His bachelor flat was decorated in fine taste with original watercolours and a Tientsin rug on the walls. Antiques were dotted about the tables. A prize possession a delicate Chün vase he'd bought by luck in a junk shop, stood on a tall ebony torchère in the hall.

Hattie admired his sketches, mainly of Cornish fishing villages he visited each summer, but there were some landscapes and a few of men mending nets or caulking boats. He drew a large pencil picture of her reclining in the nude. She liked it apart from an objection about the proportions of her backside.

"I must draw you as I see you."

"But I don't have such a *huge* bottom, Cocky."

"You can't help being the most voluptuous thing to hit London this century, Hattie. You're gorgeous!"

She forgave him.

He took her to Annabels in Berkeley Square. Frank Sinatra and entourage were at the next table. They went to Paris for a long weekend but, perhaps affected by the romance of the City of Light, spent their time in bed and saw little of the sights. They visited London's endless galleries and ate in French, Italian, and Japanese restaurants. Hattie had never been so happy.

One afternoon she was out at Holland Park. Kate had a bad cold and Hattie had brought over some galley-proofs with a few suggestions for changes. Kate was really unwell so Hattie had not stayed long. Standing on the pavement outside she looked about for a taxi since it had started to rain, but in vain. She'd get soaked at the other end. It was four o'clock, a bit of a long shot, but she'd just see if by any chance Cocky was at home. Clutching her briefcase under her arm she ran through the now squalling rain.

When she reached his front door, struggling for breath

and perspiring heavily, it was a great relief to hear music within. In fact he was playing the Sinatra record she'd bought him after that time at Annabels. Gratefully she rang the doorbell. God, she was uncomfortable. If Cocky suggested she take her clothes off she'd do it in a minute. Come to think of it, a spot of 'love in the afternoon' would go down very well. There was no reply. The music of course. She pressed her finger on the bell and left it there for at least ten seconds.

Cocky was in his Paisley dressing-gown, his hair awry.

"Oh, I'm sorry darling! Were you in bed?"

"Hattie, I . . . "

"Never mind, I'll just jump in beside you. See if you get any sleep!"

She made to enter.

"Listen, Hattie, it's . . . eh . . . not very convenient. D'you mind? . . . I . . . "

Immediately, Hattie realised what was going on but, her heart hammering and her mouth all of a sudden dry, she did not want to believe it. "Let me in, Cocky!"

She pushed past him through the hall. There, lying on the black sofa rapidly trying to pull up her skirt, was a strange yellow haired girl. Stupidly this person looked up at Hattie, smiled ingratiatingly and said, "Hello."

Cocky was now in the room. "Hattie, this is Janie from the office. We were just . . . "

"Don't tell me, Cocky. I *can see* what you've been doing!"

"Hattie, I'm sorry. I didn't really mean . . . "

"Oh, shut up, you rotten bastard!"

Hattie's throat was constricted, her eyes full of tears. She blundered back into the hall. There was a moment before Cocky caught up with her. She decided what to do. As he came towards her pleading for forgiveness she cupped her hand behind the Chün vase and swept it with all her strength against the opposite wall. It shattered. Cocky looked at her in horror.

"*You can pick up the pieces,*" she screamed and slammed the door in his face.

11

HATTIE DID NOT ALLOW her betrayal to depress her. She did, however, resolve to avoid any serious emotional entanglements for the present. But this in no way inhibited her from seeking male company. On the contrary, through Kate Loxton, she met more new friends who in turn invited her to their parties and it was an unusual event if she finished a night out without a man in bed, whether at Weymouth Mews or a variety of up and down market addresses round London. One night stands, when she felt like it, eliminated draining nervous tension and kept her body quiet. Hattie came to relish her independence of action.

There was another factor which heightened this heady feeling of detachment, of liberation, self-government. The contraceptive pill had been introduced in a limited way. It was not long before Hattie had ensured a regular supply through Dr Howard. Jane Howard was a sympathetic doctor in a fashionable practice in Wimpole Street, whom she'd met at a party. This was unbelievable freedom! Joyfully Hattie sent her stock of Durex condoms hurtling down the rubbish chute.

Kate and a few other women provided intelligent

companionship, and Hattie, recognising that she could enjoy their company too, realised she had matured considerably in the last year or so. Her mind was calmer, she saw her position in life and its potentials quite clearly. Another substantial salary boost, reflecting new, more senior editorial tasks, enabled her to move to a larger, two-bedroomed flat in Beaumont Street.

About this time someone invited her to a meeting in a Paddington church hall. The purpose was to discuss progress towards 'Women's Rights', so Hattie had a fair idea of what to expect. She went along without great enthusiasm. What she had not been prepared for was the quality of the contributions from the platform and the floor and the fact that the audience was ninety per cent women. The atmosphere was strangely exhilarating.

The topics covered were indeed well-ventilated issues – equal pay for equal work, mandatory ministerial representation of women in Parliament, more women company directors. But, in time to come, it was not so much the content of the discussions at this isolated meeting that Hattie could recall but the courage and confidence of the speakers. At moments she'd found herself unexpectedly near tears, choked by surging emotions of sisterhood and solidarity. She determined there and then to see if she could help.

It was 1963 and meetings of this kind were rare. The modern feminist movement was as yet still a loose federation of clamouring voices, often disparate and sometimes, in the matter of means towards ends, contradictory. However, feminist books had begun to be published in an increasing torrent, from the USA particularly, and private discussion groups started to spring up in London. The sense of women being on the march, although many, women included, continued to mock, Hattie found moving and exciting. She got into step eagerly.

Subtly her attitude to men hardened. With a widening circle of women friends and involvement in her editorial job confined to women authors, men were becoming increasingly peripheral in Hattie's life. Except for sex. Early on she'd noticed that there was quite a high proportion of women in the feminist movement who were obviously emotionally involved with a woman partner. It was an open secret that many of these relationships were in fact exclusively lesbian in character.

Hattie supposed that it was unsurprising that feminism should attract women with those proclivities, but she often wondered how many had in fact deliberately chosen this separate, one-sex way of life *after* throwing their lot in with the reformers. As far as she was concerned these girl couples were simply objects of curiosity. How could they find any satisfaction? A man's body, and his sexual equipment in pàrticular, had been an insistent central thought in Hattie's mind for ten years. To forego regular contacts with men now was unthinkable, however much she might otherwise despise them.

For as she became more drawn into the close society of feminist activists, Hattie's contempt grew for the men she continued to bed regularly. Rarely was one unwilling to rise to her bait. She found with repeated practice that she was able to bring a casually introduced individual to a state of almost instant sexual desire. Equally, she began to discover a mildly sadistic pleasure in leading a man on, only to lift the drawbridge of a simulated lack of interest on her part at the last moment. But she dressed attractively and made sure she could always find male company when she needed it. She became less discriminating about the social or intellectual level of her bedmates. Their qualifications were simple – to be able to quench the intermittent thirst of her lust and to be willing to do for or to her whatever might take her fancy.

Feminism now filled Hattie's mind. It was as though she'd spent her whole adult life to date in preparation for this fight. Here were hundreds of women, spirited, educated women stridently articulating the kind of protests she'd herself wanted to make publicly for years. They flatly opposed male assumptions of superiority and claimed the right of women to an equal hand in decision making in all the important areas of civilised existence.

Most importantly of all, as Hattie saw it, the cry was for increased role-sharing in the domestic sphere. In intimate meetings, hearing one speaker after another call for the male spouse to participate in household chores to enable his partner as well as himself to pursue her career, Hattie found herself sweating. She thought of her mother's life, her grandmothers' and earlier generations of her kin who'd not even dreamt of such opportunity. They should be avenged. It was clear too that the advent of the pill had given a new impetus to those with a particular interest in this field of women's protest.

Once or twice Hattie felt constrained to add her endorsement to the general theme by telling of her own family's experiences. Old Edward's expulsion from the Gothenburg home of her grandfather, James, was an especially original and vintage illustration of the primitive, unchallenged male chauvinist in all his vicious cruelty, and her account went down well. Hattie was eventually asked to give an address to the group.

In the midst of this new activity several unexpected things happened. First, Sheena wrote to say she was getting married to William Devine Shields. Sheena's mother had fallen seriously ill with cancer and so it was to be a small affair at the Chapel of the Sacred Infant Jesus. Her sister would be bridesmaid. Very few guests. Sheena was sure Hattie would understand. As she parcelled up a present of a ceramic coffee percolator, Hattie wondered fleetingly if it was possible Sheena no longer approved of her. She laughed. Poor, limited Sheena – what did it matter any more what she thought? An unreconstructed provincial Catholic, for God's sake!, just *dying* to slip into her traditional submissive housewife role.

Charlie sent a letter and it was only the American postage stamps and zip-code space on the envelope which, after a moment or two, alerted Hattie to the writer's identity. She had almost forgotten his handwriting.

> *Dear Hattie,*
>
> *You'll be surprised to hear from me. One way or another we never did communicate much, did we? Anyway, Mother was saying in a letter that you'd had a leg-up at the publishers and moved to a palatial flat, so I thought I'd just say "Congrats!" Well done, bonnie wee sister o'mine. What d'you do for kicks? Not stuck for long if I know you. Life is for living, that's what I say, Hattie, and I'm glad you got out of boring old Rutherglen too. Tell me all about it sometime.*
>
> *Me? Well, I came over here (New York anyway) for 2 months and so far I've stayed 2 years, mostly in California. I've been with Ralph Gomez, my very good friend, for over a year now and life is good, though I do miss you all sometimes quite badly. I've found a job with a small graphics outfit which keeps us in burgers and tequila! By the way, Ralph's a Hispanic, but as big and handsome as any conquistador! You knew about me, didn't you?*
>
> *Well, Hat, that's it. Give me a bell if you're ever over LA way – promise? Take good care now.*
>
> *Sincerely thine, Charlie*

An Anger Bequeathed

The letter saddened Hattie. Its jolly tone was forced. He was a lost cause. All she could hope was that he'd make the best of his warped existence, hiding in the sprawling anonymity of a vast foreign city. An old nerve twitched with sudden anger at her father. A bit of understanding, a kind word at the right moments, oh, dammit, just a bit of love and Charlie would almost certainly have turned out differently. As a little girl Hattie had thought her big brother wonderful, in adolescence she'd fallen a little in love with him. Putting the letter away in a drawer she brushed away one tear with her sleeve.

Shortly after this Charlotte visited London with a friend from her church. They'd taken advantage of a British Railways' cheap offer which included a hotel room for two nights. The first day Hattie's mother and Mrs Rankin spent at a special exhibition, *Scientific Discovery through the Ages* at the V & A Museum. On the second Charlotte and Hattie met at the Cumberland Hotel for lunch and a leisurely chat over coffee.

"Come on now, Mum. I want you to see my flat. We'll take a cab."

"Whatever you say, dear."

Hattie had by now arranged her place for maximum comfort. She'd also hung some quite avant-garde prints and placed a half-sized white plaster male nude from an original Greek classical statue in the corner of her sitting area. Near the windows stood a well-maintained fleshy cactus plant.

"Oh, what an interesting room, Hattie! It's lovely."

"Thanks, Mum. Go and inspect the rest while I make some more coffee. Here, give me your coat."

They passed a happy enough hour or two. Hattie did most of the talking, about her job, about the feminist movement.

"Yes, you always were interested in women's rights and

all that, weren't you, dear? I'm glad your job's going well anyway."

"The job's fine, Mum, and I love it. I think I'm good at it too. But the Women's Movement is actually a very important part of my life now, you know."

"I'm sure it's good work. Bless you, Hattie."

It was clear to Hattie that her mother really didn't want to discuss the subject and, as always in the past, she felt irritation rising. But it was useless getting worked up and she was much more able to control herself nowadays. She lit a cigarette, lent back and relaxed.

"I had a letter from Charlie. He seems to have a good friend over there and to be reasonably cheerful."

"Yes, I know. I wonder if he'll come back, Hattie. Your father was wondering that just the other night."

"Was he now? Tell him not to bet on it." Charlotte looked tearful so Hattie quickly added. "He misses *you* a lot." And, slightly paraphrasing her brother's message, "He said so in his letter."

"Did he? I do miss him." There was a slightly uncomfortable pause. Then, "And what about you, Hattie? Are you getting a social life as well as work and the women's group?"

"Oh, I have a busy time, Mum."

"Any men friends?" Charlotte's wan smile contained an intuitive knowledge of the type of relationships her daughter was likely to be having and, at the same time, a kind of wilful self-deluding hope that perhaps Hattie might have a special young man. "You know Sheena McHugh got married last month?"

Hattie wasn't going to deceive her mother, even if that was what Charlotte might have preferred. "Yes, I sent Sheena a present. Me, Mum? Well, look, this is 1963, the pill's been invented and I'm all grown up. I work hard, I give a lot of time to the movement and I have a good time. OK?"

Charlotte shut her eyes briefly and nodded. "Yes, dear, I'm sure you're leading a worthwhile life. And you *should* enjoy yourself. Just always take care, Hattie darling. I think of you all the time."

Hattie stood up, went over to her mother and kissed her on the forehead.

"My darling mother. I do love you, you know."

For a moment neither spoke, each afraid the effort might precipitate an embarrassing sob. Charlotte recovered first.

"Come and see us before too long, Hattie. Robert's always enquiring about you. He's not the man he was."

"No?" Hattie was not going to be drawn into an exchange of sympathy for her father. "D'you get out all right?"

"Not much. The garden's a blessing when there's a blink of sun. Robert's been doing a lot in the greenhouse since he retired. We can't go far without a car of course. I wish I'd learned to drive."

"You had a week at Nairn, didn't you?"

"Yes. That was nice. Robert always says he feels at home up there. The Murrays came from there originally, as you know."

"I remember. I've probably got dozens of distant cousins in Moray and around."

"Apart from Robert's grandfather, Edward, they seem to have been bachelors or produced girls, so it would be difficult to trace them I expect. Of course there was his first wife's side too."

"Maybe I'll try one day, Mum. It's amazing really. Your sisters were the same – one unmarried and Aunt Millie having only Gillian."

Charlotte sighed. "So, Hattie, will you visit us soon?"

"I always love seeing you, Mum."

"Can you not just be, well, neutral with Robert? We took

the bus up to Cathkin Braes not long ago. The leaves were turning and it was incredibly clear. You could see right over the city and across the river to the Campsies. Robert said then how complete it would've been if you'd been with us. D'you remember the four of us picking brambles at Cathkin, Hattie?"

"Yes, of course, but look, nothing's going to change between my father and me. There's no use pretending it might. You can come down and stay here any time, Mum."

Charlotte's shoulders sagged. "You're awfully hard, Hattie."

"Maybe so but I've told you before. Unless women are prepared to be clear-headed and consistent in today's fight for their dignity and their rights, the struggle will be lost."

For the first time Charlotte displayed some irritation.

"Yes, yes. I know the line by now, Hattie."

Winter came and with it a regular round of parties, increasingly in the company of feminist friends. The men who attended these get-togethers were sympathisers and only a few attracted Hattie. Most tended to be rather gentle types, pacifistic, often vegetarians, occasionally obvious homosexuals.

After a number of these outings Hattie knew what to expect – a plate of unpolished rice with curried vegetables, not very fresh fruit, cheap plonk and endless talk on the movement's progress. But she genuinely enjoyed the comradeship of these kindly militants and always felt calmer after an evening with them. She'd never had a sister and worked now in a highly competitive field dominated by men. It was pleasant to know people who were actually concerned for one's welfare and interested in hearing one's views, a great relief from the noisy company of eloquently bombastic males most of whose immature egos seemed to compel them to foist their own opinions on all and sundry.

But Hattie was accustomed to strong meat and found herself returning home by eleven thirty on Saturday nights tense with frustration. She needed fun, bright conversation about the arts and politics. She enjoyed chic dressing and eating well. Above all, she needed the stimulation of men around her, men who would respond to her physically, men from whom she could take her pick. So, after a month or two, she combined her interests, attending women's gatherings first, then going on to a late night party. She'd recently learned to drive and acquired a small car. By now she knew her way about London.

It was two in the morning when she met Dick Littel at a party in Hampstead. He hailed from Amsterdam and evidently had something to do with selling popular records which had brought him to London for a few days.

"Hiya, Hattie," he said hoarsely when she gave him her name. "I been yakking all night at a deadly dinner party. Business. Boring, boring. Thank Christ I had this thrash to come to. Let my hormones uncurl. Know what I mean?"

"I do, Dick."

He was dressed in a denim suit and wore an open-necked pink shirt with exaggerated collar points. A gold chain and medallion hung round his neck. Smart and à la mode enough for this crowd, thought Hattie. But there was a somehow slightly neglected, unwashed impression beneath the exterior. However, as the hour got later, Hattie drank whisky freely. By three Dick looked ready-made for her bed.

As they drove south to Marylebone neither spoke much. They were going to sleep together but there was no romance in it. Hattie guessed that Dick's sex life was much like her own. By the time they reached Beaumont Street she was suddenly tired in the bone. It was near the date of her menstrual cycle which always dragged her down like this. But Hattie made a point of allowing her period to cause the minimum interference with whatever she wanted to do. She was going to bed with this man whether she really wanted to or not.

Dick had had little sleep the night before and after an almost perfunctory coupling flopped on to his back and began to snore. Hattie prodded him and waited patiently but the stertorous breathing went on. His mouth was open and Hattie now noticed his unbrushed teeth and coated tongue. He exuded an unpleasant, stale body odour. All at once Hattie felt sick. What was this smelly, ill-graced stranger doing here in her pretty, lovingly tended and scrupulously clean flat? She dug her elbow hard into his side.

"Get up now and leave!"

"What? *Godverdomme*! What you doing, man?"

"I'm telling you to get out of my bed and leave the flat."

"But why?" Dick was sitting up now rubbing his eyes. "I thought we were . . . "

"Oh, don't argue. Just go. You're dirty."

For a moment the Dutchman looked angry but then seemed to accept the situation. He dressed quickly and left.

Hattie cleaned her teeth and stood under a warm shower. It was nearly five a.m. when she lay down again. Surprising herself she whimpered a little, salt tears running into her mouth, before she fell into an uneasy sleep.

On Wednesday morning she experienced a sharp pain when urinating. By that evening she knew something was wrong. How could she face Dr Howard? Jane was a personal friend now. No, it was too embarrassing. So Hattie reported to a central London VD clinic. Oh, the mortification of sitting on a bench with spotty, shifty-eyed teenagers and a pair of blowsy prostitutes, of submitting to examination by a totally unsympathetic pock-marked Pakistani doctor. Thankfully it was only gonorrhoea. She'd be clean again in a few days. But it had been a profound shock.

As she walked quickly away from the hospital it came to Hattie that she'd reached a crossroads in her life. But were should she go? None of the signposts was clear.

12

THE WOMEN'S MOVEMENT was Hattie's salvation. She'd established a secure and worthwhile position as a bright young editor, but she needed an additional challenge, something to take up her leisure hours, to give her purpose. The Feminist cause, now definitely developing momentum, provided her with the involvement she sought. Hattie became its industrious ally.

Kate moved further west to an old house overlooking the Thames at Strand-on-the-Green near Chiswick. She invited Hattie to join a group which met near her new place. It was convenient enough, she liked Kate and she needed a change.

As soon as she joined, Hattie realised that these women were exceedingly radical in their outlook, determined to get things done rather than simply debated. She looked out her previous speech and rewrote it. Taking a phrase of Churchill's she'd come across about the Hun always being *at your throat or at your feet,* she applied it to men's attitudes to women. Illustrating her address again with thumbnail sketches from the actual experiences of women in her family, Hattie showed how the generations of wives had suffered equally at the hands of husbands who were cruel and domineering or weak and exploitive.

Bringing her remarks up to date she claimed that men in the mid-1960s were becoming even less sensitive in their dealings with women than they had been in the past. Since the invention of the latest contraceptive methods, she explained, men seemed to think they could finally throw off the mask of decency and copulate promiscuously without restraint, like animals. Animals, she observed, actually had superior behaviourial codes. Men were spreading disease. Rape was on the increase. Perversion abounded in all its lurid glamour, reflecting the unbalanced, depraved fantasies of sex-crazed men.

Hattie's research was thorough. Having worked up the indignation of her audience she would then read out a series of apt quotations from Mary Wollstonecraft, Freud, the Pankhursts and Simone de Beauvoir, finishing up with telling words from pamphlets and books by emerging contemporary activists in America like Betty Friedan, Kate Millett or Shulamith Firestone. Soon Hattie Murray was a recognised visiting speaker on the movement's London circuit, a valued raiser of women's consciousness, particularly about their subjugated position in the home. She typed out different versions of the address, varying the order of some sections and shifting the emphases.

Hattie wondered about the politics of the movement. Everyone seemed to take it as axiomatic that Socialism, in one guise or another, was the obvious creed for Feminists. But the Marxists and their fellow travellers didn't appear to Hattie to be conspicuously preoccupied with women's rights, certainly not as a first priority anyway. If the truth could be known there were probably as many male chauvinists on the political left as on the right. The fight was against discrimination in all its subtle, and not so subtle forms – party labels were irrelevant at this stage. Hattie suspected that if women ever did truly share power with men their political views would be likely to vary every bit as much as men's. She herself had as yet an open mind on things like foreign policy and economic management.

It was strange this constantly being in the company of women. The few men helpers in the groups hardly registered with Hattie. At first, self-imposed sexual abstinence was like a denial of her very life-force. At times she fancied there was an actual vacuum in her body of aching unfulfillment. But as the months went by and her mind became fully engaged with her job and her lecturing, the fires died down. She saw more clearly now that there were many tender relationships among the feminists and that it was not uncommon for couples to be living together, for all the world as if men did not exist. Although she could not imagine herself in such a liaison, Hattie did sometimes envy these women their mutual affection and manifest contentment.

One evening she was at the flat, relaxing with a coffee as she watched a news bulletin on TV. The phone rang.

"Hattie darling! So glad you're at home. How are you sweetie?"

"Just fine, Kate."

"Oh good. Look, I appear to have gone and lost my roneoed sheet. You know, the list of meetings up till May. Am I right in thinking you're speaking somewhere tomorrow?"

"Yes, at Barnet. Hang on, I'll get you the address. It should be a bit different I think."

"Indeed! Lots of fierce ladies with names like Rachel, Gloria and Rhoda." She laughed charmingly. "Please do well, Hattie. I'm bringing someone special to hear you."

"Oh, who?"

"No, no! It's a secret."

Drusilla Slingsby-Gore had spent the last six months in the United States. The feminist movement worldwide now received its prime impulse from American women writers and leaders, and Ms Slingsby-Gore had gone there to study their working methods and to try to bind British efforts more closely to theirs. She'd been in California and her broad leonine face was tanned as she came up to Hattie after the meeting.

"My dear girl, what a speech! Do allow me to congratulate you. Simply *splendid*. You electrified your audience. Patent sincerity, and a fine intellectual grasp of the issues. We must have a private chat, Hattie. Kate, aren't you proud of your protegée?"

"Absolutely. Hattie, you really excelled yourself tonight. I always knew you could." Kate was fairly purring.

The flattery washed pleasantly over the Chiswick delegate for the rest of the evening.

Next morning Hattie took an early call at the office.

"Harriot Murray?"

"Yes."

"Oh, good morning, dear. It's Dru here. Dru Gore?"

"Hello, Dru. Yes ... I ... well, good morning to you too."

Dru laughed at her confusion. "Sorry, it is a bit early in the day, isn't it? But I didn't want to miss you in case you might scoot out to some meeting or something."

"No, it's OK. I'll be here all day."

"I wondered if you'd care to drop in here for a little chat on your way home from work tonight? For a drink perhaps, about six?"

"That'd be very nice, Dru. Where do you live?"

"Number 38 Lascelles Square. D'you know it?"

"Yes, I'll find you, Dru. Thanks for calling."

"Splendid. I'll look forward to seeing you, Hattie. Very much."

Putting the receiver down Hattie found her hand shaking. She shook her head in perplexity and hurriedly lit a cigarette.

It was late April and as Hattie walked down Sloane Street and turned into Lascelles Square the first dusting of gold on mature laburnum trees was glowing against heavy purple lilac blossom. The facade of the building's mottled brickwork looked settled and impressive – to one side of the door was a bas-relief of scollop shells and cherubs. Expensive cars were stationed all round the square, nose to bumper in reserved spaces.

"I've come to see Miss Slingsby-Gore."

The silver-haired hall porter glanced at an in/out indicator board on the wall, smiled and deferentially pointed to the antique lift. "Fourth floor, turn right. Beautiful evening, miss."

"Yes, it is. Thanks."

Drusilla greeted her warmly with a kiss on the cheek. "Come in, Hattie. There now, let me take your mac, and your briefcase. I expect you've been squashed to bits in the tube?"

"It was rather crowded."

"I know. With a figure like mine it can be *purgatory* on occasions!" She laughed in self deprecation, casually conveying new and easy intimacy between them. "I thought we'd sit over here. It's such a *heavenly* evening."

Two armchairs had been turned round to face long, floor-length windows which stood ajar. Between the chairs a delicate rosewood table supported a small dish of fresh olives. As Hattie sat down the bosky square below them was motionless in the warm air. Shadows were lengthening. At the far end of the big room Hattie noticed a grand piano.

"D'you play, Dru?"

"Rather badly I'm afraid. Now, what can I get you?"

"Have you any Martini?"

"Dry? Gin cocktail?"

"Yes please."

"I'll join you. Quite acquired the taste in America. Have an olive while I make them, won't you, Hattie."

When Dru returned Hattie enquired if she'd mind if she smoked.

"You do what you like, my dear. But you're a naughty thing. They're very bad for you."

"Sorry," said Hattie, playing her host's game for a moment by looking contrite as she flicked her lighter.

"I wouldn't like to think you were doing anything to undermine your health. Apart from all the work you're going to do for the cause you're a very pretty girl." Dru turned her face straight on to Hattie's. Her smile was openly friendly and secretly private at the same time.

They spoke of the Barnet meeting. Dru enquired about the content of Hattie's speech.

"Oh, I've only really got one script, but I rearrange it from time to time."

"How very professional. Tell me, Hattie, what about that long line of suffering women in your family?"

"Well, I couldn't know them all for obvious reasons, but from what I've heard all my life, that's how it was for them and their children."

"Monstrous behaviour. There's been a fair quota of bastards in my family too. But they're not going to get away with it for much longer, are they?"

"I hope not."

Dru picked up her glass and moved it forward to clink with Hattie's as she was about to sip. "Tell you what, Hattie. Let's not think about men for a bit and just enjoy ourselves, shall we?"

"Good idea, Dru. Cheers."

Hattie was rewarded with another of Dru's beaming, but at the same time, confidential smiles.

Soon after this Dru took Hattie and Kate to dinner in a small Italian restaurant following a meeting they'd all attended. Dru had given the group, in Kensington, an account of her American researches, a speech Hattie was to hear many times over.

Later that week Dru rang to ask Hattie to lunch at her club, the Lansdowne in Fitzmaurice Place. Hattie enjoyed the experience. In fact, she was beginning to find Dru's amusing, intelligent company and aristocratic background much to her taste.

"You've made a hit with Dru, Hattie," remarked Kate with a grin one day.

"She is an extraordinary person."

"I know. Very special. But, do be careful Hattie."

"What d'you mean?"

"Well, she's a tremendous asset to the movement of course, but she does have a colourful reputation."

"Really?"

Kate looked slightly annoyed at Hattie's puzzlement.

"Yes, you *must* have heard. She has a particular interest in intelligent, good looking young women."

"Oh!" Hattie threw her head back smiling. "As a matter of fact I haven't heard anything like that. But don't worry about *me*, Kate. My God! The very notion." She laughed loudly. Observing Kate's quizzical, sidelong glance Hattie perceived, for the first time in their acquaintance, a degree of sexual ambivalence in this sophisticated woman's nature.

She continued to meet Dru, sometimes several times a week, and Hattie found her unfailingly stimulating. Something of consuming interest had invariably just befallen, or was about to happen to, this unconventional new friend. Other women, even men, seemed dull by comparison. Slowly, with a certain wry, self-aware amusement, Hattie allowed herself to slip under the spell of the beguiling Drusilla Slingsby-Gore.

There was to be a small dinner party at Lascelles Square. Hattie was invited.

"You'll balance the table most decoratively, my dear."

"Who's coming, Dru?"

"Oh, a rather stiff old lawyer and his boring wife. The Boughtons. One has to put up with him. Absolute encyclopedia of all the out-of-the-way bits of the law which can be turned to account to enforce women's rights. A good friend of the movement."

"Is that all?"

"John Chetwynd and Caroline. Just the six of us."

Hattie's eyes widened. "You mean the Tory MP?"

"That's right. He's a poppet and, again, a strong supporter, really very radical for a Conservative. We've known each other from *babyhood*."

"Mmm," was all Hattie could manage. Chetwynd was a prominent politician, frequently in the press and on TV.

"We'll dress. More of an occasion, don't you think?" The older woman noticed her friend's quick swallow. "You've got a long frock, haven't you, Hattie sweet?"

"Yes, of course, if the moths haven't been at it."

"Excellent. I think it'll be fun, and I want you to know these men. They're important to us."

Hattie did not possess an evening dress. She hurriedly priced a few but rebelled at the outlay for what might prove an isolated occasion. One shop ran a discreet hire service. She tried on half a dozen. Either they were drab or too stagey and Hattie was becoming quite anxious when the assistant brought another model into the changing booth.

"This one isn't really for hiring. It just came in, but Miss Carney says you can have it if you like, seeing we haven't been able to suit you from the normal dresses."

It was perfect. Heavily studded in multi-coloured sequins its tight-fitting sheath was slimly flattering. Though there were straps it was cut very low with a matching deep cleavage at the back.

"If I may say so, Madam, you have just the figure for this dress. You'll look great on the night."

"If I don't pop out in front and splash the soup!"

Hattie pirouetted before the mirror. God! She did look spectacular.

Dru had never kissed her on the lips – not till that night. A butler and cook/waitress had been imported for the dinner party and the white-jacketed flunky admitted Hattie and took her wrap. She'd been asked to come early to give a hand. Dru was arranging a bowl of flowers in the drawing room. She turned round.

"Hattie darling!" Her mouth fell open. "Lord, oh Lord, what a dress! You look *gorgeous*." So saying she stepped over to Hattie, took her in her arms and kissed her squarely on the lips.

Hattie visibly shuddered. For a moment her mind whirled. There seemed to be loud music in her head, thunderous, from a distance. Then, just as suddenly she was calm again. In front of her stood Dru, smiling. Was there a hint of satisfied recognition at the effect she'd had? Perhaps Hattie was imagining too much.

"Oh sorry. I've gone and smudged your lipstick. Silly me. Run along and redo your face, sweetie. They'll be here in ten minutes or so."

Then Dru was bustling about again, putting last minute touches to the circular table in the dining room, straightening cutlery, changing the position of small silver ornaments.

The Boughtons were every bit as dry as Dru had indicated. However, John and Caro Chetwynd made a vivid contrast, he strongly built, black haired, limpid eyed, she taller than average, aquiline-nosed, haughty. Champagne was served by the butler, olives and almonds dispensed. Introductions were made.

Dru had placed Hattie next to John Chetwynd. He was charming, interested in her career and keen to talk about the Women's Movement.

"Of course, we're greatly weakened in Government with all the shenanigans of recent years. Profumo and all that. There's likely to be an election in the Autumn, so our ability to get things done at present is badly hobbled. The other side *talk* till the cows come home about international fraternity, but the Labour Party has a lot on its plate. Crazy Luddite unions for a start."

He took a mouthful of burgundy. "I'm very much afraid, Hattie, that the cause, women's equality and so on, is going to have to mark time for a year or two. That's the PM's view anyway. Naturally, some of us will keep the lobby pot boiling."

He enquired what Hattie's main interest in the movement was.

"Principally the domestic sphere. I think wives should be entitled to a minimum percentage of husband's earnings, if the wife is at home bringing up a family that is. There should be much greater provision of crêches by the State, on the Scandinavian pattern. And I'm all for a Minister of Women's Affairs, who would have to be a woman, naturally."

"Naturally," said John Chetwynd, grinning at her. He caught Dru's eye. "Drusilla, your young friend here has quite an agenda for us!"

"I know, John. Watch what you say or she'll quote you in one of her fire and brimstone speeches!"

"Really?" He looked at his fellow guest with renewed interest.

The evening was a success. The only sour note came over coffee from Caroline Chetwynd who did not seem to care for the obvious rapport between her husband and Hattie. She asked pointedly which university Hattie had attended, Oxford or Cambridge.

"Glasgow actually."

"I see." Caro looked coldly down her long nose.

Dru had heard. "What about you, Caro? Six months on the knicker counter at Harrods, wasn't it?"

There was a burst of delighted laughter. Its victim closed her eyes and nodded, admitting defeat with a smiling, thin-lipped not very good grace.

When the others had gone Dru paid off the two servants.

"Come over here and have a nightcap, Hattie sweet."

"OK Dru. I did enjoy tonight. John Chetwynd's obviously a good man. But the meal too, and the wine. Thanks for asking me."

"It was nothing, Hattie. I'm afraid I can't remember much of what was said though."

"No? The hostess has to be on her toes I suppose."

"It wasn't that."

They were sitting together on a sofa by the drawing room fireplace.

"Oh, well . . ."

"Don't you see, my darling?" Dru grasped Hattie's bare shoulders and gently turned her till their faces were close. "I couldn't take my eyes off you all night, Hattie."

13

AT TIMES HATTIE FOUND it difficult to believe what was happening to her. Outside the office Dru had become her life. They went everywhere together. It was summer and the pace of women's meetings had slackened. But Dru had friends all over the place. They attended small gallery exhibitions and met the artist, went to recitals of chamber music and spoke to the musicians. Hattie mentioned casually that it might be fun to go to a Beatles concert in the Albert Hall. The event was completely sold out but Dru managed to obtain two tickets. "Don't ask me what I paid for them, you lucky girl!" It was a heady existence.

Dru gave Hattie several valuable presents – an 18 carat gold chain and locket containing a miniature photograph of herself, an antique ruby ring, an exquisite nude female Art-Deco figure in polished copper. In return Hattie had a silver pen inscribed 'Drusilla' and bought her a flaming orange Hermes silk scarf. But it was Hattie's attention and affection that Dru really wanted.

Since the dinner party she'd become much more demonstrative, kissing Hattie on the mouth and caressing her whenever opportunity arose. That night, light-headed on champagne, wine and a large brandy which Dru pressed on her, and maybe a little euphoric at the high level of conversation she'd participated in, Hattie had allowed Dru to kiss and cuddle her for a while before going home. It was harmless, quite pleasant really to be so obviously appreciated. Perhaps Dru had even briefly fondled her more than half exposed breasts but, in the morning as she tried to dispel a fuzzy headache with unsweetened black coffee, Hattie couldn't be absolutely sure. She badly wanted a cigarette but there weren't any in the flat. She'd given them up at Dru's request.

Late one Friday in August they had tea on the House of Commons Members' terrace with John Chetwynd and afterwards shared a taxi, Hattie to clear up at the office, Dru to return to Lascelles Square. The country was in the grip of a sweltering 82 degrees heatwave. Londoners and tourists swarmed around Parliament Square, shirt-sleeved, sticky. As the cab drove along Millbank even the sluggish, polluted river managed to look inviting.

"Lord, this is like New York heat!"

"Equatorial," concurred Hattie.

"I've just had a brilliant idea."

"Oh?"

"Let's go down to Sussex for the weekend. Have you anything on?"

"No. D'you mean to your . . . "

"Yes, to Kirdstone Park. I happen to know Mummy and Daddy are away, in India of all places at their age! The rest of my kin take to the hills en masse in August. The Dordogne mainly."

"Well, it sound lovely, Dru."

"There's a pool. Thirty acres of woodland to walk in. We'll not be disturbed."

"OK. Shall I pick you up in the morning? Say about ten?"

"Perfect. I'll telephone tonight and make sure our beds are aired and that there's something to eat."

"I thought you said that nobody . . . ?"

"Just the Doregas. A Spanish couple who look after the place. They're dears."

It was already stifling by the time Hattie pulled out into Marylebone High Street next morning. The thought of a private swimming pool in green countryside was alluring indeed. She wondered again about this strange, intense friendship she'd fallen into. Hattie had always been the one to choose her friends, her lovers. It was certainly a new experience to be so hotly pursued herself. Was she making a bad mistake allowing Dru to monopolise her time? Where was their relationship leading?

Since adolescence Hattie had had periodic vivid dreams about men, dreams saturated with sexual imagery. These had not ceased since she'd stopped associating with men, but somehow, when she was in Dru's company any physical frustration seemed to melt away. They talked so much, and were always going here and there, having new experiences. Just being with Dru seemed curiously satisfying, an appreciative embrace, a warm kiss enough to keep her calm and happy. But what were Dru's inner thoughts? There was a shy inscrutability about this highly intelligent woman which, despite her voluble gregarious ways, Hattie found hard to penetrate. Driving into Lascelles Square she admitted to herself that there was a niggling anxiety at the core of her complex feelings for Drusilla Slingsby-Gore.

Dru had donned a blue-jean outfit of skirt and jacket for the occasion. It was too tight for her broad shoulders and the shortness of the skirt accentuated her large knees and massive, if shapely calves. Hattie was touched to pity by her slightly pathetic appearance. With that figure it was just impossible to dress smartly. Men must find her a joke.

"Well, you look the part, Dru!"

"D'you like it, Hattie? Oh, thank you, dear. I'm always so *unsure* about clothes."

They had some coffee together before setting forth. Traffic was not heavy and the sun poured down. It was an idyllic drive. With the roof and windows fully open they relished the rushing breeze. The wind made it difficult to converse and soon they lapsed into silence, each thinking her own thoughts.

Kirdstone Park was a fine old Jacobean house at the end of a winding drive off a minor country road. Its mature brickwork, tall chimneys and formal box-hedged gardens conveyed a comfortable stability. Dorega emerged from a small lodge near the wrought-iron gates and took their bags in. He showed Hattie her room, which was spacious and looked out over the garden towards acres of forest.

"Drinkies time, Hattie! I've found a bottle of Pimms No.3. Carmen's chopping up the bits and pieces of fruit etcetera. Will that suit you?"

"It certainly will, Dru."

"We'll sit on the terrace. What weather!"

Even the birds seemed to have been silenced by the relentless and increasing heat. Dru had taken off her jacket and now sat awkwardly on a not very robust folding canvas chair. Her breasts strained against the material of an inappropriate satin blouse and her skirt had ridden up revealing even more startlingly the huge dimensions of her knees.

"*Slàinte*, Dru"

"Oh, you and your Scotch words, Hattie! Cheers!" They drank, delighted with their Pimms and the shimmering glory of the morning. "I've asked Carmen to give us some cold meats and salad. Is that all right?"

"Ideal."

Dru wrinkled her nose at Hattie and smiled tenderly. Slowly she shook her head from side to side still holding Hattie's eye, as if marvelling that someone like Hattie Murray should exist.

Looking up from her reclining chair into that big, expressive face, Hattie again felt an acute stab of confused anxiety. There was something very close to adoration in Dru's eyes.

After lunch, during which the Spanish couple waited on them and they drank chilled white chianti, Dru suggested they go for a walk.

"Don't know about you, Hattie, but if I lie down now I'm done. Probably wouldn't come to till six, and then feel like death."

It was cool in the beech forest. After a while Dru took Hattie's hand.

"D'you mind, darling? I'm so happy with you."

Hattie's emotions were in turmoil. She had no real sexual impulse towards Dru, though for some time now she had been aware that her friend almost certainly did entertain such feelings for her. But Hattie was enjoying the clandestine ambience of the affair. There was an undeniable thrill in being the object of such a single-minded, secret passion.

They came to a sun-drenched clearing and Hattie meekly followed Dru's suggestion that they lie down and rest. For a while they lay on their backs, inert, gratefully letting the sun beat down on their bodies. Then Dru's hand reached out again to Hattie's. She moved closer and soon Hattie felt strong arms around her. Dru laid her length tight against Hattie and suddenly began kissing her, mouth open, tongue probing. Hattie allowed the initial contact but then felt compelled to resist, finally using a good deal of force to push the other woman aside.

"My God, Dru! Take it easy," she panted.

"Hattie, darling darling! You do love me, don't you? I need you *terribly*."

There was defeat in her staring eyes as well as devouring lust. Hattie experienced a renewed pity for this bright, generous woman imprisoned in an unacceptably proportioned body. But she was also deeply disturbed by Dru's driving sexual hunger. However strange the circumstances there was undoubtedly something aphrodisiac just being near her in this state. But a self-protective instinct told Hattie to stand up, to break the spell. She rose.

"Of course, Dru. You *know* I'm fond of you but . . . "

"Don't say anything more, Hattie, *please*. I couldn't bear it." She got up awkwardly, brushing grass and seeds off her ridiculously abbreviated skirt. "Look, I'm sorry if I upset you. The sun . . . I was carried away. Oh Hattie, please forgive me."

She stood there, her head bowed in contrition and embarrassment. A twig, caught in her short hair, stuck up foolishly. Hattie felt a great surge of what she could only call love of a sort for the woman before her. Dru had given her so much. She'd entertained her open-handedly, introduced her to countless fascinating people, widened her horizons beyond anything she'd ever dreamt of. Now her only sin was to have declared her need and to have kissed her passionately to show it.

"It's all right, Dru. Forget it, really. But maybe we'd better walk back."

This time it was Hattie who took Dru's hand until the safety of the house came into view.

Dru found her voice again. "Lord, it's hotter than ever. Would you like to have a swim."

"Yes please."

"Come on then. I'll show you. It's round here, through this hedge."

It was a charming old-fashioned pool, oval with marble statues at intervals round its stone rim, but the lining had been modernised. Small aquamarine tiles attractively set off dancing refractions of gold rippled light.

"It's gorgeous, Dru! I must get in."

"Go on then and put your cozzie on."

Hattie snapped her fingers in annoyance.

"Would you believe it? I've left it in London."

"Oh dear, I didn't bring one either. Anyway, I don't think mine would be much use to you!"

"Hell."

Dru turned to Hattie. "You'll simply have to swim in the altogether."

"What? I couldn't do that."

"And why on earth not? Don't tell me Hattie Murray is suddenly going to turn all bourgeois conventional on me?"

Hattie stared into the cool depths of the blue green water. She was very hot. "Well . . . listen, are you coming in too, Dru. And what about . . . ?" She jerked her thumb towards the lodge.

"The Doregas? I've sent them off for the day. Probably half-way to their daughter's in Brighton by now. We're quite alone, Hattie. It's all right."

"*Are* you coming in?"

"I'm not much of a water-baby, Hattie. I'll just sit here with a magazine. If you look behind your bathroom door they should have put out a towelling robe for you. Go on now, while it's still sunny."

"I'll go up to my room for a minute anyway, and see what I think when I get there."

"Oh, don't be ridiculous, Hattie dear. You'll enjoy it. Maybe you'll get your pretty bottom sunburned. That's not a chance that comes one's way every day!"

The white bathrobe was hanging in its place. Hattie

stripped off, put it on and stood gazing out of the window. A heat haze obscured the most distant trees. Was this madness? She'd had a demonstration of Dru's barely controlled appetite already. Probably, if she had any sense left, she should be driving back to London right now. But the prospect of airless, litter-strewn streets, an empty, enervating flat defeated her. Dru *had* calmed down, and if she did come over amorous again Hattie now felt confident she could deal with it. She'd joke her out of it. This was a fabulous place and she was damned well going to enjoy it.

If she was going to swim in her birthday suit, so what? Hardly a wildly daring thing to do in 1964. Even so, this thought gradually assumed a glamorous allure as she made her way downstairs. By the time she could see Dru, slumped on a reclining chair at the pool side reading an *Encounter* magazine, Hattie was surprised to find that she was trembling slightly.

"Well done, Hattie! I knew you'd have the courage."

"I'm not sure, Dru, but I can't resist the water. Quite honestly though, I'm a bit shy."

"For goodness sake, girl! Jump in. I promise not to look till you're under water." She returned her eyes to the magazine.

Hattie slipped off her robe. With a whoop she ran to the edge and leapt into the air. The splash as she landed in the deep end sent a shower of water over Dru.

"Rotter! I'm *soaked*." But Dru was grinning happily as she sat up to dry herself with a pocket handkerchief.

Hattie was a good swimmer, quickly completing several lengths of the small pool, her head first above water, then below. She somersaulted, she dived and finally floated contentedly on her back. The sun was lower now, but not a hint of cloud crossed Hattie's azure field of vision. The uninterrupted, burning heat on her skin was delicious. After twenty minutes she climbed out and picked up her robe.

"Don't bother with that, Hattie. Look, I've wheeled a lounger out of the changing hut."

Hattie was enjoying the sun too much to argue. She sank face down on the warm, padded mattress. There were several minutes of silence, broken only by the industrious whirring sound of a cricket in long grass nearby.

"Hattie?" Dru's voice was small.

"Mmm?"

"I think you're the most beautiful thing I've ever seen."

"Oh nonsense, Dru." Hattie remained prone, her eyes shut.

"You looked so elegant in the water. Like a slim young seal, or perhaps a mermaid even."

Hattie was aware that Dru was getting up. "You're too flattering for words, Dru," she laughed as she turned her head. Opening sun-dazzled eyes she saw that Dru had knelt down beside her. And before Hattie could move or say anything further Dru's head dropped. Hattie felt two hard kisses planted, one on each buttock.

"There!" Dru stood up immediately. "Now I'm going in to knock up something for our supper. Stay here as long as you like, but don't get cold when the sun goes behind those trees. Promise?"

"OK," Hattie grunted without moving. The wordless acceptance of such a demonstration of affection would not have been readily understood in Rutherglen, she thought with amusement. But then, who wouldn't react in some sort of unconventional way to being undressed in woody seclusion in hot sunlight? It was curiously elemental here, pagan almost, lying beside water watched only by the trees. The sun was still burning the length of Hattie's body although now there came the occasional, tentative warm breath of a little eddying zephyr. As she lay on, luxuriating, her reverie became progressively more sensual. Pictures of past sessions with men began to play through her mind cinematically. God! She'd have to find a man again, soon. Acting the nun didn't suit her at all.

And Dru? Well, Hattie silently admitted, her current relationship with this strange, fascinating woman did probably now have a sexual element in it. Even if it was only to the extent that Dru was unable to conceal her feelings, and the inevitable response which her eager pursuit produced. But Hattie simply could not imagine how any closer encounter with her could result in the kind of excitement and shattering satisfaction to be had with a man. An attractive man, available and physically well-equipped, was becoming an urgent necessity.

Hattie stood up, dry-mouthed and breathing hard. She put on her towelling robe, feeling rather foolish now at her lack of clothing, and started walking back to the house. Suddenly, she was keen to be back in London, to start reaching out again to a circle of friends, especially men. She'd been in purdah for months. That was going to end with effect Monday.

Meantime, there was Dru to contend with. Hattie supposed they'd have a quiet supper and an early night. She decided that she anyway was not going to be kept out of bed late. If Dru was still feeling hot, maybe she'd allow her a nice juicy goodnight kiss. After all, she deserved some reward for today. Surely she wouldn't suggest anything more serious.

14

TO HATTIE'S GREAT RELIEF Dru appeared to be much more at ease after they'd showered and met again on the terrace for iced sherries. A fish casserole was in the oven and, while it cooked, they found genuine pleasure discussing likely initiatives for the Women's Movement in the winter. Dru described the outline of an important new paper she was working on – *Aspects of the Androgynous Ideal*. Hattie made her laugh with cruelly accurate takeoffs of some of the more eccentric feminists known to them both.

After the meal, accompanied by a bottle of Austrian spätlese, they watched a mystery film on TV. Hattie made sure she sat in an armchair on her own. By nine the effects of a day in the sun, emotional tensions and the strong wine had them both heavy-lidded. Hattie several times fell asleep momentarily.

"Dru, I'm simply not taking this in. I'll have to say goodnight."

"I'm the same, dear. It's been a wonderful day in many ways though, hasn't it?"

"Fantastic. Terrific to get out of London for a while. Thanks very much, Dru."

"Come here a moment." This is it, thought Hattie. She knew just what she was going to permit. "I want to hear again that you've forgiven my indiscretion."

"I said so already, Dru. Let's forget it. Anyway, it's nice to be kissed sometimes."

"I do love you, Hattie."

"Try not to be so *intense*, Dru."

"Sorry. But can I please kiss you goodnight then?"

"Of course you can." And Hattie shut her eyes, offering up pursed lips obediently. She felt Dru's hands firm on each side of her head, and then the kiss, moist, lingering, their tongue tips briefly touching.

Dru sighed deeply. "I feel much better now. Off to bed with you. Breakfast nineish all right?"

"I look forward to it. Sleep well, Dru. 'Night."

Thank heaven! There wasn't going to be any difficulty. Dru had seen the warning light. Maybe a walk in the morning, then they'd get off. Perhaps stop at a village pub for lunch. She'd make it clear to Dru in the next week or two that their old exclusive relationship was over, that she must spend time with other people, that she was after all not a lesbian, not even bisexual. No hard feelings. In fact, there was no reason why they shouldn't remain friends.

She'd left a window open and the room was now pleasantly cool. Hattie undressed and slipped gratefully under the duvet. It must have been around two in the morning that she struggled out of a dead sleep to consciousness. Someone or something had entered her room. She switched on the bedside light, her heart suddenly pounding. There stood Dru, blinking in the harsh light. She was absolutely naked.

"I'm sorry, Hattie. I just couldn't . . . "

"*What the hell, Dru?*"

"Your beautiful white form . . . in the pool . . . couldn't get you out of my mind. Impossible to sleep . . . I . . . I . . . "

There was a sharp intake of breath and a strangled gasp.

Hattie's eyes had now accustomed themselves to the light. What an extraordinary spectacle the woman presented. With her huge, widely separated udder-like breasts and massive jodhpur thighs Dru Gore looked uncommonly like one of those Palaeolithic Venus carvings Hattie had seen in books about the evolution of beauty standards. But Dru was very much flesh and blood. Hattie now noticed the surprisingly flat expanse of her belly, a dark fan of pubic hair reaching towards her broad, deep navel.

Dru's hands hung by her sides. Hattie, in a state of some shock, glanced up amazed. She saw tears on the other woman's cheeks.

"God Almighty, Dru! Are you crying?"

"Oh, Hattie, Hattie! I *must* love you. For pity's sake let me in beside you."

She was so desperate, so vulnerable, obviously suffering. Hattie hesitated. She just couldn't find it in her heart to eject her from the room. And then an unbelievable thing happened. The emanation of heat from Dru's heavy body reached Hattie and she was herself suddenly racked by a wave of fierce desire, a raw longing to feel again another's skin against hers, to be touched. She shuffled to the far side of the bed.

Once under the duvet Dru's distress evaporated. She became an eager lover. Though Hattie's mind was reacting chaotically to what was now happening, resistance to its uncommonness wrestling with a rising excitement, she was soon comfortingly aware of a tender female considerateness in Dru's exploring hands.

They kissed, then Dru whispered hoarsely, "You're wonderful, Hattie darling. Now I'm going to taste you at last."

"What? Listen, Dru, I don't . . . "

But Hattie's protests faltered as Dru moved down the

bed, then ceased altogether as she felt the older woman's tongue go to work. Dru knew what she was doing. In seconds she had Hattie on the threshold of a series of orgasms, each mounting higher than the last. Hattie moaned. Dru doubled her efforts till Hattie cried out.

"Stop, Dru! For God's sake leave me alone. I've come enough."

Dru moved up the bed again and levered herself up on to all fours over Hattie.

"I'm going to make love to you now, Hattie."

"How d'you mean? I don't want . . . "

"Just wrap your legs round me like a good girl." Gently, but determinedly she guided Hattie into compliance and began to rub herself against her.

But Hattie's storm of sexual hunger had quickly abated. Lying on her back in a position of counterfeit copulation, sexually uninterested now, she began to feel not in any way ashamed but simply stupid. What *would* they look like to the proverbial fly on the wall – she, pinioned helplessly with another great lumbering woman banging and lunging at her in a ludicrous impersonation of intercourse? As Dru sighed and grunted with increasing effort a small demon of self-ridiculing laughter began to tickle somewhere in Hattie's stomach. Soon it was struggling for escape from her throat.

For a while Hattie managed to keep her giggles under control. Her partner was in no mood for mirth. Indeed, Dru was getting desperate for another kind of release, heaving herself about in ever more abandoned positions as she sought maximum clitoral friction. At one point Hattie raised her head, intending to look unobtrusively at the bedside clock. But this placed her cheek squarely in the path of Dru's swinging breasts. There was a resounding smack. Hattie fell back laughing uncontrollably, quite unable to speak for the moment.

The thrusting motion abruptly ceased. Dru froze. She waited for Hattie's giggles to subside.

"Are you laughing at me?"

"No, Dru," Hattie began, "it was just now when . . . " But she exploded again, unable to restrain herself as the slap of their recent collision re-echoed in her ears. When she had finally calmed down Dru was out of bed and on her feet.

"I'm sorry you find this all a joke. I'm afraid I was utterly serious. I thought we understood one another. Obviously I've made a terrible mistake, but don't worry, I shall never embarrass you again." Mustering what dignity she could Drusilla Slingsby-Gore, still flushed and perspiring in her nakedness, walked quickly from Hattie's room.

"Dru, come back! I'm sorry, I didn't mean to . . . "

"Don't you dare speak to me or come near me ever again." The door was slammed viciously.

The ensuing hours of silence were oppressive. Somehow Hattie got her vaulting emotions and anxieties under control and, near dawn, fell into an exhausted sleep. It was nine thirty when she awoke. Quickly she showered, dressed and, filled with apprehension, made her way downstairs. Dorega met her.

"You like eggs or just flakes, miss?"

"Some toast and coffee will do, thank you. Oh, is Miss Gore up yet?"

"You not know? She take the village taxi to London. Very early. About seven, I think. Important meeting she say."

Driving back through the country towards London there was no humour left in Hattie. At moments the breach with Dru did seem a positive release, enabling her to plan her own life again without looking over her shoulder. But then, a debilitating emptiness would overcome her, prompting perplexed tears. Once she had to pull off the road to wipe her eyes and blow her nose.

Hattie knew for certain now that all along, despite what she'd permitted to occur the night before, she'd never felt anything of real importance for Dru Gore in a physical sense. But she had found her constant attention flattering, her mind and personality extremely stimulating. It was not going to be easy to fill the void.

The flat was stuffy, even with all the windows open. She'd bought a Sunday newspaper and now settled down to read it. The afternoon stretched ahead interminably. At four o'clock she went out to a small delicatessen and bought rye bread and Polish sausage. A sandwich and coffee comforted her. She switched the radio on. Bruch's violin concerto was beautiful as always but unbearably melancholic. TV – an irritating old Abbot and Costello film, a golf tournament.

Hattie paced about the flat. When she thought about it, there was absolutely no one she could confide in, least of all Kate Loxton who had warned her something might go wrong. Did she feel ashamed? Or angry? In the end, Hattie decided, her main reaction to the events of the last day and a half was one of sadness, sadness for Dru as well as for herself.

Why, oh why had she led Dru on? For, although it had of course been Dru who had always initiated things, she *could* have stopped her dead at any time in the past months. Oh yes, it had been Dru who'd pressed her feelings on her, embraced her, kissed her, but Hattie knew very well that her responses had been ambivalent enough to keep up the hopes of a driven lesbian like Dru. Had she cynically traded a false show of affection for a vicarious share in Dru's social prestige? If so, there was unforgivable cruelty in her actions. Dru was a pitiable victim of her own nature, probably stemming from early despair about her physical shape, and Hattie had realised that quite clearly from the start. But she quickly dismissed this potential source of guilt. It had not really been as simple as that.

She made more coffee, sat down, stood up again, began walking back and forth from room to room – a caged animal indeed. But Hattie did not smile at the image. God, she was miserable.

Near five the doorbell rang, its harsh irruption unbearable on Hattie's taut nerves. Who the devil could this be? She went to the door frowning, hoping the caller had made a mistake. A few more hours of rationalisation, private wound licking, were badly needed to regain her equilibrium.

"Hi, Hat! A face from your wicked past come to haunt you! Remember me, Hat?"

"Paul Horrigan!"

"As ever was. Can I come in?"

"Of course."

The cheap suit, not very good skin, Glasgow accent. Hattie was finding the utmost difficulty adjusting her mental register to this unexpected visitor.

"How on earth did you find me, Paul?"

"Met Sheena McHugh, correction, Shields, the other day. Preg as hell. She gave me your address. Sure I'm no intruding, Hattie?"

"No, it's all right. Sit down, Paul. Coffee? There's some in the percolator."

"Thanks. See, I had to come to London for an interview with this stationery mob on Friday."

"Stationery?"

"Aye. I've been in that line of business for a couple of years now. This would be a company switch, but I'd get an area of my own to work in the south of Scotland. Probably live in Ayr. Sales, you know?"

"I thought you went into textile designing."

"Ach, I got fed up with that. Stuck in an office all day."

Hattie put down a mug and poured him a coffee.

"How did the interview go?"

"No bad. I'll probably get the job. Should hear by the end of the week." He took a mouthful of coffee. "Aren't you wondering why I didn't get the Friday night train back, Hattie?"

"Why was that, Paul?"

"I wanted to see *you*. Where the hell have you been anyway? I rang about six times on Saturday and all this morning. Eventually decided to come over and camp on the doorstep till you showed."

"I've been in the country with a friend."

"Very nice. I thought you'd caught the sun. Is this a special friend, Hattie?"

"Just a girl I know."

"Aw, that's OK then." Paul smiled broadly. His teeth needed attention.

"Tell me about the old crowd."

They chatted. Paul enquired about Hattie's work, her social life. Hattie gave him an entertaining description, proud of some of the places she'd been, people she'd met. Dru's name was eliminated from the account.

"I couldn't stand living in London."

She saw immediately, with rising irritation, that he was jealous, his shabby male feathers ruffled.

"Dr Johnson said that if you're tired of London you're tired of life."

"Aye, maybe he did, but I'd soon get tired of the bloody English. And all these blacks running around. Give me good old Glesca."

She wanted to tell him that his crushing provincial inferiority complex was pathetic. Instead she merely looked him straight in the eye and said, "Oh well, I enjoy it. I couldn't go back."

"No? Listen, Hattie, there was something I wanted to say."

"Go ahead, Paul."

"D'you remember how it used to be with you and me?"

"I've got a good memory, Paul."

"Well, I think we could say we were quite fond. Yes?"

Hattie pushed out her lower lip and raised her eyebrows in an expression of only partial agreement. "We had fun together."

"That's a pretty cool way of putting it, Hattie. Anyway, I've had a few girlfriends since those days. I don't suppose you've been sitting on your hands either, eh?"

"Granted. Paul, what are you getting at?"

"D'you mind if I smoke?"

"Carry on, Paul. I've given them up."

He lit up and inhaled deeply, blowing a long jet of smoke towards the ceiling as he collected his thoughts.

"I'm no much good at speeches, Hattie. The thing is, I'm free these days, and with this new job I should finally be able to put a few quid in the bank. I was wondering if you and me could maybe . . . "

"Just what were you wondering, Paul?"

He inhaled again and was then seized by a coughing fit. "Sorry."

"You should stop smoking, Paul."

"Maybe I will if you ask me nicely, Hattie." He leered at her and winked but, seeing this produced no reaction, proceeded with his mission. "To come to the point, I was thinking you and I could hitch up. I could come down and stay with you here. You could come up to Ayr. If we got keen, well, I noticed a registry office not far from here. Who knows, Hattie?"

She knew she must be firm. Ambivalent attitudes had landed her in enough trouble recently. "Paul, that's very nice of you but I honestly think we've grown apart. We're no longer the same kids we were nine years ago."

He got up. Grinding out his cigarette he moved across the room and sat down beside her on the couch. Without more ado he put his arms round her and began to squeeze her breasts tentatively. This was the language Hattie Murray used to understand.

"Don't, Paul! Leave me alone."

Paul Horrigan knew women better than that. They liked to play hard to get. He continued to massage her breasts, slipping one hand under Hattie's blouse.

"Come on, Hattie. I bet you haven't changed. Except for the bra."

"Paul, I asked you to leave me alone."

She tried to wriggle out of his grasp but he had a firm grip round her shoulders. With his free hand he was now struggling with her skirt zip.

"Relax, for Christ's sake, Hattie! You really turn me on. Even if we never get spliced we can still enjoy a good screw, can't we?"

The zip was giving him trouble. He removed his arm to give him two hands for the job. Not only were Hattie's nerves jumping alarmingly, she was by now thoroughly angry. Paul Horrigan may have seemed all right at eighteen, but he now struck Hattie as a shallow, coarse individual. He certainly had no proprietorial claim on her, whatever might have happened years ago. She took her opportunity, sprang up and swung a hard, back-handed slap at his face.

"Get out! I asked you twice to stop."

The shock of the blow and the realisation that he was not going to get the satisfaction he'd so keenly anticipated infuriated him.

"You bitch! Who d'you think you are? So you've been to a few snobby clubs and chatted up some toffee-nosed MP.

Doesn't mean a thing. You're still a randy cow. You'd drop your drawers for the roadsweeper if he waved his cock at you."

"*Get out, Get out!*"

"Oh aye, Sandy Watson told me all about the time you sucked him off in his father's car."

"If you don't go this minute I'll call the police."

"Aw piss off! I'm going."

Ten minutes later Hattie was lying face down on her bed weeping without restraint.

15

HATTIE WAS MORE DISTURBED by those two days than she dared admit to herself. Strangely, it was easier to come to terms with the Dru fiasco than Paul Horrigan's visit. There was pain at losing in Dru a valuable, intimate friend, but the outlandish reasons for their separation somehow neutralised its effect, for the present anyway. She was left with pity.

Paul was different. No doubt he'd coarsened with the years, but he was nevertheless a link with her past life. He seemed symbolic of much else in her original background that she'd irrecoverably jettisoned. Apart from her job, Hattie realised, her hold on friends and a coherent social life in London had again become uncomfortably tenuous. She felt bleakly lonely, hollow.

Time passed and, as it seemed to Hattie, quite justifiably, she conceived a violent hatred of Paul Horrigan. Arrogant, cheap bastard! He really had thought he could casually look her up after God knows how many years and expect her to take her clothes off in half an hour. Dirty sod. But then, wasn't he typical of men? They all wanted it, and if it wasn't available on a willing basis the thing to do was to deceive or simply bully the woman into it. That had been the way in her family all down the line. Christ! How she loathed them.

It was a barren period during which Hattie buried herself in her work. Her industry was noticed and she received another substantial salary advance. It was gratifying to be making this headway but the emptiness of her inner life persisted. She went out to Chiswick when the women's meetings started again. Kate Loxton had been in the south of France during the summer so they'd not met for almost two months. She turned up at the second meeting.

"Hello, Kate. You're brown as a nut."

"I saw Drusilla Gore the other day."

"Yes?"

"She was very evasive. If I had to guess I'd say you two had had a row. Would I be right?"

"What did Dru actually say, Kate?"

"Enough to indicate you were no longer *intimes*. I'm not going to speculate on the possible reason, but I did give you some good advice once on Ms Drusilla's special requirements. Didn't I, dear?"

"I remember, Kate. Look, it won't do any good talking behind someone's back. As far as I'm concerned Dru is a dear person who works hard for women. If she has personal problems I'm just sorry. I hope she and I will always be friends."

Kate's cat-slit eyes narrowed, unsmiling. "Really?" How much had Dru told her? Hattie's heart was hammering uncomfortably. "Well, I'm afraid you won't be seeing much of her in future."

"Why not, Kate?"

"She's going back to California. Permanently. Something about another friend with a house on the beach. Someone she knew before when she was out there meeting the Feminists."

"I hope she's happy. She'll come over from time to time

I expect."

Kate eyed Hattie coldly. "Maybe."

Sheena wrote enclosing a Polaroid picture of her month-old daughter and warmly inviting Hattie to make the child's acquaintance on her next trip north. It had been a long time since Hattie had been home so she arranged to take a week's leave the following month and sent a line to her mother with the dates. Baby Valerie's photo was propped up on Hattie's mantel at Beaumont Street.

It was quite extraordinary. When she was in the flat Hattie caught herself more than once talking in baby language to Valerie's picture. She started carrying it in her handbag, peeping at the little face while she sat on the tube and when she was alone in the office. Knitting had never been Hattie's strong point but she now took immense pleasure going into wool shops to select baby clothes' patterns. A present for Valerie had to be special.

She decided finally that she couldn't face the complicated job of producing one of these articles and settled for a little quilted pram coatee and cap. Time after time she would open the box in the evening, hold up the tiny garments and croon, "There you are, my darling wee Val. These will keep you warm as toast when the nasty cold wind blows, won't they?" She was longing to see the child.

Her father appeared unchanged to Hattie, if slightly vaguer and less forceful in his speech. Retired four years now he didn't read the papers thoroughly, didn't listen to the radio or watch much television. Most of the time was spent with his books in the sitting room or the garden according to the season. After she'd given him some account of her present editorial responsibilities Hattie found there was little else to say. These days neither wanted to risk a disagreement, which a wider conversation would almost certainly have precipitated.

Charlotte was ageing fast. Still only 48 she had put on weight, her shoulders were rounding and her fine gold hair was now almost completely grey.

"Mum, you should dress better. That cardigan and skirt are positively *dowdy*."

"It doesn't matter, Hattie. As long as clothes are warm and hardwearing I'm content. Money's not easy, you know. This awful inflation everyone's talking about? Thank the Lord, Robert had the good sense to buy this house from the bank when he did. It's paid for now."

"Yes, I know. Anyway, try to choose something a bit brighter next time."

"Robert and I go out very little now."

Hattie exhaled sharply through clenched teeth. "*He's* maybe feeling done, Mum, but you're over twenty years younger. Don't get entirely into his ways."

"Yes, dear."

Soon after her arrival she drove up to neighbouring suburban Burnside. Willie and Sheena had chosen a small, between-the-wars semi-detached bungalow. Woodend Avenue's minute divided gardens were immaculate. Sandwiches and homemade cakes were on offer with the afternoon tea. Hattie took the bundle of baby, nappy and rompersuit on her knee.

"Hello, Valerie. I feel I know you already from your nice picture."

The baby chortled happily. Sheena fussed Hattie, delighted to show her visitor round the little house and to tell her all about her daughter's progress since birth. Willie was at work but had said he hoped Hattie would return when he could be at home. The time came to leave.

"Just put Val into her pram at the back door, Hattie, would you, before you go?" Sheena was fundamentally a kind and intelligent woman. She'd seen how much Hattie was enjoying handling the baby. She'd let her do this small chore by herself.

Sheena couldn't have guessed what the experience was actually meaning to her friend. In the even smaller back garden a fine big Silver Cross pram was stationed, the diminutive coverlet turned down to receive its occupant, a protective cat net ready to be fixed. Hattie stood by the pram holding the child. Pale blue eyes blinked at her. In her arms the scrap of life was warm.

"Oh God! I can't put you down, Valerie darling. I don't want to leave you."

Hattie was crying inwardly, in real anguish of spirit. For a second or two she didn't quite know where she was. Sheena appeared.

"Well now, Miss Val, we must get you under that blanket, mustn't we? I don't think your Auntie Hattie wants to say goodbye!" She turned smiling to take the baby. "Does she?"

Hattie swallowed and got herself under control. "She's an adorable child, Sheena."

There wasn't to be a second visit. The office rang that night asking Hattie to come back early for a special editorial conference. She left next morning.

BABY SNATCHED OUTSIDE SHOP
BIG POLICE HUNT ORDERED

The sensational story was on the front pages of the national press for several days. Hattie found herself actually sweating with anxiety for the child's welfare. But at idle moments she also fantasised about the case, imagining that she had stolen the child. She pictured herself secretly feeding and bathing the baby, keeping it till the hue and cry had died down, till the child regarded her as mother.

The real-life baby was released after a few days and the

story disappeared from the newspapers. But Hattie still dreamt. One day, after shopping in a small supermarket in Marylebone High Street, she emerged clutching some purchases and noticed a pram with a baby parked outside. Impulsively she put her free hand on the shiny black handle and rocked the child. "There's a pretty, pretty baby in his nice blue jacket." Furtively she tucked the coverlet under the little chin. "Mustn't catch cold, little one." From the corner of her eye she noticed the plateglass door begin to open and walked away smartly without looking back.

Soon Hattie was compelled to recognise with reluctance that, amazingly, she was broody. Every day it became clearer to her that only a baby of her own would cure an increasing sense of painful emptiness in her life. She considered her situation carefully. Single parent families were nowadays gaining respectability in the community and more financial support from the State, but it would obviously be impossible to keep her job if there was a child to be cared for. If she chose to stay at home her career was finished, at least for several years. If she tried to pay a full-time nanny the financial strain would be severe, bad for all concerned.

The more Hattie worried at the problem the more desperate she became for a solution. As a positive gesture, she broke the routine of years and stopped taking the pill. Gradually, another unexpected factor entered Hattie's thinking. However hard she tried to reject the idea, she felt compelled to accept that her child would undoubtedly be better off with a known father at home. Almost this realisation drove thoughts of chuckling babies from Hattie's mind, but the frustrated maternal instinct was too strong. In the end she evolved a picture of the necessary male. She even wrote down a rough specification – age 30/40; politics liberal, pro-feminist; personality quiet, biddable; job flexible, able to co-operate on child's routine. There were some preferred characteristics. He should be reasonably attractive, capable in bed and have some worthwhile money in the bank. Lastly, it was essential that he had no objection to continued sexual freedom for both partners after the baby's birth.

Coolly she surveyed any candidates she knew. Almost certainly it had to be one of the men she'd met at women's meetings. Their very presence in such company automatically confirmed several qualifications. She recalled one man who was often in evidence at Chiswick. He was usually with an older male friend, both journalists she thought, but he hadn't struck her as queer like some of the others. What was his name? Foley, that was it, Roger Foley.

A week later, drinking a half pint of bitter and chatting animatedly with Harriot Murray in the City Barge pub beside the river, Roger couldn't believe his luck. For some time he'd been an admirer of Hattie's forthright speeches, her obvious courage and the articulate manner in which she marshalled her arguments. His own mother was a bit like Hattie, but too set in her class-conscious ways to do any good in the modern movement. Her attitudes and opinions had, however, greatly influenced Roger, and she encouraged him to do what he could to help in the continuing emancipation of women.

Of course, he'd spoken to Hattie before at meetings, usually to commend some point she'd been making during discussion, but their relationship had never been more than superficial. She'd not shown any interest in him and, anyway, she'd usually been with her friend, Kate Loxton, or that dragon, Drusilla Slingsby-Gore. Now, for some reason, she seemed to want to know all about him – his job at the magazine, his family, his literary tastes, where he spent his holidays etcetera. It was very flattering and Roger was delighted to tell Hattie anything she wanted to know.

Later that week they dined together at a chic West End French restaurant. Roger belonged to a cinema club and a few days later took Hattie to a rather lurid German film about the history of brothels in Europe. He was electrified when, during one particularly explicit scene, she'd grabbed his hand and squeezed it hard.

Hattie invited him up to her flat for supper while they watched a TV debate on women's rights in which Kate was a panel member. Later, she put her arm round him on the couch and a passionate, if somewhat uncomfortable session ensued. Within three weeks an ecstatic Roger found himself in Hattie's bed.

For two months nothing happened. In answer to an oblique question Dr Jane Howard informed Hattie that prolonged use of the pill sometimes inhibited pregnancy for quite a time after contraception had technically ceased. However, by January 1965 Hattie suspected the fish had bitten and by February her condition was certain.

At first Roger panicked. Full of apologies he offered to finance the best abortion to be had. Hattie seized the opportunity to enquire searchingly into his financial resources and was gratified to discover what she had begun to suspect. Roger had opted out of his family's leather tanning business in Worcester and taken his share in cash. He was modestly well off. She quickly made it clear to Roger that she had every intention of having the baby and suggested to him that he would make a good father, that he should be proud of his part in the forthcoming drama.

Before long Roger realised that indeed, if his principles really meant anything at all, he must stand by Hattie. It was agreed he'd move in with her straight away, but that they'd start looking for a better place.

It was Roger who raised the subject of marriage.

"I mean, I don't hold with many of the conventions,

Hattie. It's slavishly observing society's entrenched customs that perpetuates a good deal of exploitation and unfair discrimination. Especially where women are concerned."

"Quite. So why talk about marriage?"

"Oh, I don't know. I suppose I was thinking about the baby."

"My child will be raised a free-thinking independent person, without all the deadening intellectual and emotional baggage imposed by a male-dominated system. He or she will carry on the good fight unencumbered by restrictive social structures."

Roger swallowed. He knew he was no match for Hattie in an argument, but he had to try again.

"Of course I agree with that in principle, Hattie. It's just, well, I know my people will expect it. Mother especially." He looked apprehensively at Hattie. "We can teach the child whatever we think is right throughout its life."

This was going to be the first important test of wills and Hattie knew she must prevail.

"Am I to understand, Roger, that you are going to regard your mother's predilections as more valid than mine? Never mind our joint views about what's best for children?" He opened his mouth to reply but Hattie held up her hand. "Good God! I thought you had a mind of your own. Didn't you free yourself from family controls when you quit the business?"

"I didn't want to go into tanning. That's all. It didn't mean I . . . "

"Whatever your family may or may not mean to you, Roger, *we're* together now and you're the father of this new life growing in my womb. That's an overwhelming responsibility, and don't you dare think of sliding out of it."

"Hattie! That's not fair. You know I've no intention of doing that."

"Men are past masters at behaving utterly selfishly if they don't get their way. Just don't you try it, Roger Foley. I'm warning you."

He knew it was useless to go on. "So, you're saying we're not going to get married?"

"That's right. We never spoke about it. But that didn't stop you jumping into bed at the first possible moment, did it?"

Roger hung his head. "No," he said dully, "but we were both pretty keen."

Hattie did not respond. She let a few moments pass, then remarked, "I thought we agreed completely on the sanctity of individual liberty?"

"Yes," Roger confirmed uncertainly.

"Including sexual freedom?"

"I suppose that's logical. Although . . . "

Hattie went for the kill. "The agreed logic of our views, therefore, is that although we may live together, each accepts that the other is free to have loving relationships with others from time to time."

"But, Hattie darling, I wouldn't want to . . . "

"I'm not saying either of us is going to rush out looking for new bedmates the whole time. Nevertheless, I *am* saying that we must respect each other's freedom and right to alternative relationships, if the situation arises."

"Well, yes, *if* it ever arises, Hattie."

"As long as we understand one another, Roger."

Presently she sent him out for a bottle of milk. When he returned the resigned look on his face was what she'd expected. Their conversation for the rest of that evening was desultory. As Hattie washed up and Roger dried he said quietly, just a hint of peevishness in his tone, "You've never met Mother."

"I've not been invited."

"Oh, Hattie!" His dismay was palpable. She'd shown no interest whatsoever in being introduced to his family.

"Well, have I?"

"I suppose not formally but . . . "

Hattie clattered a saucepan noisily down on the melamine worktop. "Why don't we visit her soon? Saturday?"

"I'm sure it would be OK." Roger smiled for the first time in several hours. "I'll give her a ring shortly."

"Fine. When that particular custom has been observed, I'll take you up to Scotland."

"To meet your parents? I'd like that very much."

The appointment made with Mrs Foley for two weeks later, Hattie directed Roger's attention to a sheaf of estate agents' property leaflets she'd picked up that day. They sat examining details, finally winnowing out three possible premises. All were within walkable distance, so they went out for a preliminary reconnaissance. A scarlet-shuttered, two-storeyed, three-bedroomed house in Brodick Mews greatly took their fancy. By now Hattie knew the full extent of Roger's assets.

"It'll stretch us, Roger, but this looks just right. Don't you think so? According to this sheet there's even a tiny garden at the back. Big enough for a pram anyway."

"If you really like it, Hattie, I can't see any reason to object."

"We'll have to see inside of course, but I've a feeling we shouldn't miss it. It could be a fabulous investment too."

Her enthusiasm had communicated itself. "Right, Hattie. I'll be on the agent's doorstep at opening time."

There was another keen buyer and they had to offer a premium to secure the property, but they were both thrilled when the sale was confirmed a day later, subject to contract exchange. Hattie danced about the empty rooms eagerly planning their furnishing. The neat little garden turned out to be walled and well looked after. She gave a month's notice on the flat.

On the eve of her first visit to Roger's family in Worcester Hattie sat with him watching a TV comedy serial. Her attention wandered. Sometimes these days she thought she'd explode with excitement. Almost three months pregnant now, the unstoppable reality of approaching motherhood filled her mind. She'd become convinced it would be a girl and started thinking of names. Then, 12 Brodick Mews, W1 – they'd be moving in in a week's time to camp in one room while carpets and furniture were delivered. It had been tremendous fun choosing everything, and Roger had demonstrated an unexpectedly good taste about fabrics, light fittings and so on. He'd been a great help.

Hattie decided she'd never been so happy in her life. Her only worry was Mrs Victoria Foley. The auguries for their meeting were not good.

16

THE TANNERY WAS in the town, *Greenlawns*, the family home, a mile outside. A three hundred years old wood-frame house, it had been substantially enlarged and converted over time, till now it stood comfortably in its one and a half acre garden. They parked in a small courtyard at the back and walked to the front door, which was locked. Roger rang and they were admitted by an elderly domestic.

"Oh, it's Roger! I mean Mr Foley. Sorry, dear." This person touched Hattie's arm, smiled and said, "Can't get used to that 'Mr Foley!' I've know'd Roger since he were a young 'un."

"Hello, Mrs Carpenter. How are you?"

"Just fine, dear. Now, your mother's in the drawing room waiting, so don't you stand around gossipin' with me. I'll get some coffee on the go. Coffee all right for you, miss?"

"Lovely. Thank you, Mrs Carpenter."

Victoria Foley did not get up when they entered the room. Roger quickly greeted her with an affectionate kiss on the cheek. She held out her hand to Hattie and for a second the visitor felt a crazy impulse to curtsy. Instead, she grasped the rather podgy fingers and pumped the cardiganed arm.

"How d'you do, Mrs Foley?"

"Very well thank you . . . Miss Murray?"

"Do call me Hattie."

"Is that Harriet?"

"That's it. With an 'O'."

"I shall call you Harriot. Do sit down. Roger wrote to me about you."

"Really?"

Roger hurriedly broke in, "Just about how we met in Chiswick and so on."

"You seem to be doing splendid work for the cause of women's emancipation, Harriot."

"One tries to help."

"I think you're too modest. Many of the young feminists today I find admirable, though they can be horribly strident on occasion." Hattie warmed to this rather amusingly haughty woman. "It's important always to mind our manners, however passionate our feelings. Don't you agree, Harriot?"

"Up to a point, yes. It depends on circumstances." She quickly saw that Mrs Foley did not like a reaction other than unqualified endorsement of her opinions.

Coffee and biscuits were wheeled in on a silent trolley.

"Ah, thank you, Mrs Carpenter." Mrs Foley proceeded to fill the Spode cups from a modern cafetière. "And you're an editor too. Do tell me about that, Harriot."

Hattie obliged with a brief description of her work. There was a pause. Roger cleared his throat and put down his cup and saucer.

"Mother, in case I've not made it clear, Hattie and I are living together in Marylebone. We've found a mews house to move into soon."

Mrs Foley didn't blink. "I had gathered as much, Roger. It didn't happen in my day, but I'm not going to moralise.

I suppose these trial marriages may actually avoid a good deal of unhappiness."

Roger's next information, however, did cause his mother to sit up. "We're going to have a baby."

"Good Lord!" Mrs Foley's mouth fell open. She looked quickly at Hattie. "Are you sure?"

"There's no doubt now, Mrs Foley. It's been over three months."

"It could *still* be a mistake. You could be lucky. I remember an old school friend of mine who . . . "

"But I *want* the baby."

Victoria Foley was having difficulty understanding the situation. She took a rapid mouthful of coffee.

"But . . . but, there isn't *time*. Even if you got a special licence and married tomorrow it would still be too late, wouldn't it?" She looked, suddenly betraying anger, at her son, but Roger was staring at the carpet.

"Too late for what, Mrs Foley?"

The older woman was becoming red in the face. "Well I never! You know perfectly well what I mean! How can the child ever be, you know . . . legitimate? Properly so anyway? Good gracious! . . . what's the . . . the . . . ?" Mrs Foley was spluttering now.

"Do calm down, Mother," said Roger miserably.

"*I will not calm down!* What about the family name? What about your parents? Roger, how could you?"

Hattie looked at the agitated woman expressionlessly. "I think Roger's right. There's no point in getting yourself worked up. After all, it's his life. And mine, incidentally."

Mrs Foley ignored her, pointedly addressing her son. "When *are* you going to marry then?"

Roger glanced at Hattie. She replied, "We're not."

The effect was to produce absolute silence in the room. The sound of the front door opening and closing reached them, followed by a few steps and the rattle of the drawing room door handle. It was Mr Foley.

"Well, hello everyone! Roger. Victoria. And this must be Hattie? So pleased to meet you, my dear. Reg Foley."

"Reginald, I'm afraid there's . . . "

"D'you think I could have a cuppa, dear? I'm perished." A hearty, good-natured man, thought Hattie, observing his portly figure and fleshy, rubicund face. "Cut my game to nine holes this morning, but I still got damnably cold out there. Wasn't sorry to pack it in to tell you the truth, Hattie. Playing like a drain I was anyway." He laughed loudly.

"There's rather serious news, Reginald."

"Oh?"

"Roger, are you going to tell your father?"

"All right, Mother. Hattie and I are living together in London and we're going to have a baby."

Instinctively Reg Foley broke out in happy laughter again. "Well done! Well done! I call that *good* news. And when can I expect to be a grandfather?"

"*Reginald!*" Mrs Foley's shout of irritation at her husband had a practiced ring about it.

Mr Foley looked perplexed. Hattie made matters plain. "The baby will be born in about five and a half months' time."

"And of course they're not married. What's worse, they've no intention of doing so! Now do you understand, Reginald?"

He cocked his head on one side. "You're in a bit of a pickle then. Yes. I see. But . . . it's not the end of the world, is it? I mean, there are ways of dealing with this sort of problem nowadays." He was looking at his wife but once again Hattie replied.

"I'm not getting rid of the baby by abortion *or* adoption, if that's what you mean. It's our child and we're going to cherish it."

Foley smiled admiringly at her. "Good girl," he muttered.

This further infuriated Mrs Foley. For the first time since Hattie and Roger's arrival she got to her feet, screwing up a paper napkin and picking up her glasses case. "I will not listen to any *more* of this. I was looking forward to our lunch together but I couldn't face it now."

Reg put a hand on his wife's arm. "Steady now, Victoria. Perhaps they're just not ready. Maybe in a little while. Eh, Hattie?" He had already realised that she was the decision maker.

"We believe in personal freedom, Mr Foley. Not the shackles of matrimony."

"Oh my God!" Mrs Foley was now white with exasperation.

Her genial husband suddenly lost patience too. "D'you mean that even with the bond of a baby, my grandchild by the way, you'll both feel free to have a bit on the side whenever you get the notion?"

"If you insist on putting it that way, yes."

Mrs Foley grabbed the sleeve of her husband's checked sports jacket. "Reginald! Come out of this room immediately! If they've any decency at all, they'll leave our house and not come back unless they're prepared to try at least to act like civilized British people." She was crying with vexation. "Roger, surely we brought you up to respect the decencies? I just can't understand you."

"Times are changing, Mother. In some ways we hope to be *more* 'decent' than was often the case in the past."

It was Roger's father's turn to be angry. "Just what is that supposed to mean, boy? Your mother and I . . . "

"I meant nothing personal, Dad. But you have to understand . . . "

"Reginald, this is hopeless. I never expected to hear such heartless, cruel, downright immoral words from my own son. Of course I couldn't foresee the wicked influence he'd come under." She gave a stifled sob and left the room with her husband unhappily in tow.

Roger and Hattie moved in to the new house and by the end of April had the basic furnishing and fittings in place. They could spend the rest of the year completing the job of turning 12 Brodick Mews into a home, but already their nest was comfortable, ready for the newcomer.

"Roger, I don't feel up to Scotland. I think I'll ask my mother down here."

"Fine. What about Mr Murray?"

"He doesn't travel much these days. Anyway, we've never seen eye to eye."

Roger glanced uneasily at Hattie. "Pity."

There was a lot to explain to Charlotte and Hattie decided it would be easier to get it over with by phone.

"Mum? How are you?"

"Oh, Hattie! How lovely to hear your voice. I'm all right but Robert's a bit down at present. Mr MacKenzie, one of the church elders, has just been in to see him. That always does him good."

"I wondered if you could get away for a visit. Say, some weekend soon? Quite a few things are happening at this end."

"I expect so. It's been ages, hasn't it? What is it that's happening, Hattie?"

"Well, to begin with I've found a man. He's called Roger Foley and we've moved into a new house together."

"You mean you're living . . . ?"

"Yes, we're living together, Mum."

Quietly Charlotte's voice came down the line. "I'm sure you know what you're doing, Hattie. I hope you're well and happy."

"Affirmative on both counts, thanks, Mum. I'm going to have a baby."

"Oh, goodness! Hattie, when . . . I mean, how long . . . ?"

"We can talk about all that when we meet. Never mind just now, Mum."

Charlotte arrived by train the following Saturday morning. Hattie met her at Euston. They saved their serious talk until they were safely indoors, Charlotte drinking coffee, Hattie herb tea. Roger had tactfully found it necessary to deliver some copy to his Holborn office.

"What a perfectly lovely little house, Hattie."

"It is nice, isn't it?"

They inspected the other partially furnished rooms and the small garden.

"So much better than a flat."

"Yes. We should be straight by Christmas."

They sat down in the living room.

"Now, tell me the whole story, Hattie. Your father and I got quite a shock, as you'd imagine."

"Let's leave him out of it."

Charlotte sighed. "When did you find out, Hattie?"

"It was definitely confirmed not all that long ago, but I'd suspected it for months."

Charlotte couldn't hide her anxiety. "So, how long is it . . . I mean . . . ?"

"The baby's due in mid September, Mum, all things being equal." Hattie saw her mother's anguish. It would be best to give her all the bad news in one. "And as far as Roger and I are concerned we have no plans to marry."

"But, Hattie, the baby? Don't you think . . . ?"

"We both believe in the supreme importance of personal freedom. Our child will be taught to think that way too, not to heed the suffocating structures of a paternalistic society. Can you understand that at all, Mum?"

Watching her vital, attractive daughter that morning Charlotte realised that Hattie's present behaviour was all of a piece with the rebellious attitudes she'd developed in adolescence. The compulsion to assert total independence as a woman had eventually led her, inevitably and quite consistently, to want to produce a baby but, at the same time, to reject the conventional ties that marriage necessarily entailed. Oh yes, there was logic in Hattie's behaviour, and her courage was not in question either but, for the thousandth time in the past twelve years, Charlotte asked herself where it would all end.

She was quite prepared, if it could not be avoided, to welcome an illegitimate child into the family, to overlook what amounted to wilfully immoral behaviour on Hattie's part, in the hope that she would eventually calm down. Charlotte was no prude. What troubled her deeply was the degree of Hattie's dedication to her ideas of how a woman should behave in 1965. She perceived a disturbing element of desperation in Hattie's evolving approach to life. With a mother's intuition Charlotte foresaw dimly that there could well come a time when her daughter would badly need her. Charlie hardly ever wrote now. Maybe he'd never come back from America. She decided at that moment that, whatever might happen, whatever anybody else might say or think, she was not going to lose Hattie's affection.

"You really mustn't expect a conventional old lady like me to go along fully with these very new ideas, Hattie. But if you've thought it out with Roger and believe you're doing the right thing by yourselves and your baby, then I accept it. After all, you're twenty eight, Hattie, even if I still think of you as my darling little girl."

"I knew you'd understand, Mum. Bless you."

Mother and daughter embraced emotionally.

"Careful now," said Charlotte. "There's a little person in

there and he doesn't like being squeezed!"

"She. I'm certain it'll be a girl."

Roger returned. He was a pleasant surprise to Charlotte who realised she'd been expecting some kind of bearded eccentric. Here was an affable, polite fellow, dressed in a neat suit and yellow poloneck sweater, enquiring solicitously about her sleeper train.

"Long journeys by train are the devil I find. If you fly down next time I'll be glad to meet you at Heathrow. The new shuttle service is not too expensive I think."

He asked about Rutherglen and said he looked forward to bringing the baby up in due course. There was no embarrassment as he spoke. Charlotte wondered if this was a much commoner situation than she'd imagined. Was she even more behind the times in her provincial backwater than she'd thought?

It was when they began discussing arrangements for the child's upbringing that Charlotte saw how dominant Hattie's will was in the partnership. It emerged that she didn't anticipate being absent from her editorial desk for more than three months, one ahead of the birth, two thereafter. A nanny would live in, and Roger was clearly expected to exploit to the full the flexibility of his hours in order to be available a good deal of the time Hattie was at the office. By lunchtime it was obvious to Charlotte that, well meaning and intelligent though he undoubtedly was, Roger's bonhomie and confidence lacked depth. He looked to Hattie for a lead in everything. Maybe it was as well that way.

As she settled into her return sleeper compartment on Sunday night Charlotte's feelings were confused. And she was increasingly apprehensive about her ability to explain the position to Robert. He'd never understand. It might even break his heart.

When Roger got back from Euston he found Hattie in

bed reading. He joined her.

"I liked your mother, Hattie."

"She's sweet, isn't she?"

"Yes, and nobody's fool either."

Hattie put her book down on the duvet. "Charlotte Murray is a copybook example of a talented woman crushed by a ruthlessly exploitative husband."

"Is he a bit of an ogre then?"

"You'll never get her to admit it. She's loyal, faithful to her vows, one of the old school, but the fact is she was torn, kicking and screaming, from her educational path. On the verge of great things she was. University, then research probably. I think she could have been a scientist of some standing."

"Christ! What a pity."

"Indeed. I once heard her speaking to an afternoon group at our church in Rutherglen. Something about the history of the district, its notables, flora and fauna etcetera. She was marvellous. The audience was spellbound, in the palm of her hand. No slides or videos, no nothing except – so she told me later – a morning's research at the local library. I tell you, with further education she could have been up there with most of the TV pundits we pay attention to today. An utter waste of real talent."

"Couldn't she have . . .?"

"Oh no! Mr Robert Murray needed a wife to help his shabby little career along at the bank. So he and my grandfather simply decided matters between them and gave my mother her orders."

Roger shook his head in totally sincere disapproval. "That wasn't all that long ago. Almost *unbelievable*."

"It happened. Male chauvinism is very skilful at exerting all sorts of subtle and diabolical pressures to get its own way, Roger. Everything from crude physical bullying to emotional blackmail."

Roger had been internally much upset since the row with his mother. He'd seen the pain in Mrs Murray's eyes too, even if she did cover up very well. Coming back in the car tonight he'd decided to broach the subject of marriage again with Hattie, to see if he could extract some kind of minimum undertaking that they reconsider the question at a later date. But as he slipped down now and turned his cheek to the pillow he knew it would be pointless to risk a blazing argument again.

"Goodnight, Hattie."

"Oh, goodnight, Roger."

Hattie had picked up her book again and was reading with concentration.

17

IN RETROSPECT the next four months would always seem dreamlike to Hattie. Methodically she built up a layette of frothy little garments, stubbornly choosing everything in shades of pink. Roger found a capacious well preserved Victorian wheeled cot and lined it with white muslin, secured by broad silk ribbon. Having studied the latest evidence, pro and con, Hattie decided she would breast-feed the child. She was careful with diet and stopped any alcohol intake.

Roger was very good with her, especially during the last week or two. Nothing seemed to be too much trouble, and Hattie found herself feeling real affection for this kindly man whose principal effect, to date, had been to irritate her. She had, of course, deliberately sought out a malleable, easily-managed individual as a mate, but that did not mean she considered such characteristics particularly admirable. However, she knew now, whatever might happen to their relationship over the years, that she had been absolutely right to ensure her little girl had a father to help raise her.

At two forty five in the afternoon of September nineteenth, 1965 Sylvia Murray was born. It was not a difficult birth and she was perfect. When the little raw creature was put to her breast Hattie, already deliriously happy, felt faint from sheer joy. Sylvia responded with contented murmurs.

Roger told his mother the news by telephone but she simply cried, "Oh Roger!" dissolved in tears and then slammed down the receiver. Charlotte was restrained but she did ask about the baby's colouring, congratulate Roger and send her love to Hattie.

Mother and child were soon back at Brodick Mews. Miss Matthews, the new nanny, had already moved in. About forty and motherly, she was going to be vital to their plans. Hattie took care to cultivate her allegiance from the outset. At the original interview the question of their marital non-status had been taken head on.

"Mr Foley and I have progressive views about family life, Miss Matthews. We're not married in law but we intend to provide at least as stable and loving an environment as many conventional couples do. I take it you have no reservations."

Peggy Matthews had looked doubtful at first, but as Hattie smiled reassuringly at her she seemed suddenly to make up her mind. "I think times have changed, especially where professional ladies like yourself are concerned, Miss Murray. I've seen a deal of unhappiness and cheating in so-called respectable marriages I can tell you. If you and Mr Foley are going to make a real home and take a true interest in your little one, that's good enough for me."

"That's all right then, Peggy. As long as we understand one another we'll get on fine. I can see you're a caring person and I'm sure you're extremely capable. These references of yours are first rate."

Miss Matthews straightened her shoulders with pride. "Thank you very much indeed, Miss Murray."

"You really must call me Hattie. Everyone does. And my husband . . . I mean . . . Mr Foley, he's Roger."

They laughed together at Hattie's slip. Peggy Matthews'

goodwill had been secured.

Early in December Hattie went back to work. In her absence they'd farmed out her authors to other colleagues. Simon Hotchkiss, the senior editor, called her into his office.

"Welcome back, Hattie. We've missed your smiling face. How's the baby?"

"Sylvia's thriving, thanks, Simon. Is there still a job for me here?"

"If there wasn't you'd have us in court before we could consult counsel, wouldn't you?"

"Probably."

He gave her a thin smile. "As a matter of fact, something's come up which I think you'll find intriguing."

"Oh?"

"Let me explain." Hattie was now told about a planned new house imprint, 'Valkyrie', which would specialise in books about women's affairs, particularly their changing position in Western society. We're bringing in Judith Goldstein as managing director."

Hattie knew of her as fiftyish, at the top of her profession.

"Nothing but the best, Simon."

"That's right. This is going to be a very important market for us in the future, don't you agree?"

"Yes. You could well be right."

Hotchkiss leaned back in his swivel chair and picked up a tortoiseshell letter opener. "We know of your outside interests, Hattie, and, in my opinion, this venture could be right up your street. What d'you say?"

"It's interesting all right. What sort of position had you in mind, from the seniority point of view?"

"There'll be a board of three to begin with – Judith Goldstein of course, and me, for a year or two anyway till we see how things go. We'd like you to be the third director, Hattie. There'd be a good salary lift, naturally."

"Done, Simon."

Hattie shook his hand enthusiastically.

"The lawyers and accountants are on the job already. Articles of Association, a set of company books etcetera. Judith will be here next week. I'd say come New Year '66 Valkyrie should be in business."

On her way home by underground that evening Hattie shut her eyes as the now familiar excitement at imminent reunion with Sylvia began. Every day she was better pleased with her choice of name. S Pankhurst was probably looking down from her psephological heaven and watching the progress of her little namesake. She was going to be proud of her, as proud as she'd no doubt been of her own free child. And now this new job and a *directorship*. Hattie wondered what else she could possibly have achieved to improve her outlook. She ran most of the way home from Regents Park Station.

Charlotte came down again and said all the right flattering things. Not once did she ask about marriage, nor was Robert's name mentioned. Roger's older bachelor colleague at the magazine, John Quarry, visited, bringing an over-generous selection of toys which would be of no interest to Sylvia for at least three years. Kate Loxton called to donate a tiny antique, solid silver bell and to profess herself 'frankly astounded but very pleased indeed' at the events in Hattie's life during the past year. The Foleys did not come to Brodick Mews.

Valkyrie Ltd, held its first board meeting, and editorial attitudes and a potential author list were minuted. Appointments and salaries were confirmed. Judith Goldstein was a forceful woman and Hattie knew she'd have to produce her best work consistently to win any commendation. But it was a tremendous opportunity and Hattie determined to throw herself into it.

A domestic routine was quickly established. Roger made his own hours at the office unless a deadline had to be met, but this was a rare occurrence. So, most mornings, after Hattie had gone, he'd take a list of requirements compiled by Hattie and Peggy and go out shopping. Baby foods, disposable nappies, wine, stamps, French bread, coffee beans, fruit, toilet paper. Roger was soon an expert on the most convenient, keenest-priced sources of any item. He quite enjoyed the task. If he was home first, which was frequently the case, it was understood that he'd prepare the evening meal. Roger became quite a good cook.

Sometimes when Hattie looked at him, even as she felt a faint gratitude, another darker emotion stirred. She wanted somehow to hurt him. She could not have said what the springs of this impulse were but there was no use denying its existence. The more tolerant and helpful Roger's behaviour towards her, the more insistently came the urge to wound him. Hattie was not proud of this feeling, she could not fully understand it, but it was real.

In the shops Roger heard talk of a series of robberies in the area, some involving an unpleasant degree of threatened or actual violence.

"Hattie, I'm not happy about having no means of defence. Not with Sylvia potentially at risk anyway."

"What can we do? You'd never get a firearms licence, would you?"

"No, but I've got a shotgun at Greenlawns."

"*Have* you? I didn't know you were a slaughterer of birds."

"I'm not, and never have been. My grandfather left it to me. Actually, it's a beautiful thing, a Purdey sidelock with fine engraving. My father's a shooter of course. That was one of our early quarrels."

"You'd better go and get it then. Take the photos of Sylvia."

Roger went alone and brought back his gun and a box of cartridges.

"Father thought Sylvia looked like you."

"Did he say anything else?"

"Not much. Just that he wished we could all meet but that Mother won't have it."

"Weak fool."

"That's a bit hard, Hattie. You don't know Mother. If he tried . . . "

"Oh to *hell* with them, Roger! I don't want to hear any more."

"No. I suppose not." He went upstairs to conceal the shotgun at the back of their bedroom hanging-cupboard.

Hattie became very busy in the new enterprise. Judith Goldstein had left a good position for Valkyrie and she wanted results. However, the effects of producing Sylvia followed by months of hard work began to tell. Hattie needed a holiday.

They took a villa in the hills behind St Tropez in the Province of Var. It had a pool and she, Peggy and Roger lay in the sun all day, thinking private thoughts as they luxuriated in the heat. Now and again Sylvia was left with her nanny while they explored the silent vineyard country or shady old towns like Grimaud, the narrow streets redolent of an earlier presence – the Knights Templar. Roger and Hattie ate exquisite seafood meals or simply gorged on gargantuan ice-creams.

Once or twice they spent an afternoon on a smart beach. Hattie lay minus her bikini top with half-shut eyes, watching a constant parade of dark-skinned, perfectly sculptured male pulchritude. She was aware of the females, often breathtakingly beautiful in G-strings and bare breasts, but it was the men that she studied hungrily. The currently fashionable swimslips were so abbreviated and high on the hips that nothing was left to the imagination. And Hattie's imagination needed no stimulation to transport her from the beach to the private seclusion of a hotel room with any one of these youthful Adonises. Mainly they seemed to be German.

But, returned to the villa, it was bath-time for Sylvia and, not long after, they fell into bed, sun-exhausted. Life was full for Hattie. The memory of the sexy peacocks on the beach quickly faded.

Neither did any other memories of the holiday long endure as she became re-engulfed in the building of Valkyrie's list. In no time, it seemed, it was Christmas again. Then spring was on the way with a sprinkling of early yellow crocuses in the park. Hattie enjoyed wheeling Sylvia along the prettily bordered paths on Saturday mornings, the baby sitting up in her pram and chuckling at the antics of the ducks on the canal. Sylvia was an enchanting child.

Charlotte came down again and stayed for a few days. She was equally delighted with Sylvia and got on well with Roger. They didn't go north and it became an established routine for Granny to visit once in the spring and once in the autumn.

Both Hattie and Roger brought colleagues home from the office. They made a few friends among the neighbours and at the local pub, the Dover Castle. This hostelry was not far from the BBC studios at Portland Place and it attracted an unusually interesting clientele as a result. Once a month or so a small dinner-party was held at Brodick Mews and about as often, Hattie and Roger went out for a similar occasion. Hattie considered that they had a satisfactory social life.

Those first few years simply disappeared in a whirl of constant activity. Hardly able to believe it Hattie realised all of a sudden that Sylvia was not only an intensely curious child and a fluent talker but that she was ready for nursery school. Peggy knew from other nannies of a suitable place nearby so Hattie now went along and proudly enrolled her daughter.

Either Peggy or Roger delivered her in the mornings and collected her at midday. The well-bred young lady in charge described Sylvia as 'a highly intelligent little girl, a natural leader who should do very well.' A year later, in 1971, she was attending a private school in Bayswater. Roger drove her there and back. Among the pupils was an admixture of diplomats' and foreign businessmen's children, and Sylvia kept her parents constantly interested with a stream of African, Arabic and Oriental words. However, after a couple of years, Hattie became unsure if the school, though no doubt fashionable, was really giving Sylvia the mental fodder she needed. There was a difficult interview with the headmistress, an expensively dressed, tetchy widow, and afterwards Hattie told Roger that she'd taken Sylvia away from the school.

She consulted Judith and other professional friends with daughters. Her conclusion was that Sylvia should be sent away to Berkshire to board. The new school's prospectus spoke of 'a warm, caring atmosphere where a girl's intellectual and social capabilities are developed to the full.'

It was a miserable journey up to St James's Preparatory School for Girls, Roger driving, a white-faced seven and three quarter year old Sylvia sitting in the back. Hattie tried to cheer her up a bit when the sweeping lawns and attractive brick buildings came into view.

"Look, Sylvia, isn't it a lovely school. And, d'you know, they've got an Olympic-sized swimming pool?"

"I hate swimming."

"Oh nonsense, darling."

"You know I do."

Hattie tried again. "I've seen the dormitories, Sylvia, and they're really nice and cosy."

"I want to go home."

This went on more or less constantly until it was time to part. Hattie hugged the little girl and promised to write a letter to her that night. There was no response. Not till Roger took her in his arms and kissed her did Sylvia give way. Then the floodgates opened. Sylvia clung to her father and wouldn't let him go.

"Daddy, Daddy, I love you! Don't leave me ... *please!*"

"Darling, we must. You'll be all right when we've gone." Roger was struggling with tears.

"But I want to stay with you always."

"I know, I know, but never mind, Sylvia, you'll be home for half term in no time."

The reply to this was an inconsolable howl. Hattie was unhappily aware of the intensity of feeling between the other two. She took Roger by the elbow and they left hurriedly.

On the journey back to London they did not speak. Only as they neared home did Roger bleakly venture, "I do hope we've done the right thing. She's so young."

Hattie screwed up her lips. "She'll be as right as rain in a day or two. I want her to be independent, not hanging on to her parents' coat-tails."

But Roger was not listening. His heart was aching and all he knew was that he loved his little daughter dearly.

Peggy Matthews was paid off and suddenly the house became uncomfortably quiet. For a while they went to the Dover Castle more often in the evenings, but Hattie's workload increased remorselessly. She didn't resent this. On the contrary, Valkyrie's progress was now a national talking point in the publishing business and Hattie deeply valued her involvement. It did mean, however, that most nights her briefcase was full of papers to look through, or there was a manuscript to evaluate. If Roger went out to the Dover for a couple of hours it really suited her. She worked more quickly in his absence.

Sometimes she'd put her work aside, pour herself a drink and lie down on the couch. The house was efficiently heated and, as she lay there alone in the warm silence, Hattie found herself day-dreaming about encounters with strange men. She hadn't really felt this way for years, but, as the months went by, she had to admit to herself that she was sexually frustrated. After Sylvia's birth she'd resumed taking the pill but it had been a long time now since she and Roger had made love. The plain fact was that he bored her utterly. He'd never really been much of a bedmate. Hattie thought of all her male colleagues and friends. Mentally she undressed them one by one. Was any a candidate? In the end she decided probably not.

One darkening, rainy afternoon she happened to be in Westminster. Head down she was hurrying for the shelter of the underground.

"Hattie! It's Hattie Murray, isn't it?"

"Yes . . . I . . . "

"John Chetwynd. You remember? You came to tea once on the Terrace of the House with Drusilla Gore."

18

HATTIE OFTEN WONDERED if things might have been different had that chance meeting failed to occur. Perhaps not significantly, she eventually concluded. If John hadn't turned up she'd almost certainly have found someone else. The child was settled at boarding school and Roger seemed to have got himself into a rut that satisfied his limited aspirations, but she was full of life, pawing the ground for new adventures you might even say.

Just the same she didn't suppose either she or John Chetwynd had any real idea of what was ahead of them when he put his arm round her waist and pulled her close so that they might both be shielded by his cane-handled umbrella. It was flattering to see the rush of pleasure in his distinguished face.

"Yes, John, of course I remember you. And our conversation at that dinner party in Lascelles Square?"

"That's right. Look, there's some sort of café place over there. Have you time for a coffee?"

"All right."

How incongruous John Chetwynd was in the steamy little sandwich bar. Hattie noticed some of the defeated-looking customers staring at this handsome, immaculately suited man and whispering to one another. Probably they vaguely recognised him from his TV appearances of a few years ago. He had difficulty squeezing his person behind one of the little plastic-topped tables that were fixed to the wall. Seated opposite her at last he laughed with amused relief.

"These places are not meant for the likes of me I'm afraid."

"No," said Hattie, realising he'd intended no irony. What a frank, open face he had. His clear brown eyes looked straight into her own from under thick eyebrows, his nose was strong, his skin, although without a trace of colour, nevertheless glowed healthily. But it was John Chetwynd's mouth that Hattie found his most compelling feature. Generously Cupid's bow-shaped the full lips somehow managed to convey strength of purpose with a sensitive sensuality.

"Well, well," he smiled, "fancy running into you after all this time."

"I'm glad."

"Rather." He drank his coffee, clearly without much pleasure. "Tell me, Hattie, what happened to you? I mean, I know Drusilla went off to live in California. She sends a Christmas card every year. But you just seemed to drop out of things altogether."

"I got very busy in my job. I also had a baby."

"Well done you! Boy or girl?"

"Sylvia's eight now. At boarding school."

"And your husband? Is he . . . ?"

"No husband."

"Oh, I'm sorry, Hattie."

"That's all right, John. Roger Foley, the child's father, and I share a house in Marylebone."

"Yes, I see." He lowered his head and glanced up with

a mischievous smile. "You've always been an independent lady I think, Hattie."

"As far as is possible in this man's world."

"Are you still involved in the Women's Movement? It's certainly taken off this last year or two."

"Not really. Except via my work. I still keep in touch but there simply isn't time these days. You?"

"Oh yes. I chair an all-party committee. We're trying to get cross-bench support at the moment for proposed legislation to stop financial institutions discriminating against women. Most of them insist that a woman who wants to raise venture capital for a new business has a male partner, as an example."

He enquired about Hattie's job. She told him proudly about her directorship and the objectives of Valkyrie.

"Splendid! I thought you'd do well." He looked at his watch. "I have to go. I say, Hattie," nervously he touched his hair, "d'you think we might meet again?"

"I'd like to, John."

"Oh good. What about dinner one evening?"

Diaries were consulted and a date agreed.

"Could you possibly come to the House? I'll be tied up till seven. The Central Lobby?"

"I still get a thrill going into the House of Commons," said Hattie, nodding her assent.

At first Roger made a face when she told him of her appointment.

"What are you frowning at?"

"Nothing, Hattie, nothing."

"John Chetwynd's somebody I knew years ago. He's a great women's rights supporter and actually in a position to *do* something about it."

"I know who he is."

"Well then, I expect you to be *pleased* that he considers me sufficiently interesting to chat to over a bite of supper, It doesn't matter what you think anyway, Roger. I'm going."

"Yes, Hattie."

The meeting was a success. Both of them thoroughly enjoyed talking about their careers. There was genuine common ground in their mutual interest in the Women's Liberation movement and, undeniably, an unspoken physical attraction underlay the evening. The glamour of daily contact with the mighty and the faint redolence of expensive cigars hung like an alluring nimbus round the charismatic member for North Rollerton. Chetwynd, for his part, sensed with excitement Hattie's eager body, demurely, but at the same time provocatively clad as she was in a tight-fitting dark green fine wool dress.

Hattie asked about John's wife, Caroline.

"She spends most of her time nowadays down in Devon. Taken up riding again. And she breeds Welsh Springers. Caro hates London. Funny, she used to adore it. Actually, she's very good with the constituents."

"So how do you manage, John?"

"In the flat? Oh, I'm all right. I don't eat in much, but I can cook if I have to. A cleaning lady comes in twice a week. She sees to my laundry and dry-cleaning. I get home about every other weekend for a political clinic. The peripatetic life seems to suit me!"

Over coffee he let his hand rest for a moment on Hattie's openly, affectionately, while they continued to tell each other of their doings. He finished his cognac.

"I can't tell you how much I've enjoyed this evening, Hattie. You're so alive. I feel a new man." He squeezed her hand. "Would you dine with me again?"

"Yes please, John."

It was arranged for the same night a week later. This time

Roger raised no objection.

Another satisfying evening neared its end and Chetwynd remarked, "It wasn't easy to make a break tonight. The meeting had to carry on without me."

"You should have sent out a message. I'd have understood, John."

"How good you are, Hattie. I do admire your level-headedness. But I just told them I had an unbreakable engagement. They probably think I'm with the PM!"

"Thanks anyway."

"I was wondering . . . perhaps we could have lunch? Can you ever take a bit of time off the treadmill at Valkyrie?"

Hattie knew immediately what was going to happen. Without hesitation she replied, "Yes, easily. That's a very good idea, John." There was a bonus too. She needn't mention it to Roger.

The meal in the Savoy grillroom lasted only forty five minutes. Neither had much appetite. During the starter John had said, "I hope you won't think it naughty but I thought we might skip the pudding and coffee. I've got a percolator back at the flat in Vincent Street. It would be much easier to talk there, don't you think? These waiters make a terrible racket."

Hattie was actually trembling, suddenly desperate to be alone with this attractive, strong-bodied man. She clenched her teeth but managed to say fairly evenly, "John, you're full of good suggestions."

Chetwynd did produce a jar of ground coffee, but before he could make any further preparations Hattie pressed her lips on the back of his neck. He spun round and, embracing her hotly, sent Hattie's mind reeling with several obliterating kisses, his hard tongue forcing itself between her teeth and licking first the roof of her mouth, then the underside of her own tongue. His hands were everywhere, on her breasts, between her legs, massaging her buttocks. Hattie was aflame.

Still grasping at one another they crabwalked to the bedroom and, once inside, drew apart for just long enough to undress, helping each other in their haste. Their naked bodies brushed. Hattie dropped to her knees. Ecstatically she took his erect penis into her mouth and momentarily savoured him. Then she was under him on the bed. They thrust at one another recklessly. Hattie cried out, transported by his relentless, desperate plunging.

"John! You're wonderful . . . so *big*. Go on, go on . . . !"

"Hattie . . . Hattie . . . Now . . .now . . . aaah . . . "

They lay joined for many minutes. After a wash they slept lightly. Near five, this time with more control but just as much satisfaction, they made love again.

Before Hattie left for home at six they both knew that they had embarked on a serious long term affair.

John Chetwynd soon became the pivot of Hattie's life but, because of the nature of her relationships with men during her pre-Roger years, she found no difficulty in keeping the matter to herself. After the first few sessions she decided that John was quite a simple person. Stripped of his clothes and the seductive aura of politics, Chetwynd MP was really just a well-intentioned, hard-working party representative with a special interest in women's rights. In fact, Hattie found a number of his opinions banal, secondhand, his vision sometimes pedestrian and narrow. She realised that it was quite possible he saw women's rights as simply a useful platform to advance his own career.

But he was virile, a robust and effective lover. And he'd obviously fallen heavily for her. They were still discovering new ways of enjoying each other and Hattie had not felt so at peace with herself in years.

Because of John's public position they had to take care not to be seen in each other's company too often. Now and then, however, they went to a play and, of course, restaurants. After an opera outing in the winter of 1975 a newspaper gossip columnist reported in a piece about prominent people 'Seen at The Garden last night' that John Chetwynd MP had been accompanied by his 'regular, attractive woman companion.'

"This rag doesn't penetrate to North Devon, Hattie. Forget it."

But someone did bring it to Caro's attention.

"I told her two tickets for Fidelio had unexpectedly come my way and I'd taken one of the secretaries at short notice."

"What about the regular companion bit?"

"Oh I just brassed it out. Said the reporter got it wrong. I think she bought it."

Hattie wondered about Caroline. "John, how actually are things between you?"

"Caro's a good enough sport, but there's honestly nothing left. I think maybe the fact that she couldn't have children undermined our relationship. And she wouldn't adopt. We've had separate beds for years, if you want the truth."

"Too bad."

"But I've got you now, my darling, haven't I?"

"Up to a point, John. We'd better keep out of the limelight in future."

It became irksome confining their meetings to small restaurants and Chetwynd's Westminster flat, even though Hattie now had a key. She voiced her annoyance. Next time they met he was jubilant.

"We're going to have a fortnight's complete freedom, Hattie!"

"How, for goodness sake?"

"Well, a very old friend of mine from Oxford days has just sent me an invitation. He's an unbelievably rich American called Harrison Bellchamber."

"Wow! That's some appellation."

"I know, but Harry's a great character. You'll like him. Anyway, he's made millions in the plastics industry over there and now he's bought this fabulous yacht. He's going to be cruising in the Med all summer and he's asked me and Caro to join him."

"So where so where do I come in, John?"

"Caro doesn't want to go. She's not keen on the heat and the second half of July is a bad time for the dogs apparently. Getting rid of the end of the litters. But that's when I'm free. Any chance of your getting away, Hattie?"

"Maybe. But if Mr Bellchamber is a friend of Caro's . . . I mean . . ."

"No problem there. I've got too much on him! No, seriously, Harry's broadminded and utterly discreet." Hattie wondered fleetingly what previous experience had so convinced John. "He'd much prefer I turned up with a charming, intelligent and decorative lady like you than come on my own and sit ogling his."

"So he'll have a friend too?"

"Undoubtedly. He's been divorced twice but it hasn't put him off. Apart from his three-man crew there'll probably be another one or two couples as well. Fun."

"I can arrange it at work I'm sure. But I'll have to think of a way to fix Roger."

"Well, let me know. I can't imagine anything nicer."

"I'll ring you at the flat this evening."

It was about eight p.m. when she broached the subject.

"Roger, I received a nice invitation today."

"Yes?"

"You know my friend John Chetwynd?"

"Of course. Have you been seeing him again?"

"Off and on. The point is he's got an amazingly rich Yank pal who's bought a luxury yacht in the Mediterranean.

John's taking a party down to cruise around with this character in the latter half of July. He's asked me."

"Are you thinking of accepting?"

"Yes I am."

"But Sylvia will be at home."

"There's all the rest of the summer. We could take her for a week to Brittany perhaps. There's probably a music camp or something she can attend while I'm away."

"What about me?" In trying to sound potentially angry he succeeded merely in conveying a wounded petulance.

"Roger, you're free to do what you like."

"I *like* my family. I don't want to swan around on boats with strangers."

"So be it, but let me just remind you once again that the bargain always was that we are free to pursue our own lives. That's exactly what I'm going to do, Roger."

A few minutes later, without a word, he went out to the Dover Castle. Hattie picked up the phone and confirmed to Chetwynd that she'd be with him on the Mediterranean jaunt.

During the next three months Hattie prepared for the trip, buying several daring swimsuits, filmy, see-through beach wraps, deck shoes, shorts and halter-tops, a cheeky yachting cap. At night she lay imagining sun-filled days, fruits de mer and chilled wine, passionate tussles with John in a gently bobbing luxury cabin.

Sylvia came home a few days before she was leaving and expressed surprise that the whole family was not going. But her father's promises of a sail on the river and a visit to a safari park quickly consoled her. At nearly eleven Sylvia was neither a little girl, nor yet adolescent. Her moods alternated unpredictably between a childish joi de vivre and the dreamy abstractions of growing up. She was at a lovely stage. Despite Hattie's eagerness to be off, she felt reluctant to leave her daughter.

"I'm sorry this trip came up at this time, Sylvia, but it was too good a chance to miss. You do understand, don't you, darling?"

"Yes, Mummy."

"I wish I could take you with me."

"It's all right. I'll be fine with Daddy."

"I'll miss you, Sylvia."

But the child had already turned to study a leaflet Roger had given her about alternative sails on the Thames.

The last evening before departure the telephone rang. It was ten o'clock and Sylvia had not long gone up to bed.

"Hello, Hattie?" It was unusual for Charlotte to call so late.

"Mum! Is something wrong?"

"It's Robert, Hattie. He's not been at all well lately. I don't *think* it's anything new but he's nearly eighty, you know."

"I know. What does Dr Cowan say?"

"Just that it's old age. He gave him some stronger tablets the other day. Digitalis."

"I'm sorry, Mum."

"Hattie, is there any chance of a visit? I know you're busy but Robert keeps asking for news of you and saying he wishes things were different. Maybe if you came . . . ?"

"Things will never be different, Mum, and you and I know it. I'm afraid I'm away from tomorrow for two weeks anyway."

"I see. Where will you be?"

"Cruising on a yacht in the Mediterranean as a matter of fact."

"How lovely! Sylvia *will* enjoy it."

"I'm going on my own, with a group of friends. Roger's looking after Sylvia."

"Oh."

"Look, Mum, try not to worry. I'll call you as soon as I get back. All right? Maybe I can dash up for a weekend or something. It's about time you came down to see us too." There was no reply. "Mum, are you still there?"

Very quietly Charlotte said, "Have a good holiday, Hattie," and put the phone down.

19

THE QUAINTLY NAMED *Au Mal Assis* restaurant on the chic Cannes Waterfront was the rendezvous. John had travelled on an earlier flight and was already half way through a spectacular looking bouillabaise when Hattie walked in. He rose and kissed her warmly.

"It's wonderful to see you, Hattie darling. Here, sit down and have some of this. Absolutely delicious."

"Where are the others?"

"I've seen Harry and I know where the yacht's parked. Not far. Let's finish this off and get-over there. It's a terrific craft."

The sweeping, graceful lines of *American Beauty* were in marked contrast to those of its owner. Harrison Bellchamber looked older than his forty eight years. Almost hairless, he was running seriously to fat. Resplendent in a voluminous pair of apple-green Bermuda shorts he sat on deck in a reclining chair, glass in hand, welcoming the new arrivals. It seemed he had brought two personal companions, one a tall blond Californian girl, the other a very young friend he'd apparently met in the Caribbean earlier that summer. 'Black Lolita' were the words that occurred to Hattie as she shook hands with this simpering dusky child-woman.

"Hiya, Johnny! So this is the fair Harriot? Come right in, Harriot. Jake here's our steward. He'll show you and John where to dump your things. Then come up and grab yourself a glass of bubbly. Get in the groove right off, OK?"

He laughed, a jolly fat man bellow.

"Thanks, Harry. It's a beautiful boat."

"You like her? Pride of my life, Harriot."

"I'm usually called Hattie."

"That's nice. Listen, Hattie, we're going to have a ball. So just you relax and enjoy. Right?"

"Right, Harry."

It would have been hard to do otherwise, being piloted lazily from port to port along the Riviera. The blue wavelet crests were gilded by the sun, whose remorseless rays brought the teak decking to a temperature which Hattie found required her espadrilles. They ate and drank sumptuously. Conversation dwindled in the disorientation of heat and constant, brilliant dappling light.

Some evenings they went ashore for an hour or two on dry land. The yacht's radio telephone had developed a fault, so John checked in to his office occasionally from various bars and hotels on the Cote D'Azur. There were two other couples, both American, neither married, and John and Hattie joined up with each in turn on these expeditions. But everyone was preoccupied with his or her partner and frankly relieved to get back to *American Beauty* and the prospect of a night's love in a cool cabin. Bellchamber didn't bother to stir from his floating comfort. Garbed in Brooks Brothers' reefer jacket and captain's cap, he enjoyed chatting with neighbouring boat owners. He also took care to show off his girlfriends.

Hattie and John fairly wallowed in sex. Head to tail they licked and sucked each other nightly to a frenzy before coupling their bodies for a glorious, lunging climax. By now they had the orgasmic measure of one another and each session was skilfully prolonged, leaving them both panting and drained.

Only one episode disturbed Hattie. They'd spent the afternoon in a small lagoon sunbathing and swimming. Even Bellchamber had flopped into the water. At one point Hattie was lying on deck, topless, deepening her already dark tan. She was aware, vaguely, of Cheryl, Harry Bellchamber's Californian friend, stretched out near her. Suddenly she realised Cheryl had taken her hand. She turned her head. The girl was smiling, her light blue eyes, toothpaste white smile and sleek blonde hair a startlingly attractive assemblage. Then Cheryl winked.

"Don't know 'bout you, honey, but all this sun and seafood's gotten me real horny."

"Mmm. I know what you mean, Cheryl."

Hattie felt her hand being gently squeezed.

"How about you and me go below for a minute?"

Now Hattie knew what was happening.

"No Cheryl, I'm not . . ."

"Aw, come on, Hat. I'm all goose-pimples for you. Mr Harry's a selfish bastard. He just don't care to waste his goddam time satisfying a girl. All he wants is Baby and me jerk him off."

"Sorry about that, Cheryl, but I don't . . ."

"See, it don't matter nowadays. I enjoy a man with a nice big dick same as you, Hattie, but back home I got lots of girlfriends too. You come down now I'll show you how we please each other."

Cheryl poked out her long pink tongue and flicked it languorously. For a second Hattie was near panic. The sheer animal magnetism of Cheryl's uninhibited sexuality was overpowering. Hattie knew she was not far from doing her bidding. But the moment passed. John's reassuring patrician laugh floated up from the water. She rose and patted Cheryl's sun-bleached hair.

"I don't go in for that, Cheryl. Sorry. You need a good man."

"Get lost, honey," came the languid reply.

But as she jumped into the sea with the others, Hattie was decidedly uneasy. If she hadn't had a man on hand, would she have gone with Cheryl? How secure was her heterosexual preference? Perhaps she was becoming decadent? Or was it that her basic contempt for men, or her distrust of them at least, had inevitably created a certain instability in her sexual attitudes?

By evening she was jumpy. Bellchamber gave her a small black cheroot and she found it calmed her. Following another ravishing meal she felt better. That night she clung to John and pled with him to penetrate her more deeply than ever. He did his manful best, but he had swum an unusual amount that day and was soon exhausted. As he slept profoundly John Chetwynd would have been amazed to learn that the handsome thirty nine year old woman lying silently at his side was unaccountably weeping, great salt tears gliding down her cheeks to terminate, undried, in her mouth, her ears, or on the pillow.

They disembarked next morning back at Cannes. Farewells were taken and Hattie and John clambered on to the quay. Both were returning to London that day but by different airlines. John was annoyed by a persistent photographer.

"Buzz off! *Allez, allez!* We don't want your damned pictures."

Eventually the man went away tamely enough. They summoned a taxi for the airport.

It was mid-afternoon when Hattie reached Brodick Mews.

Nobody at home. Roger must have taken Sylvia out for a trip somewhere. But they knew roughly when she was due back. No doubt they'd be in soon. Then she saw a sealed envelope bearing her name on the dining table.

> *Dear Hattie,*
> *Sorry to say your father died of a heart attack last week. The funeral was this Tuesday. I organised some flowers from 'Hattie and family,' which I hope you approve. I tried to contact you but the yacht phone didn't work.*
>   *I've taken Sylvia to an exhibition tennis match at the Queen's Club (she's keen on tennis at school). Should be home about 6.30/7.*
> *Roger*

She made a strong cup of tea and smoked a cigarette. Damn and blast him! He would choose to expire at the wrong time. Well, it was Thursday now and there was nothing she could do about it. As soon as she'd drunk this tea she'd phone her mother. Should she offer to go up? Hell, there must be a mountain of work on her desk. Anyway, what good would it do? No use trying to fake grief. Mum knew the score. She lit another cigarette and dialled Rutherglen.

"Mum? Hattie."

"Hello, Hattie."

"Mum, what can I say? I . . . "

"Say whatever you like, Hattie. It won't bring back Robert."

"Now, Mum, I know you must be feeling rotten. I'm so sorry and I wish I'd been able to come up to attend . . . "

"Do you, Hattie? I don't think so."

"Now, Mum . . . "

"I should think it was rather convenient for you to be out

of the country. You didn't have to force yourself to come here and pretend a love and respect you didn't feel."

"I've always been honest about that."

"Oh *yes*, don't we know it? I wonder if you've any conception, Hattie, of just how selfish and hurtful that kind of 'honesty' can be."

Charlotte was understandably wrought up, her husband of forty one years only two days in his grave. "Mum, this isn't doing either of us any good. Would you like me to come up this weekend?"

"No, Hattie. I need some time on my own now. God will comfort me I know."

"But, Mum . . . "

"I'll let you know if I need to see you, Hattie. I want to go now. I'm so tired."

"All right then. Oh, did Charlie know?"

"He sent a wreath and spoke to me from Los Angeles on the telephone. I don't think he's too fit. By the way, please give Sylvia my love. I spoke to her and told her her grandfather was dead. I must go now. Goodbye, Hattie."

The phone clicked. Hattie stood stupidly with the receiver in her hand. As she replaced it and began to pace from room to room a choking animus against her father set her heart racing. She lit a cigarette and screamed through clenched teeth. "I HATE YOU! YOU ROTTEN *MAN*. I HOPE YOU ROAST IN HELL!" Her words were simple but the venom in her voice lanced viciously through the empty house that sunny afternoon.

Hattie poured a large measure of whisky and drank it quickly. Just half past four. Two hours till Sylvia would be back. In the bathroom her sun-tanned face looked back stonily at her, somehow curiously out of place. Oh God! She *felt* utterly out of place.

Later, examining her accumulated mail, she thought of

John. He was probably feeling fairly peculiar too. You couldn't go through a fortnight such as they'd just spent together, and then simply break off, without being shattered. Oh well, they'd agreed it might be prudent to stay apart for a week at least. He'd be half-way to Devon by now.

Promptly at six thirty an enthusiastic Sylvia burst in.

"Oh hello, Mummy. Gosh! You should have seen those players' serves. Absolutely brill!"

"Sounds terrific, Sylvia. How are you, my darling?"

"Fine."

"Have you had a good time with Daddy?"

"Oh yes! We went to the safari park and shopping and a sail on the river to Greenwich and . . . what else? Yes, at the safari park at Windsor we saw a *killer* whale and dolphins! It's been *super*, hasn't it, Daddy?"

Roger smiled fondly at his daughter. "We've had a lot of fun, Sylvia. Well, Hattie, are you all right?"

"Yes thanks. Sylvia, I've brought you a present."

The child unwrapped a small, rather expensive green malachite ornament, bought after some haggling in a jewellery shop in Nice.

"What is it?"

"It's a copy of a tiny, very old carving dug up in the south of France. You could keep it on your dressing table, Sylvia."

"Thanks." She put it and its packaging unceremoniously to one side. "What are we going to do tomorrow, Daddy?"

"We could have another sail up the Thames, in the other direction."

"Oh yes, that's right. Let's."

After a while the child went upstairs to wash before supper. Hattie explained to Roger about the defective yacht phone and that she'd already spoken to her mother.

"How is she, Hattie?"

"Pretty sad, naturally."

"She was very upset that neither you nor your brother were going to be at the funeral. I gather one of her sisters and her husband were the only family there."

"I couldn't help it, Roger."

As he looked at her his eyes were without expression. "I suppose you couldn't."

At bedtime Hattie tried to draw Sylvia out a bit more but received mainly monosyllabic responses. The girl didn't seem to be actually antagonistic, simply distant. She held her pretty little mouth up politely enough for her mother's goodnight kiss but, again, Hattie ached at a lack of warmth in the gesture. She might have been one of Sylvia's school matrons. Hattie knew she should try to spend more time with her daughter, get to know her better, but it was so difficult, being at the office all day.

Simon Hotchkiss was glad to see her back.

"First Judith was away, then you, then Judith *again* with a bug. I'm on my knees, Hattie. Anyhow, did you enjoy the Med?"

"I had a super time, Simon."

"Good. You'll be ready for the fray. We should be gearing up for the Book Fair like mad. Can you sort out your desk quickly please? Then the three of us must confer." Hattie prepared to leave his room. "Incidentally, one piece of not such good news – Kate Loxton's taken her business elsewhere. No explanations. No warnings. But final, I'm afraid."

"Strange. I'll have a word with her. Of course I haven't handled children's books for ages now."

"Judith said she made a specific point about 'not wanting Harriot Murray crawling to her and begging.' Words to that effect. A lost cause by the sound of it."

"How *nice* it is to be back!"

Hattie found she was glad to plunge into the job again. In half an hour she'd sifted out the letters which required early attention and was dictating replies to her secretary between a series of internal phone calls which erupted once the word was out that she'd returned.

Judith, Simon and she had a working sandwich and wine lunch in the boardroom. By three Hattie began to see daylight. By four she felt once again abreast of events, on top of her job. Pausing at four thirty for a cup of tea and a biscuit she took yet another allegedly urgent call.

"Hello, hello . . . is that Miss Murray?"

"That's you, John, isn't it?" They had a pact not to call each other at work or at home.

"Yes. I'm sorry about this, Hattie, but it's imperative I see you as soon as possible."

"Where?"

"I've just driven up from Devon. This phone is at one of these places on the motorway. I should be at the flat in an hour or so, traffic permitting."

"I'll come over at six. OK?"

"Thanks. Till then."

As she taxied across London Hattie knew with a dull premonition that John's news would not be good. But what could it be? A sudden diagnosis of disease? John was one of the healthiest specimens she knew. Something adverse in his political career? He was unlikely to be rushing like this to impart such tidings. As she paid off the cabbie it came to Hattie that only one possible source of malevolence remained – Caroline. But what did she know? What could she do?

In five days the poised, confident John Chetwynd had turned into a quaking mass of sunburned anxiety.

"Hattie *darling*! Come in, come in. Christ, I'm so glad to see you."

"Calm down, John! What on earth's happened?"

"It's Caroline."

"I thought as much. Has she found out something?"

"Everything! Hattie, it's *ghastly*!"

His story then unfolded. Evidently Caroline had had a letter from Drusilla Slingsby-Gore in California months before with the information that her husband was seeing Hattie Murray. Drusilla had said she was only keeping faith with mistreated women, that it gave her no pleasure to pass on such facts and that her source could not be revealed. Caroline had immediately engaged a private detective who had been recording their movements ever since, culminating in a set of photographs of them entering the flat in Vincent Street or hand in hand at Cannes harbour.

"I wonder he didn't poke his lens into our cabin on the yacht. That's where he'd really have got a scoop!"

"It's not funny, Hattie. Caro's man evidently got the lowdown about our sharing a cabin from a Miss Neilson. That was that Californian bitch, wasn't it?"

"It was."

They stared at one another bleakly.

"Could I have whisky, John?"

"Of course."

She lit a cigarette and thought quickly while he made them each a drink. When he returned she said, "So, is she making threats?"

"It's divorce for sure. We haven't got on for a long time now, and with all her evidence..."

"She'll cost you a lot to go away?"

"Oh I'm sure of that. Maybe I could survive that but..."

"But what, John?"

"It's the constituency."

"What can she do to damage you? I mean people, even MPs, get divorced rather frequently these days."

"It's the local Party Selection Committee. The chairman's a woman. An old battle-axe called Florence Dashwood. She's a bosom pal of Caro's."

"Go on."

"Well, I've told you before how popular Caro is down there. If this Dashwood female takes it into her head to do it she could destroy me."

"By fixing it so you wouldn't be selected again for North Rollerton?"

"Correct."

"But couldn't you stand somewhere else if that happened?"

"If the publicity was bad enough I might never be adopted as a candidate again."

"Good God!" Hattie was genuinely amazed. "I can't believe it. In 1976?"

"I assure you it's eminently possible. Judging by Caro's rage when she finally brought all this out yesterday I'd say it looks a certainty. Hattie, what am I going to do?"

She was not impressed to note the tears in his eyes. "I would recommend, first off, that you keep your nerve. And your dignity."

"Hattie darling?"

"Yes?"

He lent forward and took her hand. "If this does blow up in my face will you stay with me all the way?"

"What exactly does that mean, John?"

"I mean, my dear, that, when the dust settles, will you marry me?"

"*WHAT?*"

20

THE *DAILY TELEGRAPH* CARRIED the fullest report.

> MP FORCED TO RESIGN
> Mr John Chetwynd has resigned his seat as a member of Parliament for the Tory constituency of North Rollerton, Devon, following pressure to quit from the local party faithful. He is being sued for divorce by his wife, Caroline, amid a scandal involving colourful rumours of private detectives, nights at the opera and an expensive Mediterranean jaunt on a luxury yacht. The grounds for divorce are reportedly Mr Chetwynd's adultery with an attractive younger woman, Harriot Murray, believed to be a London publishing executive.
>
> A spokeswoman for the North Rollerton Selection Committee, Mrs Florence Dashwood, said, "This is a sad day, but we are a bit old-fashioned down here and do not approve of illicit liaisons, especially where trusted public figures are concerned. Caroline Chetwynd is extremely well

liked in the area and there is much sympathy for her. It's laughable that our former Member has always protested his great interest in Women's Rights."

A former Guards officer, John Chetwynd, 48, first entered Parliament in 1960. The couple married in 1957. His wife is the daughter of the late Brigadier Eustace Lewington, Lord Lieutenant of Devon from 1952 to 1959. There are no children. A by-election is expected in the autumn.

Hattie still found the whole thing incredible. Surely a Parliamentarian's position shouldn't be so vulnerable? But, as a now regularly tearful John eventually made clear, Caroline's popularity and high visibility in the constituency had been indispensable factors in his vote garnering over the years. More devastating was the ridicule to which his avowed feminist sympathies had been exposed. Several long time opponents of his views had seized the opportunity to humiliate him. Cutting jokes in the smoking room about the Honourable Member for North Rollerton's well known dedication to uplifting the status of women, or should it be lifting up their something else . . . ?, or in the Chamber, 'Mr Speaker, might I enquire whether the Honourable Member's feminist principles have as an aim polygamous arrangements on the Polynesian pattern?' – this kind of ruthless hounding finally made his position untenable.

Of course it must have been Kate who'd told Dru, knowing of her friendship with the Chetwynds. She knew many journalists, and must have checked after that Covent Garden report. Bloody bitch! Just because she, Kate, couldn't make up her mind whether she liked men or women didn't entitle her to lash out at other people who had no doubts.

Kate was eaten up with jealousy about Sylvia too, and had never come near since that visit just after she'd been born. Kate Loxton was very good at patronising the less fortunate, but she obviously couldn't cope with them once they succeeded. What was the use of seeking her out, having a showdown? The damage was well and truly done. Let her enjoy her miserable triumph.

John had been shaken by Hattie's absolute dismissal of his proposal of marriage. She would not even discuss it. For her part, Hattie had been astonished by his bland arrogance.

"You're not serious, John, surely?"

"I need a wife, Hattie, and I love you."

"Well, I'm damned! As long as you had a wife keeping a cosy house for you it was all right to use me as a bloody mistress. But now wifey wants out I'm expected to swap roles without blinking. You take my breath away, John Chetwynd!"

She'd taken his breath away too. He was suddenly white, the black smudges of sleepless nights very noticeable, one eye bloodshot.

"Hattie! You *know* it wasn't like that."

"Wasn't it?"

"No. I've always respected you."

There was an anger sprouting uncontrollably in Hattie's innards. Respect be damned!

"Have you forgotten that I have a household already?"

"No, but . . . well, I mean, you and Roger are not married so . . ."

"So I should simply desert him, throw my lifetime principles down the lavatory and waltz up to the alter with you? My God, John . . ."

"Hattie, please . . . I . . ."

"Oh, shut up! You and your whining are making me sick. You're just like all the other chauvinist pigs when we get down to it aren't you? You want all the trappings of respectability *and* the right to go on screwing whoever takes your fancy."

"Hattie, you were the first. Honestly, I'm not . . . "

She wasn't listening. "What really riles me is that you and your type simply don't take women seriously, whatever you may *say*. You know my views on marriage but they haven't registered at all as an actual option I'm prepared to live by. We're finished, John." He was quietly weeping. "I'm sorry of course, that all this had to happen, but you're unbelievably selfish you know. Not once have you expressed any anxiety about how *my* name in the papers might affect *my* career, *my* life."

"I'm so sorry, Hattie."

"It's too late, John."

She left the flat for the last time.

Roger's reaction was a surprise. Naturally he was tense in the days following the newspaper stories but there was never a real shouting match. It seemed he'd discussed the whole thing at length with his old friend and counsellor, John Quarry, who worked with him at the magazine.

"I think you've behaved like an idiot, Hattie, but my only real concern is for Sylvia. I don't want her hurt."

"We've no need to tell her."

"People talk. I wish we could get her away somewhere for a while."

"Good idea. I'll think about it."

Roger drew his head down into his shoulders in a gesture she recognised as habitual when he was mettling himself to say something of importance.

"I need hardly say how disgusted I am by all this. If it weren't for Sylvia I would have cleared off long ago, but I will not let her down. I happen to think she needs a father's support, particularly with a mother she cannot rely on."

"I resent that. It's simply not accurate anyway. All that's happened . . . "

"For the love of God, Hattie! What d'you think a little girl is supposed to make of a mother who sees nothing wrong in sleeping with another man and getting it plastered all over the national press?"

"You're exaggerating. I . . . "

He waved her aside. "I've moved my things into the spare bedroom. All I ask is that you keep your squalid affairs out of the papers in future."

Unbelievably, coolly he was actually getting the better of her. Without warning Hattie's face was suddenly suffused with red anger. Her temples throbbed wildly.

"What a perfect little Lord Fauntleroy you are, Roger! You make me puke. We had a bargain right from the word go that we were both to stay free in our sexual relationships. Remember?"

"Yes, but all I ever really wanted was you, Hattie, and Sylvia to love."

She couldn't stand his calmness.

"Another way of putting it could be that you're a wimp, Roger. Why don't *you* go out and get yourself a bloody woman?"

He looked levelly at her. He had not once raised his voice.

"Are you finished?"

"Yes, yes."

"I'm going over to the Dover Castle. I need a few friends to help me face the world."

When he'd gone Hattie tip-toed upstairs to check on Sylvia. She was sleeping peacefully. Hattie thought anxiously about the effect the publicity might have if Sylvia somehow heard it. Then she had an inspiration. Her granny. She picked up the phone immediately.

"Mum, this is Hattie." There was silence. "Mum, if you're there, I know how bad you must feel about these newspaper stories."

"Well?"

"Listen, I'm not going to debate the thing on the phone. I had an affair, the man's wife turned out to be an avenging hellcat and the papers got in on the act. It's over and Roger and I are picking up the pieces."

"He's staying with you?"

"Of course." Silence again. "Mum, our main worry is Sylvia. We'd like to shield her from this. I had an idea. Would you take her for the rest of the holidays? Just under three weeks."

"Poor little thing."

"Yes, well . . . I could put her on a plane. The stewardesses would see her safely into Glasgow. You could meet her there. Will you do it, Mum?"

"I'll do anything to protect that darling little girl."

It was arranged. Roger drove her out to Heathrow next morning. Sylvia was thrilled by this new adventure.

While her daughter was excitedly settling in her seat, the nice air-hostess showing her how to strap herself in for the one hour flight, Hattie was sitting behind closed doors with Simon Hotchkiss and Judith Goldstein.

"For Heaven's sake, Hattie, we're not exactly regular attenders at Sunday School round here ourselves! But it's the company's name, you know. Chairman's fanatical about that."

"The name of the company was never mentioned in the damned newspapers as far as I'm aware."

"No, that's quite right, Hattie," said Judith in her normal, always reasonable voice. "Simon's simply referring to the risk of it."

"Yes, Judith, that's it really. The thing is, Hattie, we're all grown-ups and living in 1976, so that makes us free agents in our personal lives, thank goodness. But we do owe the jolly old company something beyond that, to wit, we must take care not to attract bad publicity."

"I've just emerged from a rather unusual situation which is not likely to be repeated."

"Quite, quite. Let's forget it then, Hattie. I had to promise the Chairman I'd have a word. No offence?"

"It's all right, Simon."

"Good. Now, Judith, what about this ruddy Book Fair? Are we on schedule?"

It had not been pleasant and, inwardly, Hattie cursed Kate Loxton. Of course, neither Simon nor Judith would have twigged that connection.

Life could now be safely resumed, but Hattie was troubled. Had she been unreasonable in her savage reaction to John Chetwynd's plea that she marry him? No doubt her emotional support would have been welcome, even if only until the scandal's reverberations had died away, but his craven self-centred whining had infuriated her. Roger and Sylvia might not have existed as far as he was concerned. Chauvinist pig if ever was! No, it was better to have a surgical cut, to end their liaison cleanly.

And yet, was it fair of her to complain about John's insensitivity to the fact that she already had a domestic ménage? After all, she'd been quite willing to betray Roger repeatedly, indeed with no holds barred. At least that was how a basically conventional character like John would have interpreted her behaviour. She supposed she'd rarely mentioned Sylvia. What was her lover to think? Well, that her ties meant little, that a new alliance with someone of his standing might not only be an attractive proposition but a relatively simple matter to achieve, involving no pain or especial problems for her. Doubtless John would've enjoyed the role of affectionate stepfather. Uncomfortably Hattie was now able to see the whole episode from his perspective. She asked Belinda, her secretary, to make another mug of strong black coffee.

Should she contemplate meeting him again, perhaps just a few times, to steady his nerve, to help him through the crisis? For a moment a small pity welled within her, an instinct, she thought wryly, akin to sympathy for a handsome stag brought down by one deadly shot. But this emotion was quickly eclipsed, indeed utterly blotted out in her mind by a flood of bitter resentment. She remembered his total lack of concern for *her* situation. Mr John high-and-bloody-mighty Chetwynd hadn't given a thought to a the very real danger which threatened *her* career. It probably hadn't occurred to him that she, as well as he, was going to have to live down the publicity which only *his* position in Parliament had attracted.

Hattie decided that her action in discarding this weak man, whose self-preoccupation she found unforgivable, was fully justified, but she remained anxious and inwardly unsure of herself for weeks. As time passed, however, she could tell that the shock and debilitating embarrassment were wearing off. Sexual hunger was beginning to impinge anew.

Strictly speaking she wasn't needed at the Frankfurt Book Fair. However, Valkyrie had issued several controversial new titles for its autumn list and all three of them were curious to know their reception. Sylvia had returned from Scotland, delighted with her granny and the plane trips, and was now safely ensconced at her senior boarding school, Queen Mary's. So Hattie agreed to accompany the other two to Germany.

The Fair was huge, the variety of publishers and publications bewildering. Valkyrie's stand was well patronised, however, and Hattie and her colleagues soon found themselves pressed, alongside the sales staff, into answering constant questions and gleefully writing out order confirmations. It was all most exhilarating but by ten p.m., back at the Frankfurter Hof Hotel, they were exhausted. After several drinks they revived sufficiently to eat steak sandwiches, but at eleven thirty Judith announced she'd had enough and left them to a final nightcap.

"It's nice to be with you, Hattie, out of the office environment."

"*D'accord*, Simon."

"You're not sore about my little speech the other day?"

"I'd have done the same in your shoes."

"Hard-headed Hattie."

"Only when I have to be, Simon."

"Meaning?"

"Up to you."

There was no particular relationship between the two of them. Only a good measure of mutual professional respect. The occasional kiss at the annual Christmas party hardly signified a burning lust. But they were both on the loose. Hattie had not had a man touch her since Cannes. Simon's marriage, though soundly enough based, was nowadays perfunctory, passionless.

They said little more and presently left the bar. Going up in the lift Simon took Hattie's hand.

"Which floor are you on, Hattie?"

"Fourth." The lift slowed. "We're here. Coming?"

"Just for a final, final drink. D'you have a room fridge?"

"I do." Hattie grinned.

Sitting in separate armchairs they sipped whiskies and chatted desultorily about the Fair. After a bit Simon said, "Why don't you come and sit over here, Hattie? You're looking very pretty tonight."

"We'd be much more comfortable over there." She nodded towards the bed. "What d'you think, Simon?"

He needed no second bidding. They undressed without undue rush, he carefully hanging his trousers over a chair back. Soon they were naked in the bed on their sides, Hattie's breasts responding to his enfolding arms and caressing hands. She turned to face him, he kissed her on the mouth and, without removing his lips, manoeuvred himself over her body. With a sensation almost of gratitude she opened herself to him.

They were both experienced and there was no hurry in their lovemaking. Simon's strokes were slow but searching, Hattie's buttock thrusts timed for maximum effect. Only at the last moment did they give way to frantic, climax-producing lunges.

"God, Hattie, that was *indescribable!*"

"Me too. We'll have to arrange a replay."

"Don't quite know when. We'll see."

Simon left shortly afterwards and as Hattie drifted contentedly into sleep she knew that this had been a casual encounter only. They had to work together after all. There would be no difficulty.

On the plane home and even when they chanced to be alone in the office neither made any further reference to the events of that night. If an opportunity arose in the future they might, or might not, take it.

Early in December Hattie came in from the office one evening to discover Roger in a state of some agitation. Conversation was kept at a minimum these days and, as often as not, he was out at the Dover Castle or some other pub with a group of cronies. Hattie had noticed that his beer intake was resulting in a steady weight gain. She was mildly surprised to see him.

"Hello, Roger."

"I was just on my way out when the phone rang. It was Sylvia."

"Anything wrong?"

"Some child's been told by her mother about you and Chetwynd. She's being teased."

"Oh hell."

"Also, Sylvia wanted to know if we were really married. She said she won't be home for the Christmas holidays because she's going to *kill herself*."

21

HATTIE INSISTED THEY drive out to Berkshire there and then. Miss Armour, the house mistress, was not at all pleased to see them but granted an interview since they'd made the effort.

"Sylvia darling!" Hattie put her arms around the haunted looking twelve year old. She was pushed away.

"Is it true you and Daddy are not married? Daddy wouldn't say on the phone."

"Well, darling, your Daddy and I were not married in a church or a court or anything like that. We don't really believe in that any more. But we're just as truly your parents as any of the other girls' mummies and daddies.

"But Amanda Barrington-Smythe says that means I'm illegal."

"No it doesn't, Sylvia," said Roger, looking pale and desperately unhappy. "You have exactly the same rights as everybody else. What Mummy says is correct. We're your legal parents and we love you very much. Just you tell Miss Armour if anybody tries to tease you again."

Although reassured by these statements the troubled girl

had clearly suffered much. She looked from Hattie to Roger with uncertain eyes, then flew to her father, sobbing.

"Oh, Daddy, Daddy, I love you so much! Please take me away with you."

Roger was swallowing hard. "I can't do that, darling. You must finish your term. But it's only another week or so, isn't it?"

"I know, but I hate it here. I want to come home with you tonight."

Hattie was not enjoying the very obvious demonstration of where Sylvia's affections lay. Her brain raced.

"Sylvia?"

"Yes, Mummy."

"How would you like to go skiing this Christmas? Perhaps in Austria?"

The child was taken aback by the sheer unexpected novelty of the suggestion.

"What? Oh, that would be *lovely*."

"Well, if you go back to your dorm now and promise to be a good sensible girl I promise you I'll arrange it."

After some further comforting Sylvia left them. As they walked back to the car they again met Miss Armour.

"Sorry for the upset," said Hattie as cheerfully as she could manage. "Sylvia's all right now."

The form mistress, a spinster in her fifties, did not return Hattie's smile. "You must realise, Mrs . . . eh, Miss Murray, that this sort of thing is bound to affect a child very much. Even *profoundly*." She eyed Hattie with undisguised distaste.

"Your job is to provide the girl with love and security, Miss Armour, for which you are well paid. Am I right?"

"Yes. Well . . . I . . . good gracious me. I never . . . "

"Goodnight, Miss Armour."

She left the woman stuttering angrily. Nothing was said for a while until there were on the motorway.

"Sylvia will be all right. The others will tire of tormenting her."

"I suppose so. You shouldn't have antagonised Miss Armour though. It'll only rebound on Sylvia."

"Dried-up old bitch!" was Hattie's reply.

They went to Kitzbühl that Christmas and were happy enough together in the snow and sun. Sylvia showed herself a natural skier and, by the end of the holiday, they were able to enjoy their outings to the slopes together. At supper in the evenings they joined in the sing-songs and all fell into bed at about the same hour. This was to be a regular annual event for the next few years.

Another routine was for Sylvia to spend a good part of her summer holidays each year in Scotland with her granny. Roger took her up by car and stayed a few days. Hattie visited Rutherglen occasionally, but things were not right between her and Charlotte. She never stayed more than one night.

As Sylvia progressed from an awkward, leggy puberty into adolescence a calm, self-assured personality emerged. It also became apparent that she was going to possess an arresting dark-haired beauty, her rather broad face lit with intelligence from bold hazel-green eyes. Her fine textured skin was an outstanding feature. She was already a tall girl. Hattie watched her with pride and admiration, but there was pain in it too. Try as she might, she could not get as close to Sylvia as she would have liked. Perhaps, she hoped wistfully, intimacy would come with the years.

While Sylvia blossomed Hattie had to admit that Roger was moving in the opposite direction. She wondered if he was becoming dangerously alcoholic. His daily intake of beer would have been enough for a week when she'd first known him. At home he disposed of the best part of two bottles of whisky a week. He'd put on a good deal of weight and now had a permanent, slightly bloated look. Always rather thin on top he was rapidly balding. He'd become careless about his clothes, too, but most of his journalist friends also dressed scruffily so she didn't say anything to him.

Hattie herself was not immune to the passage of years. Moving into her early forties she tried dieting for a while to restrain her figure, but it made her irritable and didn't seem particularly effective. She joked that her now thirty a day cigarette consumption kept her weight in check, and ate and drank more or less as she pleased. She also started wearing an abbreviated boned under-garment to cinch her waist. Her fingernails seemed to break more easily and some had become nicotine-stained, so she painted them with blood-red varnish. This became one of her trademarks, as did a pair of rather large gold hoop earrings. She had her hair cut shorter in the new 'Afro' style. Hattie was creating a mature persona for herself.

For there was something fresh on the horizon. Judith Goldstein had announced her wish to retire and go with her husband to live in Jersey. He'd sold out a prosperous wholesale jewellery business and they were well placed financially. Simon Hotchkiss had ensured that Hattie was confirmed as Managing Director designate of Valkyrie Ltd, and her appointment was expected to be made public by the end of 1980. Meantime, Hattie was gradually taking over Judith's MD functions. It was all rather thrilling.

Good old Simon. He must be over sixty now but he was still game. Over the years, after that first time in Frankfurt, there had been occasional business trips and the odd seminar involving an overnight stay when they'd slept together. He was a competent lover and obviously appreciated Hattie's techniques. Simon was refreshingly straightforward about the essentially physical character of their periodic encounters and made no emotional demands on her whatsoever. Even so, her willingness to go to bed with him, on an equally arm's length basis as it were, had clearly done her career no harm. He *could* have discreetly advised the Chairman to bring in another well known name to replace Judith.

But Simon was not always available and, as the list lengthened of the men with whom she took her pleasure, Hattie became increasingly detached in her attitude to them. On their last skiing holiday there had been a difficult moment. One of the instructors, a young muscular Austrian named Volker, had taken her fancy. Volker quickly responded to the sexy Scottish lady and lost no opportunity to flaunt his powerful physique whenever he caught her eye. It was an easy matter for him to indicate a morning when he was off duty, for Hattie to feign a sprained ankle and ask him to come to her room to massage it. They wasted no time. Volker's performance fully lived up to the promise of his powerful body and, when he'd done with her, Hattie was too spent to get up.

Ironically Roger did sprain an ankle that morning. He came limping back on Sylvia's arm just as the departing Volker closed the door of their room.

"What was he doing here?"

"Nothing. Just put his head round the door to enquire very kindly about my ankle."

Roger regarded her with a mixture of suspicion and resignation in his eyes.

"Mummy, I thought you got up this morning?"

"My ankle, Sylvia. Felt miserable so I just came back to bed to rest it."

"Oh."

"Roger, what have you done?"

"Obviously I've twisted my ankle as well. Sylvia, would you call the doctor please. I'd better have it bound."

Then, in early 1980, there had been a one night stand at

his bachelor flat in South Kensington with a beautiful young man she met at a party. He'd been surprisingly inexperienced and Hattie had enjoyed herself advancing his sexual education by a quantum leap. Later that year she'd taken a risk and invited a lawyer, down from Birmingham on a summer visit and staying with friends in Marylebone, to come to Brodick Mews for a drink. Roger and Sylvia were up in Scotland but there were always curious neighbours. He'd been boringly nervous about the whole thing and not much good in bed as a result.

Hattie knew her behaviour was not wholly normal, that she ought to have been satisfied with her career, Roger's undemanding presence, the interest of Sylvia's maturing. But she needed sex. There was much talk about spreading drug addiction and Hattie often felt that sex, for her, was certainly as powerful a tyrant. As the years passed she was driven ever more cruelly, not less, to seek out encounters with men, to keep changing partners, always ensuring that no dangerous emotional link developed. Sometimes, in self disgust she'd determine to give up her shabby secret life of passing liaisons, but then a new opportunity would occur, her body would scream for sexual contact and she'd fall again. Pride in her outside achievements struggled with increasingly wounding blows to Hattie's inner self esteem. What would she do in the future as her body aged? Hattie shuddered. Alone, sometimes these days she'd weep helplessly. She'd never be able to change. How in God's name was she going to end up?

That winter she had a desperate experience. There was a strike of air traffic controllers. Coming back on the overnight car ferry from Le Havre after a Paris meeting with the translators of a new feminist work, she'd picked up a good-looking Fenchman in the bar. He spoke no English and she never did learn his name, but she was unlikely ever to forget him. At first all was normal, the only unusual feature as they undressed in her swaying, narrow cabin being that she saw he was covered all over with a mass of thick curling black hair. He didn't seem to want to get into the bunk, roughly indicating that she should turn away from him and bend over.

It became a nightmare. The man quickly made it plain that his exclusive interest was anal intercourse. Hattie resisted as best she could. Twisting in his vice-like grasp she did everything possible to deny him but, murderous with frustrated lust, he punched the side of her head. Gripping her throat with one hand he ruthlessly forced her buttocks apart with the fingers of the other. Hattie didn't scream. Apart from the fact that the fiend was effectively preventing her from uttering a sound anyway, she was overcome by a debilitating, bitterly mortifying shame. Eventually, she had to give up fighting and let him have his way.

For several weeks fits of weeping overcame her when she was alone. She doctored herself with creams, but it was spring before she'd fully recovered, physically and mentally, from the trauma of that night.

Hattie was now approaching forty four years of age. She identified deeply with feminist philosophy. Women's Liberation had achieved giant strides in the seventies and Hattie felt proud that her work with the pioneers of the sixties and then at Valkyrie had made an important contribution. In public dealings with men her habitual attitude had crystallised into one of breezy camaraderie. Inwardly, she nursed turbulent shifting emotions compounded of jealousy, reluctant admiration, contempt and a realisation of her sexual dependence. Often she was seized by a devouring anger, not far from hatred.

A sad letter came from Charlotte enclosing one received from Los Angeles.

Mrs Murry,
I found your address in Charlies things so I thought I'll right you.

Me and Charlie were together eight years and we had a great time! I got no proper edication but Charlie's a real gentleman with his learning and all. So we were happy like I say.

He got the aids and went down very quick but I seen him in the hospice three times a week. See, fact is I loved Charlie a hell of a lot and I'm still crying fit to flood the Missippi.
Your sincerely,
Jerome A Phillipson

Charlie and Hattie had never been close, but she felt diminished and mourned his loss. She blamed her father totally for the course her brother's life had taken. As far as she was concerned it was one more instance of great unhappiness attributable to self-righteous male insensitivity.

Hattie took over the reins at Valkyrie with enthusiasm. Judith was a methodical woman and had left her a compendium of the year's routines as Managing Director, plus a long list of business contacts and their phone numbers. Simon stepped aside and two younger executives, both women, were vetted by Hattie and appointed. She called her first board meeting and laid down future policy. The two excited newcomers learned that the Managing Director wanted to see a harder-hitting title list, reflecting a more clear-cut dedication to the cause of modern women's emancipation. She intended to commission several authors to produce a series of short autobiographical works. These would deal with real life experiences in the sexual field as well as the social and economic, and no punches would be pulled. They would be high volume sellers. The new directors were as much impressed by their boss's competence and vision as by her reputation for a fearless, unconventional private life.

Hattie set herself to implement these ideas and, for most of 1981, thought of little else. In the evenings she'd pore over likely manuscripts, wearing the plastic-framed half-lensed glasses she now needed for reading, while Roger was out boozing as usual. Only when a rough publishing schedule for the next twelve months was in place did she relax a little.

During the summer holidays Sylvia had been on a musical course to develop her skills on the clarinet and to a tough Outward Bound camp in Wales. The rest of the time she and Roger had spent with Charlotte in Scotland. Now she was back at school for her final year. She'd go on to university, perhaps to study chemistry about which she'd lately become enthusiastic.

Sylvia was growing into a delightful young lady and Hattie yearned for her affection. Being away at boarding school had meant inevitably that she and Hattie had not shared the mother and daughter intimacies of puberty. Sylvia had made it clear that her house-mistress's practical guidance was quite sufficient. Hattie tried to interest the girl in her work at Valkyrie but, although polite enough, Sylvia showed no enthusiasm, no curiosity. It was hurtful, therefore, to overhear an animated conversation between Sylvia and her father about Roger's job. He took her to visit the magazine's office at her request.

At times Hattie felt frantic to win her daughter's love. She determined to make a bid for at least a better understanding and arranged to take Sylvia out of school for a Saturday exeat. She was frank with Roger.

"I just can't seem to get through to Sylvia, Roger. I suppose it's being out at the office so much in the early days."

"Yes, perhaps."

Roger wasn't communicative but she felt impelled to continue. "I mean, you were around much more when she was small. It's only natural she identified with you rather more."

"Yes."

"Anyhow, she's my daughter too and I love her. I can't bear her being so distant with me. Not now she's older. I just don't understand her coldness."

"Don't you, Hattie?"

"No I do not. It's an irrational attitude towards her own mother and I'm going to have it out with her."

Roger looked up. "Oh yes? When?"

"I'll take her out next Saturday. Just the two of us. I thought she'd like a sail on the river."

Roger's smile was faint. "I wish you luck, Hattie."

Sylvia tried to put her mother off. She was tired, had too much revision to do. But Hattie insisted.

"I'll have you back at school by supper time, darling. Is *that* all right?"

"Oh OK, Mother."

Hattie squirmed, annoyance wrestling with a painful realisation that her company was really not wanted.

They drove to Windsor and bought pleasure boat return tickets to Kew. It was a day of drizzle and so there were few others aboard, some retired couples, an American or two and the inevitable knot of becameraed Japanese. Hattie bought two paper cups of hot tea and found a quiet corner for them under the stern awning.

"This is nice, Sylvia, isn't it?"

The girl smiled politely, looking directly at her mother for only a moment. Her manners would never be found wanting. Hattie was glad of that. But Sylvia said nothing.

"Listen, darling, I want to talk to you about us. You know I love you very much, don't you?"

Sylvia smiled silently again. Perhaps she nodded affirmatively.

"Well, I know we've not seen as much of each other as I'd have liked these past few years, but it's been my job, Sylvia, that's kept me busy. You do understand that?"

"Yes, of course, Mother."

"Don't think I haven't had you in my thoughts every minute. What you've been doing, what's been happening at school. D'you ever think about me, Sylvia?"

"Maybe. Sometimes."

Again Hattie experienced a twinge of irritation. "That's not very reassuring for a mother to hear, you know. Not one who's always wondering what her daughter's thinking."

"In between," said Sylvia enigmatically.

"What d'you mean, darling? In between what?"

Hattie was taken aback by the sheer ferocity in her daughter's eyes as she faced her squarely and spat out one word – "Men!" Sylvia turned away and stared into the distance, lips pursed.

Hattie's instinct was to reprimand Sylvia for impudence, but her mission was to win the girl.

"Now look, Sylvia, I'm just going to disregard that. At least the way I think you meant it. I'm not going to deny I've had a good many men friends over the years. You're a young lady now and I'm sure you understand these things."

"Oh, I understand."

"Well then, we needn't quarrel about it. In any case, nobody has ever meant much to me except you, my darling. But I've never willingly hurt anyone else."

"What about Daddy?"

Hattie lit a cigarette and inhaled deeply. She sensed that the next few minutes were going to be of the utmost importance for her relationship with Sylvia.

"Daddy and I have had an agreement from the start that

each of us was free to have outside friends at any time. We have always . . . "

"Why don't you speak honestly? You mean lover boys on the side. Don't soil the beautiful word 'friend', Mother."

Hattie controlled herself. The rain began to squall and they had to move quickly into the small glassed-in saloon. Now it was necessary to keep their voices down.

"Sylvia, do try to be civil."

"Poor Daddy's been treated rottenly."

"He's got no grounds for complaint. Just because he didn't have the guts to . . . "

Sylvia shook her head vigorously from side to side. "Oh shut up, Mother! Your special pleading will get you nowhere. I really don't want to hear any more of it."

To her surprise Hattie found that her earlier indignation had melted away. All she knew now was that her fine young daughter was slipping away from her, perhaps forever. Her eyes filled with tears.

"Oh God, Sylvia! Please don't turn away from me. I love you. I need you my darling." She attempted to put her arms round the girl.

"Leave me alone, will you. And please don't make an embarrassing spectacle of yourself."

"Oh, Sylvia. Can't we . . . ?"

"I think I'll get off at the next pier. I've enough money in my purse for a taxi back to school."

"You wouldn't, Sylvia? *Please* don't."

Hattie talked her daughter into completing the round trip but the rest of the journey was a misery. Back at Queen Mary's Sylvia immediately jumped out of the car and ran gracefully into the sixth form house.

As she drove away Hattie's mind was in chaos. At the first suitably sheltered spot she parked and switched off the engine. Tears coursed down her cheeks. Her chest heaved as painful sobs possessed her whole body. Harriot Murray wept in desolation. Repeatedly she whispered, "Sylvia, oh my darling baby Sylvia."

22

BY NOVEMBER HATTIE felt confident she could leave the office for a few days. She arranged to visit New York. A coming American author was showing herself less than keen to visit London so Hattie determined to visit her.

She'd been to the city once before with Simon and quickly found that the Big Apple had lost nothing of its ability to set the pulse jumping. The cacophony of taxi horns and the street babble of its citizens seemed to go on round the clock. Though dwarfed by the monstrous glass and concrete buildings Hattie felt, like everyone else she supposed, curiously unthreatened. New York seemed somehow much smaller than London. A quite manageable town which she could get to know intimately in a short time. Probably something to do with the grid street plan, she thought.

The morning air was crisp as she stepped from the Pierre Hotel. She'd slept badly, her body-clock rebelling at its enforced five hour stall, so she took a stroll through Central Park. Multi-coloured joggers everywhere. Skate-boarders. Roller-skaters. Ivy League-suited young business in a hurry. Winos with nowhere to go. Glad of this oasis Hattie walked on, her mind in neutral.

A statue loomed farther down the path she was on. What, who was it? An odd familiarity, at once homely and uneasy, communicated itself. As she moved towards the sculpture its outlines became clearer. Good Lord! Who'd have believed it? It was Rab all right. The inscription confirmed that the New York City Government had erected this memorial to the poet Robert Burns in 1880 on the occasion of the 121st anniversary of his birth.

As so often in the past Hattie wondered at her father's devotion to the life and work of this man, surely the archetypal rebel and libertarian. Robert Murray could not have been as steeped as he had been in Burns's poetry without identifying himself to an extent with the poet's free-thinking, egalitarian courage. And yet, he'd been such a conformist all his life. It was a mystery Hattie knew she'd never fathom.

She left the park and was about to hail a cab to take her to her ten o'clock meeting in downtown Manhattan when a young coloured woman in kaftan and headband approached and thrust a leaflet into her hand. Under a banner headline, *Sisters Unite!*, it announced a public rally of the *Militant Women for Equality* movement that evening at a hall on the West Side. Hattie stuffed it into her leather coat pocket with an encouraging smile at the girl.

Within a few minutes in the plush chromium-furnished and pile-carpeted publisher's office it was obvious that the author was in no position to negotiate. A humourless, silver-haired Sales Vice President made it clear that Sadie Mastrovitch's European rights were currently not for sale, and that when the time was right they would almost certainly go to a rival company. Already thoroughly uncomfortable in the overheated room, Hattie told the author and her patronising patron what she thought of people who had the bad manners to bring someone all the way over the Atlantic on false pretences. It had no effect, so she left.

She could have gone straight out to Kennedy Airport and tried for an immediate return flight but, at that moment, the prospect of collecting her things, struggling out through the traffic again so soon, followed by the strain of being processed on to the plane, Hattie found too daunting. What she needed was a long undisturbed sleep at the hotel. She caught a taxi back to the Pierre feeling crumpled and edgy.

With a Do Not Disturb card hanging on the handle of her locked door and all her clothes off, Hattie sighed with relief. Now for three or four hours of blissful unconsciousness. She decided to take a warm shower first. There was a full length mirror in the bathroom and, walking towards the bath, she paused to examine her figure. The picture did not much please her.

The undeniable beginnings of sagging flesh showed on her thighs. Her stomach no longer pouted attractively, it fairly bulged. Her breasts seemed to be flattening and a vein near the left nipple was becoming noticeable. Her wrists and hands were podgy, the scarlet nails looked cheap. Then her face. No doubt it was an interesting face, but she hated the wrinkles and blotches that called for increasing cosmetic disguise. Her short, frizzed hair-style suddenly seemed stupidly youthful. Oh God, she muttered savagely, and hurried to get under the shower. As she stood in the warm pattering comfort Hattie wondered what she'd look like in five years time, probably with the menopause behind her. 'A raddled old whore' – the ugly description came from nowhere, but it smote her cruelly.

As she unhappily dried herself then used the hotel's free talcum, there was a final shock. She discovered evidence of grey among her pubic hairs. Grabbing a pair of tweezers from her toilet-case she put on her reading glasses and dragged a chair under the main overhead light. Angrily she set herself to deal with this new embarrassment. When she'd finished, her hands were shaking. Jesus! She had to find a man soon to prove she was still in the running. Taking two brandy miniatures from the fridge she tipped them into a glass.

The liquor and her time-dislocated exhaustion quickly took over and it was in fact nearly six when she awoke again. Hattie stretched luxuriously in the soft, king-sized bed. She felt quite recovered and keen to be up and doing. But doing what? Then she remembered the women's rally. Jumping up she pulled the leaflet from her coat pocket. Seven thirty kick-off. Time for something to eat and then a taxi over to West 117th Street. It would be fascinating to see what was going on over here, at the grassroots.

Hattie rang room service and ordered some sandwiches and a bottle of white Californian wine. As she ate and drank with relish a thought suddenly struck her. This meeting sounded rather a big affair – was it conceivable that Drusilla Slingsby-Gore might be there?

As soon as she entered the meeting Hattie decided it was highly improbable that Dru Gore would be anywhere near it. First of all, ninety percent of the delegates, as well as the audience, was non-white. Most were New York blacks and coloureds but there was a good number of Hispanics too, mainly Puerto Ricans it seemed, and a sprinkling of Orientals. But it wasn't so much the racial composition of the rally that Hattie was noticing. It was the weird character and clothing of the people around her.

Lesbians Marry Ladies, read a large lapel button worn by a hefty, be-jeaned black woman sitting behind Hattie. *We're Better Off Without 'Em* was the enigmatic legend on another. An exotic looking crowd of men and women occupied a block of seats on Hattie's left. The nearest had a square plastic badge pinned to his electric-blue silk shirt. Hattie peered and finally made out, *Bronx Gays Union*. As she studied this group she suspected that a few of the women were in fact men, male transvestites. She wondered what on earth they were doing there at all.

"Wild bunch, eh?"

The speaker was a widely grinning black man, young, conventionally dressed and, by the appearance of his very long legs jutting out into the passageway, extremely tall.

"Yes, fascinating! Not quite what I expected, to tell you the truth."

"You English?"

"Scottish, actually."

"Yeah? I'm Chester Diamond. Hi."

He offered Hattie his large boney hand.

"Hello, Chester. My name's Hattie Murray. I'm a visitor from London."

"Hiya, Hattie. You mean London's in Scotland?"

"No, no! I just live there."

A gravel-voiced chairwoman with an unreliable microphone which, without warning, emitted terrifying squeals and howls, was attempting to call the meeting to order. Obediently Hattie smiled at Chester and turned to give the platform her full attention.

"You on vacation, Hattie?"

"No, business," she repled in a whisper. But she saw that no-one else appeared to be concerned, and conversations were continuing unabated on all sides.

"Well now, that sure impresses me!"

Was he serious, or being gratuitously sarcastic? Hattie decided to give him the benefit of the doubt.

"It was an abortive trip, I'm afraid."

"Oh, too bad. When d'you fly back over the Pond?"

"Tomorrow."

"That ain't long to get acquainted, Hattie."

Chester raised his eyebrows surprisingly far, creases of black skin appearing on his normally smooth forehead. The directness of his message took Hattie by surprise. Suddenly she was sweating, but she contrived merely to smile sweetly again and affect to be trying to make out what the first speaker was saying.

The speeches were abysmally poor in intellectual content. One after the other a series of women of various shapes, colours and ages made short personal statements, usually giving a lurid description of some male employer who'd exploited her labour for low pay, interfered with her sexually and finally sacked her without compensation. Hattie felt sympathy for these rather pitiful characters but couldn't help doubting whether every case had actually happened as the meeting was being asked to believe.

Latterly, some very special pleading took place. One speaker wanted homosexual marriages to be legitimised, another that there be senior appointees in the Washington administration with responsibility for Gay Affairs, one for each community. And so on. It was not a feminist meeting as Hattie understood it. This motley crowd of misfits was not concerned to address the difficult areas of equal job opportunity, pension rights, State-funded child day-care and the like. Their protest, doubtless well justified in many instances, was mainly confined to the specific issues of sexual harassment and discrimination against homosexuals. There appeared to be an extraordinary number of deviants present. Hattie supposed that in the great US of A there were likely to be many echelons in the advancing army of women.

The haranguing showed no signs of ending but Hattie decided she'd had enough and stood up to leave.

"You sick of this, Hattie?"

"I think I'll go now, Chester."

"Mind if I walk you to the subway? Can be creepy round here."

"Thank you very much." They emerged into the dark

street. "Actually, I think I'll take a taxi if I can find one."

"Oh, OK." Did he look disappointed or was he acting again? "Where you putting up, Hattie?"

"The Pierre Hotel."

In the shadows his large eyes showed a spectacular amount of white. "Pierre? Christ, man, that's cool!"

Hattie was reacting to her cheerful escort's loping, easy stride. She couldn't check her imagination. What *would* he look like stripped off? Her closest experience of male black bodies to date had been a somewhat vague admiration of the rippling physiques of boxers and athletes seen on TV.

"There's a Yellow Cab, Hattie. I'll flag him down for you. Pierre, wow! That must be some business of yours."

Hattie made her decision. The Pierre seemed free and easy about who went in and out. She'd be back in London tomorrow. Why not?

"Chester, would you like to join me for a nightcap, maybe a late snack?"

"At the Pierre?"

"Sure. That's no problem."

"Well . . . " Chester Diamond was a highly intelligent sociology student at Columbia University. In intellectual matters he was a confident debater, not afraid to challenge others, black or white, but he was not in the habit of mixing with the sophisticated in the city's top hotels. "Gee, Hattie, I'm not sure. See . . . "

Before he knew it Chester was on his way to a world he'd so far only ever glimpsed from the sidewalk, with a rich pretty woman from England who was holding his hand and snucking up real close.

"That was some meeting, Chester! What took you there for heaven's sake?"

"Fraternal delegate. I'm on the NAACP Committee at Columbia."

"I see. What are you studying?"

He told her, mentioning at the same time that he was 22 and that his father was a school janitor. "That's my story. Except one thing."

"What's that, Chester?"

"I just sat an exam could take me over to England next year. Extra course at the London School of Economics."

"Well done. So I might see you again?"

"It's a long shot. There's about a hundred went in. Only three'll make it."

"Best of luck, anyway. Here's the hotel."

The elderly taxi driver slammed back his reinforced glass screen. "Nine bucks fifty, miss." He ignored Chester.

Sitting down at the table they drew curious glances. After a while Hattie thought she saw a woman at the bar whispering and giggling with her friend. One was middle aged with inefficiently dyed red hair and bad teeth, the other, slant-eyed and probably half-Vietnamese, wore a gold lurex leotard and a wide-brimmed black hat. Chester told Hattie about his daily jogging routine.

"You must be fit, Chester."

"Reckon so."

But the tittering women and the bartender's condescending attitude were producing an uncomfortable atmosphere.

"This isn't very nice, is it, Chester?"

"Those damn hookers got no damn right to laugh at decent folks." He spoke with a vehemence she hadn't suspected.

"Finish your drink then."

He obeyed. They left the bar and began to cross the lobby. The swing-doors to the street were straight ahead, the room elevators to the right. Chester hesitated. Hattie took his hand.

"This way. I've got my key."

"Listen, Hattie, I . . . "

"We can't say goodbye properly standing here, can we? Come up for a little while and chat some more. I won't keep you late."

Chester was overwhelmed by the opulence of the room. "Hey, this is like Lady Pompadoor's palace!" He laughed with delight at the bathroom and immediately whipped off his shirt and had a good wash. "Goddam! Doesn't that soap smell something else? And them towels are soft, man!"

He made to put his shirt back on. Hattie was staring hungrily at the flawless black skin.

"Don't bother with your shirt, Chester. It's warm. Come over here."

He walked to her. The soap's sandalwood aroma was strong but it did not mask his healthy, animal smell. Trembling slightly Hattie looked up at him and smiled.

"I want to kiss you, Chester, but you're too tall . . . Over here now."

She led him to the bed and pulled him down with her. Kissing him urgently she ran her hands up and down his smooth back. She felt the long, flexible spine, the wide, muscular shoulders. Pushing him slightly from her she fumbled with his trousers' belt.

"I'll do that, Hattie. You get your own things off. Say you don't mess, do you, Hat?" He was grinning merrily.

"I need you badly, Chester," she stammered through quick breaths.

"Me too, crazy lady!"

He was naked in seconds.

"Get under that sheet." She was struggling with her own clothes. Finally she peeled off her tights and began to unhook her little corset.

"Hey, man! What you got there?"

"Oh, it's just to give me a waist."

"I never saw nothing like that before. Not outside porno mags and stuff. You're some sexy lady, Hattie!"

She fell on him and, with a perfunctory kiss to the lips and his well developed chest, slid quickly down the bed. She took his penis in her hands. Its glistening black hardness excited her insupportably. Using her mouth for only a moment she swung on to her back and clamped her legs round the narrow hips and tight haunches of her youthful lover.

Given his age, he displayed remarkable control. Holding himself clear of her on stiff arms he worked steadily. Hattie switched her bottom from side to side in breathless pleasure. He went on and on. She looked up at his smiling face.

"My God, Chester, you've got staying power."

"Practice, Hat."

"D'you have a girlfriend?"

"No. Plenty when I was a teenager. Don't bother much with chicks, since I got into real studies and all."

"You know what a woman likes."

"That you don't forget. OK, baby, we done the laps. Now we go for the tape."

He lay on her and spread his big hands under her buttocks for leverage. The climax was completely satisfying and mutual. As they rested he remarked, "You gonna sleep deep tonight. Hat. Right?"

"I will, thanks to you, Chester."

"Listen, I got a kick out of it too, y'know! But, Hattie, I have to go now. My old mom don't approve me staying out nights."

Hattie laughed. She was sorry to show him out. Apart from his considerable sexual athleticism, Chester Diamond was a thoroughly nice young fellow.

As she sipped her Buck's Fizz on the plane after take-off next morning Hattie was barely aware of the businessman concentratedly tapping on the keyboard of his laptop computer beside her. She closed her eyes and gratefully pictured again the supple length of her companion the night before.

Roger was at home when she got in to Brodick Mews that evening. She could see he'd been drinking.

"Well, well, Ms Murray returns." He sniggered pointlessly.

"You're drunk. Why haven't you gone out? You're not usually hanging around for a chat at this hour."

"There was a TV documen ... documentat ... a thing about education and university courses I was interested in. Sylvia was asking ... But never fear, I'm going ... I'm going."

He put on his old raglan coat and scarf and was about to leave when suddenly he turned to face Hattie.

"I nearly forgot. A very funny thing happened to me yesterday. You should hear it."

"What, Roger, for goodness sake?"

"Well, I was a bit off my normal beat at lunchtime. I'd had some research to do for an article over in the Wimbledon area and popped into a hostelry near the Common. For a lip-stiffener you know."

"Roger, I'm whacked. Never mind the build-up. What's the punchline?"

"Well, this rather tatty looking individual was giving the barman his worries. Divorce, loss of big job, money problems. I couldn't help overhearing. Then he said something about parliament and women's rights and I began to take an interest."

"Was it ... surely it wasn't ... ?"

"Oh yes it was. I chatted him up and out it all came. Years ago he's in line for a Cabinet appointment till this *fascinating* woman comes along and smashes up his career. You should have heard ... "

"I'd rather not. So you met John Chetwynd. Did you tell

him who you were."

"Didn't seem to be any point."

"No. What's he doing for a living?"

"Trying to sell greetings cards and calendars. When he's not on the bottle by the looks of him."

"Damned fool."

"Quite. Well, hello and goodbye, as they say."

Roger never actually slammed doors, but Hattie could still gauge when he was angry by the degree of firmness with which he closed them. Tonight he was very angry. His description of John Chetwynd disturbed Hattie more than she cared to admit to herself, but there was nothing to be done.

Christmas came. Sylvia went on a tour of Belgium and Holland with the Queen Mary's School choir. For dinner on the twenty fifth the three of them ate out at the Mandeville Hotel. Roger had drunk too much before they walked down to the hotel and was morose and objectionable by turn during the meal. With Sylvia at her most prickly, the occasion was a miserable failure.

The weeks sped by. It had been decided that Sylvia would apply for admission to Aberdeen university to read chemistry. A natural inclination towards science had been much encouraged by Charlotte who perhaps saw a chance of yet participating in research work, her own early longing, if vicariously. Sylvia did not come home for weekends, though at sixteen she could have done so, saying she wanted to study hard for a good exam result.

One Monday just after Easter Hattie was going over some galleys with one of Valkyrie's authors when the phone rang.

"Hattie? Know who's here?"

She knew immediately. "It's Chester, isn't it?"

23

THAT EVENING SHE WENT round to the students' Hall of Residence where Chester had a spartan room. There were strict rules about visitors so they found a nearby pub and had several drinks together. However, after a few jokes and a description from Chester of his sociology course, there really wasn't much else to say.

"I'll try to think of somewhere private to meet next time."

"Suits me, sexy lady." He grinned good-naturedly, large, perfect white teeth, startling in the dark face.

Next day she took him by taxi to a small hotel off Oxford Street which she'd once before been to with John Chetwynd when his wife had been in residence at Vincent Street. Chester performed beautifully and they arranged for another assignation later in the week. Hattie noticed that he had few clothes. His student grant was meagre so she gave him money to buy a suit, some shirts and ties.

It was exciting to have this source of exotic, competent sex on tap, but Hattie found herself becoming physically impatient between sessions. She was also increasingly embarrassed at the necessary charade with the hotel staff. What could she possibly do? Then the solution struck her.

Get Chester to come and live at Brodick Mews! The more she thought about it the more she liked the idea. Not only would it mean that, with judicious opportunity taking, Chester would be available more or less whenever she felt like it but, surely, taking her young, black lover in under the same roof as the father of her child constituted an unusually powerful statement of feminist independence. Laughing inwardly at her liberated audacity she determined to do it.

"Roger, d'you remember that mad women's meeting in New York I told you about."

"Uh-huh."

"One of the delegates I met rang me today. Nice young chap called Chester Diamond."

"Typical Yank handle."

"Yes. Anyway, Chester's over on a sociology course at the LSE. He's evidently in one of those student hostels and thoroughly uncomfortable. I thought I might invite him to move in here. Say for a couple of months till Sylvia's due home. 'Hands across the Ocean', as you might say."

"Hattie, I don't think . . . "

"Maybe we'll have some conversation round here for a change. He might even cheer you up, Roger."

Any possible objection was quickly stifled by Hattie.

She put it to Chester.

"Hey! You crazy, Hat? You say you been living with this guy for years and you expect him to turn around and kiss my ass. Spit in my face is more like it."

"Roger's a docile type. Anyhow, I told you, Chester, there's *nothing* between us except our daughter. We hardly *speak*, let alone anything else."

"Well, I dunno."

"As far as he's concerned you're just a young friend who's short of cash and needs a decent place to lay his head. OK?"

"If you think the guy really don't care, Hattie."

"We'll have to watch and not make it obvious when we decide to hop into bed, won't we, Chester?"

A wide youthful grin lit up his face. "Wow! You're something, Hat."

That weekend he dumped his books and tote-bag in Sylvia's room, carefully hanging up his new suit, which was a rather lighter blue than Hattie would have chosen. When he was introduced to Roger he addressed him as 'Sir.'

Hattie laughed. "Plain 'Roger' will do, Chester! Now, let's all have a drink and get to know each other. Roger, will you do the honours please?"

Roger's natural good manners asserted themselves and he chatted amiably with Chester about his studies and the American university system. But he was not at ease. Catching Hattie alone in the kitchen he grabbed her arm.

"Why the hell didn't you mention that . . . you know . . ." he jerked his thumb over his shoulder.

"What, Roger? D'you mean the fact that Chester's black?"

"Well, yes."

"You're not betraying a prejudice, *surely*, Roger?"

"No, of course not. But I just think you might have warned me. That's all." His voice trailed away.

"I'm afraid I simply don't understand you sometimes, Roger. Now, if you don't mind, I'm going to prepare something for us to eat."

A routine of sorts developed. They breakfasted together, then, if he had an early lecture, Chester left with Hattie. Roger cleared up the dishes and departed an hour later. In the evenings they ate at seven, the cooking usually being done by Roger, before Hattie and Chester settled down to work on their respective papers. Roger regularly went out to the Dover Castle. He was not deceived. Chester was too transparent a character for Roger to entertain any real doubt that he'd slept with Hattie, but it was easier to shut his mind to the effrontery. As long as they were discreet he supposed he'd put up with it for the remaining six weeks or so.

With Chester at hand Hattie's sexual fretfulness disappeared, to be replaced by a more controlled, delicious sybaritism. All she had to do was lay aside her work, take off her glasses and reach out to touch the ever willing Chester to an instant erection. They played games. Once she got him to walk around the house all evening with nothing on, forcing herself not to lay a finger on him. Of course, they wound up on the floor eventually, hammering at each other with abandon. Another time she led him up to the bathroom and told him to sit on the WC. Squatting to face him she took her pleasure until overwhelmed by a shuddering orgasm.

"Gee, Hat. You sure like to screw!"

"I don't hear any objections."

"I *can* go without." He smiled at her a little wistfully. "Guess I'm your personal sex toy or something, Hat."

Always they ensured they were back in their chairs or in their own rooms when Roger returned.

Near the end of Chester's stay Hattie became increasingly nervous. His impending absence had her frantic at moments, particularly as she lay in bed, thoughts churning. One night, a few days before he was due to leave, she woke at three, suddenly desperate for the feeling of Chester's hard, engorged penis in her hand, the strong male smell of his body in her nostrils. Dare she go to him now?" It was risky but, Christ!, would this not be the *ultimate* liberated act? Hattie's heart was thumping heavily.

She got up and slipped silently out on to the landing. Through Roger's door came the sound of steady, open-mouthed snoring. Well anaesthetised, she reckoned, and tip-toed on to Sylvia's room. She forgot to avoid a loose parquet block and, as her bare foot now depressed it, the noise of its shifting sounded like a pistol shot in the confined space.

Hattie stood motionless, perspiring as she listened intently. There was a rasp of a dry throat being cleared from Roger's room and then utter silence again.

She slid into bed with Chester.

"Jesus, Hat, you mad?"

"Please do it, Chester," she urged. "I want you inside me. Go on, you're ready now. Don't take too long."

It was soon over. Hattie licked her parched lips.

"Thanks, Chester. You were wonderful."

"OK, baby. You better get outa here."

In the morning Hattie left early for a breakfast meeting at the Hilton Hotel with an Australian publisher. Chester had not yet emerged by the time she stepped out into Brodick Mews. It was sunny but the air was cool and pleasant to breathe. The secret thrill of her daring behaviour quickly faded as her mind grappled with the points to be negotiated with Mr Potter.

As soon as she reached Valkyrie about eleven Hattie knew something was wrong. The building's commissionaire failed to salute her and give his customary greeting. The girls at the reception desk were not their usual smiling selves. One of them motioned to her.

"Miss Murray, there's an Inspector Kenton and another policeman to see you in Waiting Room Number 2. I hope nothing bad's happened?"

"How long have they been here?"

"About an hour."

It could only be Roger or Sylvia. But what, *what*? In an agony of anxiety she walked to the waiting room with as much calm as she could muster.

"Miss Harriot Browne Murray?"

"Yes."

"I'm Inspector Charles Kenton and this is Sergeant Wilson."

"What's wrong?"

"Miss Murray, do you reside at Number 12 Brodick Mews in Marylebone?"

"Yes."

"And has Mr Roger Reginald Foley been your companion, also living at that address?"

"Yes, he lives there. We own the house jointly. Why?"

Inspector Kenton touched Hattie's upper forearm. "Please sit down, Miss Murray." All three sat down.

"Inspector, d'you mind coming to the point?"

"I'm sorry to have to inform you, Miss Murray, that there's been a serious incident this morning at Brodick Mews."

"Incident?"

"Is it correct that there was also a young black male person living at your house?"

"Yes. Chester Diamond. A family friend."

Inspector Kenton indicated to his subordinate that he should make a note of this information.

"Mr Diamond is dead, Miss Murray, apparently shot about seven thirty this morning with your husband's . . . that is, Mr Foley's shotgun."

"Oh, my God! And Roger . . . ?"

"I'm afraid I must advise you, Miss Murray, that Mr Foley is also dead. Our preliminary investigations would indicate that he shot Mr Diamond with one cartridge and then turned the weapon on himself. Of course nothing is yet final."

There was wild music raging in Hattie's head. Roger must have heard them last night. Did he lie awake in the dark for hours, waiting for her to go in the morning before . . . ? Distantly she heard the Inspector telling her that it was necessary for her to come now to the station to give a statement. Thereafter she'd be required to make identifications. An incubus of numbing terror gripped Hattie.

At the police station she learned that a neighbour had been getting into his car when he'd heard the two shots. The police had been called and they'd formed the opinion that Chester Diamond had been shot while in bed through the base of the skull, as if he'd been sleeping on his side at the time. Roger Foley looked to have taken his own life by shooting himself through the roof of the mouth in the bathroom. Hattie, distressed as she was, maintained that she could think of no motive. She gave it as her view that Roger, who was a heavy drinker, must have had a brainstorm.

"You have a daughter, Miss Murray?"

"Yes, Sylvia."

"Sylvia Murray, aged 16, presently being educated at Queen Mary's Girls' School, near Reading?"

"Yes, yes."

"We'll send along one of our women constables from the local force this afternoon to advise her of the tragedy, Miss Murray. They're very kind and sympathetic."

"I want Sylvia to come home."

"In a day or two, Miss Murray, I'd advise. There's a nasty mess to clear up at Brodick Mews. And procedures."

Oh God! This was turning into some sort of ghastly Agatha Christie scenario.

The bodies were removed, blood-soaked sheets disposed of, walls and floors cleaned to the best of Hattie's ability. She was moving about in a trance.

Before she eventually spoke to Simon Hotchkiss on the phone he'd read the grisly details in the evening paper.

"Hattie, I'm so sorry. You must be out of your mind."

"Just about, Simon."

There was a long pause. "As soon as you feel up to it please come in. Obviously the Chairman will want to speak to you."

Hattie rang Charlotte. She gave her version of events but found her mother unsympathetic, uncommunicative almost.

Then Sylvia arrived, driven in from Berkshire by her science mistress.

"Darling!" Hattie came out of the front door, arms extended.

Sylvia turned away without a word, lifted her bags out of the car and put them on the pavement. Hattie heard her say, "Thanks for the lift and, oh, everything, Miss Richards. I'll come to see you later on."

The older woman was out of the car now, embracing her pupil affectionately.

"Au revoir, Sylvia my dear girl. Remember always to keep your head. Many people love you at Queen Mary's, you know."

Then the car was gone and mother and daughter left to confront one another inside the house.

"Sylvia, this is *terrible*. I don't know what's to be said. But at least we have each other, don't we?"

"I suppose this Diamond person was another of your lover boys?"

"Sylvia!"

"Well? Don't bother lying. It's too late and it won't do any good."

"I hope we can still show some mutual respect, Sylvia."

"Respect? You don't know the meaning of the word."

The atmosphere was brittle. Naturally the girl was overwrought. Her father had just committed suicide. Hattie wasn't going to lose her temper if she could possibly avoid it. She needed Sylvia as never before.

"Now look here, Sylvia, we must control ourselves. There's enough to contend with already. Let's not fall out." She tried a smile. "How about some tea? We'll have lunch a bit later."

The response was a hard stare. "How can you talk like that?"

"You *are* my daughter, Sylvia."

"No I'm not. I'll never call you Mother ever again."

"Sylvia, don't be unkind. I . . . "

"My God! You who drove my father to his death want me to be *kind*?"

"What are you *saying*, Sylvia?" Despite herself Hattie's anger was rising.

"What I'm saying, in case it's not clear, is that you and your so-called principles, you and your string of rotten men sent my father out of his mind. You deserve . . . "

"Roger was weak, Sylvia, and a drunk as well. He pushed *himself* round the bend."

"How I *hate* you! My father was a kind, gentle man who never meant anyone any harm. You and your crazy ideas *destroyed* him. He was my darling Daddy and I loved him with all my heart. He often told me he'd have married you but that you wouldn't have it. So you made me a bastard. *And* cut me off from my Foley grandparents. Daddy always said they'd have loved me. What *principles*!"

Hattie's brain was suggesting all manner of cutting rebuttals, but the pain of what she was hearing bridled her tongue.

"For Heaven's sake calm down, Sylvia. You're still young but you'll find out. Men are selfish monsters, weak fools. Bullies. You cannot expect fairness from them. You *must* stay independent and stand on your own feet to have any hope of equal treatment."

"Claptrap! You've been peddling those out of date *idées fixes* of yours all my life. Women have every opportunity today. I'm telling you, if you're the least bit interested in the truth, which I very much doubt, YOU'RE *the monster! Not decent men like my poor Daddy.*" She was screaming through her tears.

"Sylvia, get hold of yourself! You don't understand . . . "

"Yes I do. Men and women *are* different and it's just plain stupid to pretend otherwise. There'll always be arguments. But that doesn't stop us being friends, respecting each other and co-operating. Women's hostility will simply make men *more* chauvinistic."

"Have you any idea of the struggle that's taken place this century?"

"Of course I have, but I'm talking about today. Thousands are dying all over the world every day from starvation and disease, and all you and your feminist friends can do is contemplate your navels and whine about men. You disgust me."

Hattie stared at her articulate daughter. What she said was so straight-forward, so simple, apparently unarguable. Had her own vision ever been so clear, free from prejudice? She tried once or twice more to calm Sylvia, but the girl merely grew angrier. The brick wall she'd erected was impenetrable.

Eventually, Hattie allowed her to go up to her room. Maybe she'd be more tractable by lunchtime. Sylvia was particularly fond of steak and green salad with a special home-made dressing, and Hattie had the ingredients ready. She'd bought a bottle of light red wine too. Surely after a glass of Macon Sylvia would come off her high horse. If only they could comfort one another.

The horror of the last three days was still on Hattie and it was only when she was doing something domestic that she seemed able to forget for a moment or two. She'd not yet been to the office. In the kitchen now she set herself to prepare a tasty meal. Sylvia's footsteps sounded on the stairs. Hattie carried on chopping vegetables. She wouldn't call the girl. Let her come to herself for a bit.

But after about ten minutes Sylvia still hadn't appeared.

Hattie glanced out of the kitchen. No sign of her. She called up the stairs that lunch was nearly ready. No reply. She ran up to Sylvia's room and saw immediately that many of her things had been removed. She'd slipped out of the house. Then Hattie noticed a scribbled note on Sylvia's dressing table.

*I NEVER WANT TO SEE YOU AGAIN.
I MEAN IT – S.*

For the next few hours Hattie roamed around the house in torment. What could she do? What should she do? Who could she talk to? The idea of ringing the police occurred to her. But what would she say? A row with her daughter resulting in her leaving the house a few hours earlier hardly justified a report to the Missing Persons Bureau. In any case, Hattie had no desire to advertise to anyone the depth to which her relationship with Sylvia had sunk.

As the cruel light of July persisted on into the evening Hattie's nerves began to jump. The Coroner's Enquiry next week was going to be hell. She'd have to face the Chairman too. There was unlikely to be any chance of keeping her job. He'd given a clear warning after the John Chetwynd publicity. This was a hundred times worse. And who else would take her on in anything like a comparable position? She realised how important her job had been, the one truly stable element in her life for over twenty years. And now Sylvia had gone. Alternately, Hattie cursed her luck, particularly the men who'd contributed to it, and whimpered self-pityingly.

When the phone rang at eight forty five she leapt at it like a pouncing cat.

24

"HATTIE?"

"Oh, Mum, it's you."

"You should know that Sylvia is with me."

"*Sylvia*! How did she . . . I mean . . . ?"

"She flew up on the shuttle."

"Mum, let me speak to her."

"Oh no, Hattie. She has nothing to say to you."

"Listen, Mum, . . . "

"As a matter of fact, that goes for me too, Hattie. Please don't bother us."

Hattie found herself talking to a dead line and decided that, for the moment anyway, there was no point in ringing back. She had to think.

But her mind was in hopeless confusion, her thoughts incoherent, flitting from one subject to another uncontrollably. She drank several whiskies, smoked incessantly and stared uncomprehendingly at one TV programme after another. Perhaps about 1 p.m. she fell into an exhausted sleep sitting upright.

In the morning she was cold and stiff but, after hot coffee and toast, she felt better. The letter-box flap rattled. An envelope dropped on to the hall carpet. Hattie recognised Simon Hotchkiss's writing.

My dear Hattie,
You must be suffering greatly and, whatever the outcome is going to be for you, I just wanted to let you know I'm constantly thinking of you.

We've known each other a long time now and there aren't many secrets left, are there? I'm a humdrum sort of fellow but I've got enough experience of life to recognise that you are a very special person, Hattie. And I'm grateful to have been your friend.

The world is cruel and I suppose our ways have to part, but if there's anything I can do in the future (off the record recommendations or whatever) just let me know. But your capabilities in this racket are widely recognised of course, so I doubt I can help particularly.

That's the practical side of things – what I really want to say, my dear dear Hattie, is much more personal. It is, I truly do understand you. Can you believe that? Different demons drive each of us and I know that you have been implacably intent on righting the wrongs women have endured at the hands of men for centuries. You've had no option but to do those demons' bidding all your life. Strange that in your militancy men have nevertheless found pleasure with you – I'm sure often a degree of ecstatic fulfilment they've never experienced elsewhere. I know. And I'm sure also that many must have wished they'd had the courage to hold you to a true partnership. But your rare type is used ruthlessly by fate to achieve important things. In your case that has been a strong contribution to the momentum of the Women's Movement at a critical point in its progress, for which all women should be eternally grateful. But that's not the way of the world, which is inclined to respond with baleful ingratitude and convenient amnesia. And a facile pointing to the casualties inescapable in such a titanic struggle.

I ache for you, Hattie. Yes, I'm going to say it, my feelings for you are those of real love. If I knew how to pray for you I'd do it. Just keep your head, my dear, let those awful upcoming events take their course and then make a new start. There are many, I assure you, who will cheer loudly when that day comes.

If you are ever really desperate you know where to find me. The best way of concluding this is with an utterly genuine,
Yours sincerely,
Simon

Hattie was undone. She was bad news, a disgrace to the profession, about to go to court, to appear in lurid press reports, a pariah, and yet here was this cautious, sophisticated publisher telling her he loved her, and in writing too. Warm gratitude flooded through her. Simon's bigness of heart constricted her throat. She had never loved a man. Hattie perceived the crippling disability of spirit which had always inhibited such a possibility. Oh God! At that moment she felt a half-woman only. It was a novel and highly unwelcome intimation. She wiped her moist eyes and lit a cigarette.

Had other men in her life, even if they were less articulate than Simon, really understood her, truly loved her? She thought of young Nicholas Whiteford, so long ago. Roger, John Chetwynd? Might others have wanted her as a loving mate but been frozen off by her underlying hostility? And what of her father? Could she, should she have tried harder, later on anyway when she was settled in London, to understand *him* rather than excluding him totally from her affections because of an adolescent perception that he did not understand *her*? Suddenly, for the first time in years, she felt an impulse to try to repair their relationship. But it was too late.

Hattie drew fiercely on her cigarette. Now she was not only lonely and unhappy, Simon's letter had confused her. Nevertheless she blessed him for his percipience, his sympathy, his generosity.

It was Saturday. She decided to seek the normality of other human beings in the busy High Street. Indeed, she found simply walking about among the shopping crowd reassuring. Glancing into the window of a bookshop she and Roger had patronised a good deal over the years her eye was taken by a familiar face. Atop a pyramid display of books in the corner one had been reversed to show a photograph of the author. It was Dru Gore.

Hattie entered the shop and lifted a copy of the new book. Published by Valkyrie's main competitor it was a comprehensive selection of feminist essays, illustrating various aspects of the Women's Liberation struggle, with a connecting commentary by Dru. There was a short biography on the dust jacket.

> *Drusilla Slingsby-Gore was born in Sussex, England in 1926 and worked for Women's Rights in that country before moving to California in 1964. She has been active in the Liberation Movement in the USA, lecturing widely and*

contributing articles to feminist journals. This is her first book. Ms Slingsby-Gore is unmarried.

Hattie bought the book and took it home to add to her collection of feminist literature. She was glad Dru had found a worthwhile outlet for her talents and hoped she'd achieved some peace in her private life. Hattie felt again the heat that day at Kirdstone Park. How long ago it all was. Despite everything she still missed the stimulation of Dru's sharp mind, the glamour and style of her aristocratic ways, her vitality.

She ate some biscuits and cheese, an apple. The wine she'd intended for Sylvia stood opened but recorked on the kitchen worktop. Was it her imagination or did it really taste bitter? Hattie poured most of it down the sink.

She read Dru's *The Good Fight* for a while but, although the connecting passages were wise, the ground was tediously familiar. The tone of the contributions seemed excessively shrill, some academically nit-picking. Outside, the Mews was deserted. It was a sunny day and people had probably made for the country. The afternoon stretched ahead. She laid the book aside.

Hattie went out again and walked up to Regents Park. She'd always loved the place but now, as memories of pushing Sylvia in her pram came back, she felt somehow cruelly mocked. Even the mallards swam away at her approach, as if shunning her. Hattie knew her nerves were in tatters. Maybe she'd go over to Wimpole Street on Monday morning and ask Jane Howard for some valium. She walked on but her melancholy did not diminish. Most of the other strollers seemed to be young couples, in their early twenties, holding hands, oblivious of others. Hattie felt fat and unattractive, tartily passée behind her heavy make-up.

She went back to Brodick Mews. On the way the traffic

forced her to pause just outside the park gates in the Marylebone Road. Suddenly she remembered Karl Pietersen's bear-hug as he kissed her on that exact spot, picking him up in the Tropicana coffee-house and the shattering bed session they'd had in her first little flat. It must have been 1959. She'd gleefully kept her secret adventure to herself, never mentioned it to anyone. But there had been so many others since, she'd not thought of Karl for years. Hattie found there was no longer any amusement in the recollection.

She watched a TV film and made herself a light meal. By nine in the evening she at last began to feel heavy-eyed and gratefully went to bed early. She slept deeply till one in the morning but thereafter, in the silent darkness, the desperate realities of her situation attacked her again. Voices whispered, ghostly faces flickered, out of sequence in her mind – Roger, her father, Harrison Bellchamber, Kate Loxton, Nick Whiteford, Chester, John Chetwynd, her mother, Dick Littel from Amsterdam, Dru, Karl, the hairy man on the ferry, Paul Horrigan, Cocky Thompson and Sylvia. "Oh, Sylvia! my darling baby, *I love you, I love you.* You mustn't reject me. I'm your mother. You grew in my body. I gave you suck. Darling, *darling Sylvia*! You're all I have. Don't leave me." Hattie wept unrestrainedly, speaking aloud, then shouting, as if she believed her daughter could hear.

At two thirty she got up, made a mug of tea and smoked a cigarette. As she sat in the kitchen, wretched and forlorn, it came to Hattie that she must do something immediately about Sylvia. Phone calls were no good, letters would probably not be answered. She had to see the girl, to try again to reason with her face to face. Why delay? She'd drive up to Scotland straight away. With minimal traffic on the roads she'd make good time.

Dressing quickly she grabbed her raincoat and handbag and was soon backing the car out of the Mews and driving up an empty Harley Street. She didn't stop for a hundred miles. There were several tapes in the car and these she played at high volume one after the other in an attempt to crowd out her misery – Pavarotti bawling operatic arias, some Beethoven sonatas, an ear-splitting American pop thing of Chester's. It began to rain heavily and Hattie wasn't able to make as rapid progress as she'd hoped.

In Cumbria around eight she stopped for fuel and a cup of coffee. The service station had had an early delivery of Sunday newspapers. There it was on the front page of the *News of the World*.

> *BRUTAL MURDER AND SUICIDE*
> *BY CUCKOLDED JOURNALIST*
> *– THE WORM THAT TURNED*

Hattie read on, her heart beating painfully, nausea threatening to choke her.

> *Roger Foley, 46, a London journalist, is thought to have taken his shotgun and killed Chester Diamond, 22, as he slept, before killing himself in the early hours of last Wednesday morning. He had lived at the fashionable Mews cottage in Marylebone, where the tragedy occurred, since 1966 with Harriot Murray, a prominent editor in the field of feminist publishing, by whom he had a daughter, Sylvia.*
>
> *Miss Murray, 45 has so far refused to discuss the bizarre case, stating repeatedly to reporters that, as far as she is concerned, the crime was motiveless and that Foley "must have had a brainstorm." However, our representatives have learnt from journalist colleagues and regular*

drinking companions at Foley's local, the Dover Castle, that there may well have been a clear motive.

Requesting anonymity, one close friend said, "Roger was a really nice chap but he couldn't stand up to Hattie Murray. He'd been drinking too much for a long time in an effort to forget that he was treated like dirt. He'd once before forgiven Miss Murray when she was involved in a scandal with the Tory MP, John Chetwynd, who had to resign from Parliament as a result. But when she brought that young American black to live right in their house Roger just couldn't take it any longer. He'd threatened to kill himself more than once."

It looks as if Harriot Murray will have some explaining to do to the Coroner next Thursday, whether she likes it or not.

Hattie drove on through the rain, her quick anger at the jackal press soon giving way to an acute sensation of tearful vulnerability. Painfully she realised there was nowhere to look for sympathy. As she crossed the Border into the Southern Uplands the rain intensified and she had to keep her speed down. By ten, however, she was in the environs of Glasgow. The mining towns of Blantyre and Cambuslang looked damply desolate at this hour on a Sunday morning. Hattie shuddered. How run-down these places were. High unemployment, vandalism. With relief she eventually turned into Oakside Avenue and parked outside number 47. The dashboard clock registered ten forty five.

She got out and stretched tired, stiff muscles, but her fatigue was forgotten as she strove to arrange the words in her mind that she'd have to say if her mission was to stand any chance of success. She did have the advantage of complete surprise.

Noiselessly she opened and closed the garden gate. Now she stood in the familiar porch with its striped sun-blind. The well-polished bell-push was cold on the tip of her index finger. She rang. There was no response. She rang again. then she remembered – Sunday morning service. Her mother never missed and would have left home five or ten minutes ago. But Sylvia? Could she still be sleeping? Hattie rang for a third time, with no result. She went round to the back door. Locked. She banged several times, but there was simply no sign of life.

Back in the car she sat smoking a cigarette. Mum wouldn't return till after twelve. She couldn't just sit here, and she certainly couldn't call on any neighbours who by now must be well up with the details of her predicament. The best thing seemed to be to go for a drive.

Slowly she toured Rutherglen, memories of her early life surprising her with their vividness. She'd fallen off her bike here. They'd pinched plums from that garden there. That was the clubhouse inside which she'd first discovered sex with Johnny MacGregor. And there was that overhung, dark place beside Overton Park where she'd gone with Sandy Watson in his father's car. Up in Burnside she glanced at the tiny, semi-detached bungalow where Sheena McHugh and Willie Shields had started their married life, where she'd held little Valerie so tightly. They weren't in the district any longer. She thought she'd heard they were somewhere in Fife, or was it Stirling? They'd lost touch years ago.

At noon Hattie parked again in Oakside Avenue. She'd just sit and wait now. Maybe she dozed for a few minutes but the next thing she knew was Charlotte tapping, her face close. She wound the window down.

"Hello, Mum."

"What are you doing here? I told you . . . "

"What d'you think? Where's Sylvia?"

"She's not here."

"Well, where *is* she for heaven's sake, Mum?"

"You'd better come inside. I'm getting soaked."

Once inside Hattie tried again to ask about Sylvia but Charlotte brushed her aside.

"I need a cup of tea. I presume you'd like one too?"

"Thanks, Mum. Now please tell me . . . "

"Sylvia recognised your car. She's gone home with a friend of mine. We went to Church together."

"*Church*?"

"Yes. Sylvia's often gone with me when she's been up staying. She told me chapel at Queen Mary's meant a lot to her, and I'm not surprised."

"Which friend is she with?"

"I'm not going to tell you, Hattie. You don't know her anyway."

"You can't do this, Mum." Hattie could feel a cold anger drying her mouth and bringing tears to her eyes.

"Oh yes I can. Sylvia will stay where she is until I telephone to say you've gone."

Hattie exploded. "Jesus Christ! I've come to *see* her. Sylvia is *my* daughter!"

"I'll thank you not to blaspheme in this house. Sylvia is of course your legal child but I'm telling you, Hattie, you're not fit to be a mother. You're a *disgrace* to your family, to . . . all women!"

"Mum!"

"Oh just go away, Hattie."

Somehow Hattie kept her balance. "And Sylvia? What's going to happen to her, may I ask?"

"You probably don't know, but her entry to Aberdeen University to study chemistry has been confirmed."

"You're right. I didn't. Of course we expected..."

Charlotte was not listening. "She'll stay here with me in the vacation time. I'm only sixty five and quite fit. I'll give her the kind of loving and secure home she's never had."

"So, you've got it all worked out?"

"Somebody had to, or the girl might have ended up like her poor father."

"And what about money?"

"We can manage. Anyway Sylvia says her father told her he'd put quite a few of his assets into her name in case anything happened to him. If you ask me he'd been planning to do away with himself for some time. Poor, poor Roger."

They'd been sitting in the kitchen. Charlotte stood up.

"Mum...?"

"The sooner you're gone the better, Hattie. Your selfishness broke your father's heart and it's broken mine. It was bad enough about Charlie, but it was *your* brazen behaviour that really finished Robert. Now it's killed Roger and another man too, and deeply disturbed Sylvia. Goodness knows how many other lives have been ruined. Can't you understand? We don't want to have anything more to do with you, *ever*." Hattie's head hung. She was utterly spent. "If you don't leave within ten minutes, I warn you I'll call the police."

Dry-eyed now Hattie knew it was useless to argue further. She had a final request.

"D'you mind if I take a look at my old room?"

"I suppose not, if you're not too long. Sylvia's things are in there. Don't you dare touch them."

She mounted the stairs. How narrow they were. Her room seemed unbelievably small too. She closed the door. The old cheval mirror was still in the corner. From habit she stood sideways to study the reflection of her figure – paunchy, bottomy, round-shouldered. In this little room the shock of how she really looked now was somehow greater than usual. So often in the past she'd gazed with pleasure at her image in this very mirror, sensually caressed her firm young breasts, her bewitching womanly contours.

She turned away and stared out of the window. What in God's name had gone wrong? She'd always expected a turbulent life – love, lack of love, success, failure, fun, boredom – but not this corroding despair and isolation. It seemed she'd lost the only two people who'd ever truly mattered to her, her mother and her daughter. Why, oh why? Something like panic forced her to sit down on the bed edge and to shut her eyes tightly. Oh God! This was unbearable. Did no-one in the entire world care about her? Did *everyone* hate her? She whimpered for a minute or so in miserable perplexity.

Gradually, in this unanswering silence, the sharpness of the pain in her heart necessarily ebbed a little. She rose and went to the window again. But her eyes were on an undefined distance now as she thought once more of Sylvia, viewing her, as it were, from afar. Whatever anyone might say of her upbringing, Sylvia had turned out a lovely young woman. She'd do well at university, maybe brilliantly if her eager spirit and her grandmother's encouragement had anything to do with it. She'd probably marry too and have several healthy children. It would be a 1980s partnership of equality and Hattie's guess was that, in Sylvia's case, it would last. Anyway, she had all the options open to her – career without limits, marriage and family, or both, as she chose.

Hattie's puffy, muddy-complexioned face mocked her a second time from the mirror. Her courage began to shrivel within her. What on earth was she going to do with herself in the years ahead? For a moment Sylvia's longed for presence seemed almost to materialise. Hattie noticed an angora sweater which she'd bought for the girl's sixteenth birthday. Reaching out to the chair where it lay she touched it lovingly.

She rejoiced for her daughter and the freedom of her future life. Many of the liberations which Sylvia and her generation would enjoy had legally been achieved years ago of course, but they'd had to be fought for and time had had to pass before society took them for granted.

Bleakly Hattie wondered if she could take some of the credit. She wasn't really sure if her own life, the battered, wilful, self-indulgent record of Harriot Murray's life, could decently stand as a testament with others to that necessary struggle. That was the agony of it. In the past the men in her family had behaved unforgivably, and her commitment to the Women's Movement and her hard work in publishing must have helped in ensuring that that sort of cruelty was now simply not acceptable.

She thought of Isabella Murray of Penick House, mistress of a fine estate but not thought worthy of adequate instruction in the matters of reading and writing. Her daughter-in-law Jean Creighton, imprisoned in another fine house in Gothenburg, had known no love, only her husband's unrelenting derision and abuse. Her solace, a beloved son, had been torn from her by that same tyrannical husband, driving her to despair and an early death. Then there was Martha Byrnie in the slums of Glasgow, dragged down to hopeless poverty by the fecklessness of James Murray. And Hattie's namesake grandmother, Harriot Browne at Burton-on-Trent, allowed no say in the future of her brilliant daughter Charlotte, whose talents were to be forcibly sacrificed to the self-centred wishes of older men. Hadn't they all been avenged in a really constructive way? Surely all that had been worthwhile? Surely she could be proud of her own involvement?

But what of today's Hattie Murray? There was no escape from the world's accusation of some terrible things. Could she defend herself on the grounds that she'd been willing to be broken on the wheel of women's progress, that she'd only ever acted in ways that her instinct told her would further the cause of women's rights? Was that honest? Hattie was no fool. For a long time now she'd realised that her mind had been poisoned against men at an early age. She was aware too that her passionate nature had often led her into dark sexual byways, and that this had not been without its effect on her judgement. She knew that during her time she'd been caught up in shifting tides of opinion about the proper relationship between men and women. And she'd always recognised that, however they might seem now, the men of earlier generations had equally, up to a point anyway, been prisoners of the culture and attitudes of *their* time. Well, she'd done what she had to do and, whatever the world's verdict, Sylvia, her own beautiful darling Sylvia, would go on in life, upright, free and unprejudiced. That was reward enough. And, Good heavens! – Britain now had its first woman Prime Minister running the country, and from the party of the right too. Hattie smiled wanly. She lifted the angora sweater into her arms and kissed it.

Outside the dank air was rent by the staccato notes of a musical car-horn. 'Dada . . . da da da *da* da da,' sounded the third and fourth bars of *Colonel Bogey* as a little red Morgan sports car raced through Oakside Avenue. The occupants were two carefree young couples laughing at the sheer fun of their escapade. The pair behind half stood in the cramped back seat space with their arms round one another for support, the girl's long blonde hair streaming out in the rain. Then they were gone. Something in the scene clutched at Hattie's heart. Her eyes were suddenly full of tears. But they were tears of vicarious joy as much as of personal remorse. Had there been anyone to observe it, an unselfish nobility shone at that moment in Harriot Murray's ravaged face.

It was time to leave. Sunday lunch was cooking and its

teasing aroma now reached her nostrils. She hoped Sylvia would enjoy it. Hattie took a last lingering look from her bedroom window. The rain was driving now and, although not yet one o'clock, the sky had turned so dark that lights had had to be switched on in some of the houses opposite. In the granite street gutters water swirled, sweeping away unwanted debris.

For a full list of
Argyll Publishing titles,
send S.A.E. to

Argyll Publishing
Glendaruel
Argyll
Scotland
PA23 3AE